SHADOWS OF LIGHT

THE SHADOW REALMS
BOOK 6

BRENDA K DAVIES

Copyright © 2022 Brenda K. Davies
All rights reserved.

Warning: All rights reserved. The unauthorized reproduction or distribution of this copyrighted work, in whole or part, in any form by any electronic, mechanical, or other means, is illegal and forbidden, without the written permission of the author.

This is a work of fiction. Characters, settings, names, and occurrences are a product of the author's imagination and bear no resemblance to any actual person, living or dead, places or settings, and/or occurrences. Any incidences of resemblance are purely coincidental.

CHAPTER ONE

THE RUSTLE of wings alerted Lexi that one of the dragons was descending into the throne room, but she didn't turn to look. *It's Alina.*

She wasn't sure how she knew, but Lexi was certain the speaker had arrived. It came through the bond that formed to connect her and the dragons when she ascended the arach throne.

That was two days ago, and she hadn't seen Alina since becoming queen, but Lexi hadn't spent any time exploring Dragonia or calling the dragons to her. She'd been too exhausted and heartbroken to do anything like that.

But today, she had no other choice. She could give herself one day to recuperate and wallow in self-pity and sorrow, but she couldn't allow two. She had to get up and learn more about the realm she would rule.

Now that she'd claimed the Dragonian throne and sealed her birthright to rule over the realms, she had to deal with her responsibilities. The only problem was she had no idea where to start with everything she had to do.

She'd already been to the infirmary and assisted with the wounded, but there were so many of them. She did what she could with the worst injuries before retreating from the suffering that filled the room.

There was little more she could do there, but she *had* to do something to keep herself occupied. So, she settled on something small, necessary, and that she could do—clean.

"You should *not* be doing that," Alina said.

She wasn't the first immortal to tell her this, but, as Lexi had told her aunt and Orin, the problem was… "Who else is going to do it? All those who lived and worked in this palace were loyal to the Lord. They've all fled, been killed, or are in the dungeon."

Lexi threw her bloody sponge into the wooden bucket before turning to face the red dragon. Alina's golden eyes studied her from their slitted pupils as she rose to reveal the yellow flecks along her belly.

Blood stained the ground and walls around Lexi, but she'd made some progress in removing the carnage she and Cole had left in their wake. Maybe she should do something besides scrubbing the blood from the throne room, but she couldn't focus on anything else.

Besides, there was *no way* she could sit in this room, and on that throne, with all the blood and scorch marks still marring the floor. And soon, she would have to sit on the arach throne and welcome others to the realm she ruled.

The scorch marks weren't coming off, and she suspected they'd forever scar the floor. Maybe they should remain to remind her of what could happen if someone else took the throne.

They could also serve as a deterrent against those who came here seeking to overthrow her. It would not be an easy fight.

"The immortals in your army should do this," Alina said.

"Most have left to either rebuild their realms or find new ones to settle. They have lives to rebuild, and they didn't agree to fight with us so they could work for me afterward."

Alina looked affronted by this. "*You* are the queen of *all* the realms. They do not *work* for you; they *serve* you. They are also yours to command."

"The dragons were the Lord's to command, too; how did that work out for you?"

Twin spirals of smoke coiled out of Alina's nostrils. "You must have an army in this realm and immortals to serve you. It is the way of things."

"You're right about the army," Lexi told her. "But I don't need servants."

"Of course you do. You will one day entertain here; there will be balls and parties again. Immortals will come to you for things, for help, to speak with you, and to pledge their allegiance. You *must* have servants to greet them."

Lexi grabbed the bloody sponge from the bucket before tossing it back into the red water. She pushed the bucket aside and pulled another one closer. Before starting, she'd carried in a dozen buckets, each with a different sponge, to prepare for this chore.

She'd already made three trips to refill the buckets and carry them back. Cleaning this mess helped her to have something other than missing Cole to focus on.

She couldn't cry as much if she was scrubbing, but it was still nearly impossible to breathe, and her eyes burned incessantly. He was gone. The shadows had taken control of him, and he was gone.

Her chest constricted, and she had to wait until it eased enough for her to breathe again. She blinked away the tears in her eyes, but they clung to her lashes and briefly blurred her vision.

Lexi removed a clean sponge from the water and returned to working on the stone floor. "That is a problem for later."

"There must be others to help with this," Alina said.

"They're removing the bodies from the battlefield, identifying them, and returning them to their loved ones. That's more important than helping me with this."

She should have been there to help them, but her father and Orin insisted she stay inside until they removed any lingering threats and it was safe for her to roam outside. As queen, she could have vetoed their decision, but she preferred not to fight with anyone again so soon.

Besides, it would put others at risk if she was out there too. They'd focus on keeping her safe, and someone who might not have attacked could decide to if they believed they had a chance of killing her.

So here she was, scrubbing a floor while some of Maverick's pack guarded the door. His pack had insisted on staying to rebuild and protect her.

Without their alpha and realm, they were lost and required something to focus on. She understood completely.

Her heart ached again at the reminder of Cole's uncle. He was one of the many they lost during the battle, but his and Niall's deaths hurt more as she'd known and liked them. They'd fought to ensure her place on the throne, stood staunchly by her and Cole's sides, and paid for their bravery with their lives.

Her chest constricted again, and she inhaled a small, sharp breath as her head bowed. She had to get it together if she was going to rule this realm and protect the immortals and humans whose lives were thrown into chaos by the Lord.

Focusing on the floor, Lexi scrubbed harder.

"You don't have to stay," Lexi said. "You and the other dragons can have your freedom. I won't keep you chained like the Lord did."

She could practically hear Orin calling her an idiot and her father's admonishment for offering such a thing; she'd be easy prey without the dragons. But she couldn't do to them what the Lord did. They were beautiful, powerful creatures; she was connected to them, a part of them, and would miss them, but they deserved their freedom if they chose it.

"We are not chained to you; we are bound to you by birth. It is the way of things," Alina said.

"Those ways could change. I'm offering you, and all the dragons, that change."

Alina hesitated before asking, "And what of you? What will you do when your enemies come for you if we're not here?"

"Fight."

"And die."

"We'll have to wait to see."

"We are where we are supposed to be. Your offer only solidifies that. The dragons will defend you with honor."

"Shouldn't you discuss it with them first? Maybe some of them would like to leave."

"There is no need. We are all proud to serve the last arach."

"You're not serving me; if you ever decide you'd prefer to leave, let me know."

"We will remain at your side always, my queen."

Lexi couldn't stop the relief that washed through her; she smiled a little as she returned to scrubbing the floor.

CHAPTER TWO

A SMALL YELP proceeded a tiny snout shoving into her face and brushing her nose. Lexi reeled back and released the sponge as she recoiled from the small creature before realizing it was a baby dragon.

It hopped toward her, squeaking while its tiny wings flapped in the air, and its head tilted to study her. Too surprised to react at first, Lexi blinked at the beautiful, orange creature no bigger than a cat. She swore it smiled as it hopped up and down.

When she sat on her ass, the tiny creature jumped into her arms. Despite the sadness suffocating her, Lexi laughed as the baby dragon peered into her face and released another squeak.

"Astarot," Alina chided.

The baby dragon ignored the speaker as it snuggled under Lexi's chin and plopped onto her lap. Two red dragons followed the orange one. Their tiny tails swished as one leapt onto her shoulder, and the other pounced on the orange one.

They shrieked and nipped at each other before the red one rose to brush Lexi's cheek. The orange one turned and kneaded her like a cat looking for a good place to lie before settling again.

When the red one's warm breath caressed her skin, Lexi

laughed. Cole's absence, and the loss of her friends, made it feel like someone had carved out her heart and stomped on it, but these babies were so cute it was impossible not to find joy in them.

Lifting her head, Lexi looked up as Alina sat and stared proudly down at her offspring. "How old are they?" she asked.

"They hatched the night you took the throne."

Lexi leaned her face into the tiny body as the one on her shoulder nuzzled her cheek. It was as if they felt her anguish and sought to comfort her.

"They're beautiful," Lexi said. "What are their names?"

"My son, Astarot, is the one nibbling on your finger; he is the future speaker should something happen to me. My daughter, Belindo, is on your shoulder, and my other daughter, Nithe, is licking you."

Lexi giggled when Nithe's tongue tickled her cheek. "Congratulations."

"Thank you. You should know they're the first dragons born into this realm in a thousand years."

So lost in dragon snuggles, it took a second for Alina's words to register. When they did, Lexi looked up at Alina. "I don't understand."

"I laid their eggs a thousand years ago, shortly before the arach lost the throne."

"It takes *that* much time for dragon eggs to hatch?" Lexi asked incredulously.

"No, it normally takes about three months."

Astarot stopped nibbling her finger and hopped onto her other shoulder. He curled against her face, yawned loudly, and went to sleep. His sisters continued to play, but Nithe yawned too.

"So why did it take these three so long?" she asked.

"No dragons have laid eggs and no eggs have hatched while the usurpers sat the throne. Your ascension to the throne has brought healing and *life* back to Dragonia. We dragons feared we would die out one day, but now, that will not happen."

Unexpected tears burned Lexi's eyes as Belindo settled onto her lap. She stroked the dragon's soft scales as she ran her hands down Belindo's back and across the small spikes on her tail.

"You are meant to be here; *this* is another reason why we'll follow you. You are our queen," Alina said. "You have sacrificed much and will sacrifice more throughout your life, but this is your home and rightful place in the realms."

"I know."

There was still so much to do and accomplish. So many would try to take the throne from her, but it was *hers,* and she would fight for it.

This was where she was supposed to be… even if it had cost her Cole.

CHAPTER THREE

Cole's feet didn't touch the ground as he glided naked through the darkness. He didn't bother to dress, there were no clothes for him here, and he didn't care about his nudity as he moved toward the surface.

The shadows churned and screamed around him. They still sought blood and hammered incessantly at him to satisfy their ravenous appetite.

It would have been better if he stayed below, where the darkness suppressed the shadows more. But even below the earth, where there was no light for the shadows to live, he couldn't shut them out completely.

He required access to their knowledge of the world outside his cave so he could protect Lexi. Minutes ago, they started whispering about a new danger to her.

There would be many threats to her, and it would be better if he were at her side to destroy them, but he didn't have enough control over the shadows to stand next to her. They were monstrous, ravenous things that battered his mind and sanity with their bloodlust.

She'd seen enough death and destruction; she didn't need to experience anymore.

And that was what he'd become.

He was death, and he embraced it.

As the shadows carried him out of the cave, he emerged into blinding sunshine that chased away some of the shadows. Lifting his hand, he shaded his eyes to block out the sun while his eyes adjusted to its light.

He smiled as he cloaked himself with the remaining shadows and made his way toward the portal. The shadows would take him to the threat, and he would eradicate it.

~

"You have breathed *life* back into this realm," Alina continued. "A miracle none of us expected. It is time to start acting like a queen, and queens do *not* scrub floors."

"It's time you get used to a new type of queen," Lexi said.

Before Alina could reply, a loud thud came from outside, and the earth quaked. When the walls rattled, Lexi looked at the open ceiling above.

Dragons roared as they soared overhead, but that's not where the sound and vibrations came from. When another thud reverberated outside, more dragons bellowed as they broke away.

"What—?"

Before she could finish her sentence, the doors at the end of the hall flew open, and Brokk rushed inside. "There's a giant in Dragonia! We have to get you somewhere safe."

Lexi scooped Belindo into her arms as she rose. "I'm not going anywhere."

A few feet away from her, Brokk skidded to a halt. "You can't be out and about while a giant is loose in the realm."

Lexi held Belindo against her chest as she threw her shoulders back and met Brokk's aqua-blue eyes. His blond hair was in tussled disarray around his handsome, dirt-streaked face. More dirt and blood stained his green, fae tunic and pants.

Lexi debated his words as Belindo nuzzled her chin. She'd let them keep her hidden because she wasn't ready to face the world. It had been cowardly of her, and she wouldn't let it continue.

This was *her* realm; if a giant was here, she would deal with it. "I'm the queen of Dragonia and the Shadow Realms. I will *not* hide. Besides, if the giant was here to fight, there would be more than one, and is there?"

Brokk frowned at her before reluctantly admitting, "No."

When Belindo let out a tiny roar, a puff of smoke spiraled from her nostrils. The look on Brokk's face was one of amusement and awe.

"Cute dragon," he muttered.

"The story of her existence is interesting," Lexi said.

When Brokk went to touch Belindo, the dragon gave him a disgruntled look and growled. Belindo looked about as intimidating as a grasshopper, but she was trying, and, one day, most would tremble before her.

"And that is?" Brokk inquired as Belindo relented to his petting behind her ear.

When another thud sounded from outside, Lexi sighed. "I'll tell you later. Now, let's see why the giant is here. I suspect it's their queen."

"Where is their queen?"

"You and Orin worked to release the prisoners from the Lord's dungeon; she wasn't there?"

One of the first things Lexi did as queen, even before she went upstairs to scrub herself clean and put on clothes, was order the release of all the Lord's prisoners. Standing there, naked and drenched in blood, she watched as one lycan and a dwarf trudged up from that monster's dungeon.

There were countless other prisoners at one time, but the

Lord slaughtered most as soon as they entered the dungeon. The blood for the Lord's fountain had to come from somewhere, and he'd used his enemies to feed it.

Now, the dungeon was crammed full of the Lord's men. She had to order their execution, but the idea of giving the order turned her stomach.

She wasn't ready for that, and while letting them sit down there wallowing in uncertainty was also unkind, the Lord's men belonged there. They'd helped that monster terrorize countless others for centuries.

"I didn't see a giant queen below, and I doubt they're easy to miss," Brokk said.

"They are easily detectable," Alina agreed.

"She wouldn't fit down there anyway. It's the largest dungeon I've ever seen, but there's nowhere to put a giant."

Lexi shifted her attention to Alina. "Do you know where the giant queen is?"

"I do," the speaker replied. "It isn't good."

"Of course it's not," Brokk muttered.

"Is she alive?" Lexi asked Alina.

"I'm not sure. It's been a while since I last saw her, but I would assume so."

Lexi scratched Belindo's chin. The giants were not going to be happy to hear that. "Let's get this over with."

"You have all the dragons behind you," Alina promised. "No one will attack you inside of Dragonia. If they try, they *will* face our wrath."

"I don't think the giant is here to attack; they want their queen back. It's all they've ever wanted and why they fought for the Lord when we went to war against him. Do you wish to take your children home before joining us outside?"

"We call them wyrmlings, and no, they can remain here if you allow it."

When Belindo turned her head toward Lexi, the tiny bundle

of joy rubbed Lexi's nose with hers. Lexi giggled as they exchanged this small sign of affection before the dragon spread her wings and hopped down.

She watched as Belindo hopped over to join her siblings before shifting her attention to Alina. "Of course they can stay. Are you going to stay with them?"

"I will go with my queen."

Lexi turned to Brokk. "Are you ready to get this over with?"

"I'll be right by your side."

CHAPTER FOUR

Cole emerged from the portal and into an outer realm with a dark red sun and black clouds floating across a purple sky. The shadows released him from their dark embrace and slithered across the ground.

Some swirled up to surround him as he moved, but they didn't cloak him from view again. Their power coursed through his veins, thrummed across his skin, and swelled within his muscles.

He couldn't feel all the shadows in *all* the realms—there were far too many realms for that. And they didn't all communicate with him, but the shadows he'd assigned to watch over Lexi when he left, continued to do so. They would alert him if she was in jeopardy.

He was aware a giant had entered Dragonia, but between the shadows and the dragons, she would remain safe. The shadows didn't think the giant was there to harm her, and neither did he. The man was there for his queen; he wouldn't cause any problems. If he did, the shadows would make him pay.

There was a bigger threat brewing here. The shadows pulsed

with excitement as Cole stalked toward the large building only two hundred feet away.

The shadows would get the chance to kill again, and they *loved* it. But then, so did Cole. That wasn't always the case, but he wouldn't feel any remorse over what he would unleash here.

He'd been to this establishment before. Aurora was a place of hedonism and decadence. One where he'd spent countless hours and days.

It had also become a place for traitors to gather.

Women and men danced on the large, wooden structure's different balconies and outcroppings. Some danced on the roof, stripping off what little clothes they wore and tossing them at those who entered.

A steady flow of immortals flowed into the building. Most of them played with themselves as they moved, while others openly fucked each other.

This place was one of the many dark fae pleasure houses he'd visited. Many of the dancers had been shadow kissed by the dark fae; they now craved sex all the time and would do anything to get it.

The shadow kissed didn't care who they screwed as long as they screwed someone. But then, the same could be said for the dark fae who created them… or at least most of the dark fae.

He and a few rare other dark fae had fallen in love, found the ones they would marry, and never stray from; most fae didn't. They were quite content with that, as he once was but would never be again.

Cole recognized one of them as a woman he'd shadow kissed. She wore nothing more than stars on her nipples and a see-through thong. When she spotted him, she waved before turning and vanishing from the balcony where she danced.

The shadow kissed the dark fae left in their wake often went on to screw countless others, but no matter how many other lovers they had, they still favored the one who made them. Cole couldn't remember the woman's name, but she stood at the open doors when he reached them.

"You're back!" she exclaimed as she threw herself into his arms.

The shadows around him hissed in revulsion, and a chill slid over his skin as he pushed the woman away. The look he gave her caused the woman to recoil, and her smile vanished as she edged away from him.

"Aren't you here for me?" she whimpered.

"Not unless you want to die," the shadows and Cole said.

The woman's eyes widened before she scampered inside. Red light, cast by the crimson candles on the tables and enhanced by the sheer burgundy gauze covering the windows, bathed the bottom floor.

No one here noticed him. Many didn't care who their partner was—male, female, dwarf, or a couple of shifted lycans. But then, more than half of them were openly having some form of sex with one, two, or more partners.

Swings drooped from the ceiling, toys dangled from the walls, and ropes hung from the rafters. There were private rooms in the back, and more immortals probably filled them, but many never bothered with those private rooms.

When he visited here, Cole had never cared where he was either. Now, the dark fae was ravenous, but he wanted nothing to do with this place or what happened here… other than finding the traitors.

There was a time when entering this place would have caused excitement to race through him, but now, his only reaction was his increasing need to find those who were a menace to Lexi. The shadows coiled around him before spreading out in search of those they sought to destroy.

Most didn't notice when he cloaked himself in shadows and vanished.

CHAPTER FIVE

As Lexi had expected, Gibborim was the giant who entered Dragonia. The massive man easily stood a hundred feet tall, and the sun behind him illuminated his mop of brown and orange hair.

She and Cole encountered him when they visited Colossal, where the giants resided. A black patch covered one of his brown eyes, and he'd donned clean, brown clothes since they last saw him while fighting for the Lord during the war.

The giants had chosen the other side; Niall died because of a giant, but she understood why they fought for the Lord. Their loyalty and love for their queen propelled them to become the enemy.

And now Gibborim was here to ask for his queen locked somewhere in Dragonia. Lexi could turn him away; she had every right to after what the giants decided. Or she could forgive them, find their queen, and work to repair the relationship between the realms.

She recalled Niall's easy smile and fierce loyalty to Cole. He'd been a trusted friend and a good man who might still be here if not for a giant.

But how many more will die if I continue a feud that could end today?

As much as she'd prefer to make everyone who turned against them pay, the giants had their reasons. And if anyone could understand loyalty, it was Niall... and her.

Besides, she didn't have it in her to continue that kind of grudge. She was supposed to be repairing the Shadow Realms, not dividing them further, and she would do it.

Lexi still had no idea where the Lord had put the giant queen; Alina had flown out of the throne room before revealing this vital information. The speaker now circled overhead with dozens of other dragons.

They all swooped down to soar in front of the giant. The show of strength would show the giant they'd kill him if he tried anything.

Orin had joined her and Brokk as soon as they exited the palace; they flanked her now. Behind them stood what little of her army remained.

Gibborim studied the dragons before shifting his attention to her. "I am not here to fight, little one."

When she first encountered him, she let his *little one* name for her slide. Mainly because she was a flea compared to this man, but she couldn't let it slide anymore. She'd *never* wanted to be a queen, but she was, and it was time to start acting like one.

This was *her* realm, and she had claimed *her* ancestors' throne. She couldn't allow anyone to treat her as anything other than the queen of *all* the realms.

"I know why you're here," Lexi replied, "and I am Queen Elexiandra of Dragonia and ruler of all the Shadow Realms; you will *not* call me 'little one' again."

Beside her, Brokk shifted uneasily, and Orin chuckled, but he was crazy enough, or asshole enough, not to realize Gibborim could squash them with one step. Lexi clasped her hands before her and lifted her chin; her heart raced, and she *really* didn't feel like being smushed, but she refused to let Gibborim see her apprehension.

CHAPTER SIX

Gibborim gave a laugh that giants probably considered a chuckle, but it was more like a huge guffaw here. The breeze it created stirred her hair.

Alina swooped down to settle behind Lexi with a rustle of wings. She lifted her head high as the rest of the dragons bellowed.

"Your dragons have nothing to fear from me, Queen Elexiandra," Gibborim said.

He knelt before her and rested his hand on the ground. Only fifty feet separated them, and he could swat them aside as easily as she batted flies from the air, but Lexi didn't give any ground.

This close, she could see the concern and hope in his brown eye as he studied her. "I came here hoping we could heal our realms by agreeing to work together."

"Now he'd prefer to work together," Orin retorted.

"Orin," Lexi warned. "Continued fighting will only get more of us killed and never heal the realms."

"And rewarding those who fought on the Lord's side will make us look weak."

"Mending old wounds is not a sign of weakness," her dad

said as he strolled toward them. "It's a sign of forgiveness, moving on, and learning to live with each other."

She didn't know where her dad was before this, but dirt streaked his face and blood stained his clothes. He must have been working to help bury the dead, but she was surprised he didn't come as soon as a giant entered the realm.

Something more than the dead must have kept him occupied. When she frowned questioningly at him, he gave a subtle shake of his head and rested a hand on her arm before releasing her.

Lexi shifted her attention back to Gibborim when he spoke again. "You're right, vampire, and the Shadow Realms need mending after the Lord's rule."

"A rule you helped him keep," Orin retorted.

"That is enough," Brokk cautioned.

Lexi rolled her eyes when he and Orin glared at each other. They would each kill anyone who tried to hurt the other, but sometimes, they would gladly murder each other.

"It is enough," Lexi said before turning to Gibborim. "You want your queen."

Gibborim bowed his head. "We would like our queen. You know why we didn't stand with you against the Lord, though we did hope for you to win. Now, we ask you to find it in your heart to forgive us for choosing to save our queen from the Lord's wrath.

"Our king is dead—the Lord killed him—but our queen lives, and we want to bring her home. She's a fair ruler, loyal, and kindhearted. In return, if you should require anything at all, the giants will help you."

"Who are you to promise such a thing?" Orin inquired.

Lexi wanted to tell him to shut up and stop trying to cause problems, but he had a point. She almost looked to her dad, but she couldn't rely on others to help her rule.

Kings and queens had advisors, and she would have them too, but in the end, the final decision would always come down to her and Cole… if he ever returned. Besides, she already knew her dad's opinion on this; he'd stated it as he approached.

"She is my sister, and while you're right, I cannot promise she will follow what the others and I have all agreed to pledge to you, but I can promise to talk to her about it… if she disagrees. I don't think she will."

"Things will be challenging for her without her husband. She'll require time to come to terms with the loss, but she'll also seek peace in the realms. It's all she's ever wanted. It's why the Lord punished her and her husband and put the rest of us under his thumb."

Lexi pondered this information. "And will you all turn against us if she does?"

Gibborim closed his eye and bowed his head. "No."

He could easily break his promise, but it was something, and most immortals took their vows *very* seriously, which was why marriage was so sacred amongst them. But in the game of politics and pawns, things were much different than matters of the heart.

However, she believed Gibborim was a man of honor and his word. It would upset him to go against his queen and sister, but he would.

"I'm not sure where your queen is," Lexi admitted, "but we will find her."

"I will take you to her," Alina said.

Gibborim's eyebrows rose when Alina spoke. He might topple over if someone climbed up to push on his shoulder. She understood how he felt; she'd experienced the same shock when she first heard Alina talk.

"Thank you," Lexi said.

Alina unfurled her wings and launched into the air. As she rose, two other dragons landed to stand near Lexi. They each took a position of guard and eyed the giant like they were about to slice out his other eye.

Alina turned to the side and headed back toward the palace. Her bright red scales shone in the sunlight, and her yellow belly glistened. She was a beautiful dragon, and pride swelled in Lexi as she watched her soar.

"Thank you," Gibborim said before rising.

"Don't thank me yet," Lexi replied. "I have no idea what the Lord has done with her or *to* her."

A pained expression crossed Gibborim's face before he nodded.

"Let's go," Lexi said.

They all turned to follow Alina up the hill, toward the palace, and around the back as Alina vanished behind the towering structure with all its golden peaks and turrets.

CHAPTER SEVEN

Cole unwrapped himself from the shadows as he glided down the hall. Some of the immortals closest to him gasped when he emerged from the darkness; he ignored them as they turned to watch him pass.

The shadows monitored them as he continued forward, but no one would be foolish enough to attack him. If they were, they wouldn't live to regret it.

At the end of the hall, he turned right and strode to the last door. He didn't bother to knock before grasping the knob, breaking it off in his hand, and using his shoulder to open the door with little noise.

He barely paid attention to the large room with its numerous whips, chains, ball gags, and other assorted toys covering one wall. The other side of the room had ropes hanging from the wall, and at the back were a couple of beds with different apparatus sticking out from them.

He'd spent some time in this room but couldn't recall a single woman who accompanied him. They were a blur of memories he had no desire to remember.

The shadows drew him toward a small back room. As he walked, he cloaked himself in darkness again.

Voices drifted to him before he turned the corner and entered a small room, bathed in red light and built for carnality and pain. The room's occupants hadn't bothered to close the door; they'd mistakenly believed the outer door would keep them safe and their treachery private.

He found three dark fae, two warlocks, and a vampire. He smiled grimly when he saw that one of the dark fae was Alston.

He'd been looking forward to killing this man for months. Alston was once a member of the dark fae council; he'd entered his young son, Eoghan, as a candidate to become king during the dark fae trials.

Alston had to have known his son didn't stand a chance of surviving those trials, but in *his* desire to place his flesh and blood on the throne and rule through him, he hadn't cared. Eoghan never made it through the first trial before he died a vicious death.

Cole would make Alston pay for that.

The shadows had whispered some of what was happening here to him, but his blood boiled when he stopped to listen. Alston had taken the lead as he plotted with these other fools to take Lexi down.

"She's weak without Cole," Alston said. "Now's the time to go after her. She may be in power, but she's nothing more than a child."

"She still has the dragons," a lycan said.

"And Cole's brothers are still with her," another said. "Orin and Brokk are formidable foes. Not to mention, she also has Del and Varo."

"Varo is a weakling," Alston retorted. "His half light fae heritage makes him almost useless."

Cole bristled against this summation of his youngest brother.

Varo wasn't as ruthless as the rest, but he was lethal and could easily destroy any of the idiots in this room.

Alston rubbed his chin as he stared at the far wall. "Cole's brothers were never stronger than him and are lost without him. She's barely assumed control, is weak, and Dragonia is still scrambling. We have to move now.

"If we attack right now, we can seize control without much fight. The war decimated most of their army; the ones who didn't die have started returning home, and she's lost Cole. We can get to her."

Cole didn't like how much Alston knew about what was happening in Dragonia; immortals loved to talk. He was sure all the details of the war and Dragonia had spread throughout all the realms.

"Maverick is also dead, which means his pack is scrambling too," another lycan said.

Cole winced at this reminder. He knew of Maverick and Niall's deaths, the shadows had whispered about them, but he often forgot about it in the madness and whispers spinning through his mind.

It was impossible to keep control of any thought when the shadows constantly sought violence. As grief started to rise within him, the shadows slithered deeper, and a throbbing fury replaced any other emotion.

Beneath the shadows' demand for blood, they reported on Lexi, who was now searching for the giant queen. None of those in Dragonia knew it, but the shadows had formed a noose around the neck of the giant with only one eye. One wrong move and they would decapitate the beast.

For now, he kept them from doing so. They were impatient to slice through the giant's flesh, but Lexi was rebuilding the realms; he couldn't allow the shadows to start another war.

The shadows resented him for this and berated him with their displeasure, but they calmed a little when he promised them this kill. He had to keep them under control, or he *would* be the reason all the realms fell, and he refused to let the prophecy come true, even if the shadows became increasingly demanding and blood hungry with every passing day.

CHAPTER EIGHT

"We won't need an army," Alston continued. "I was on the dark fae council. Brokk won't eagerly welcome me into the realm, but he won't turn me away, especially if I bring some of the dark fae who lived on my lands with me. I know where most of them are; they don't have to know my plan. They simply have to come too.

"The queen and her followers are looking for peace and to repair Dragonia's relationship with all the realms; they'll have no choice but to talk to me. The Gloaming may be gone, but I am still a powerful, well-respected dark fae. Once I'm inside the realm and close enough, I'll kill her."

Cole's blood boiled at the casual ease with which this man spoke of destroying his mate.

"That could work," the vampire said.

"And I assume you plan on taking the throne afterward," the other lycan said.

"Of course, someone has to, and I will be putting myself at risk to do so," Alston said.

Alston must believe killing Lexi was a far easier challenge

than the trials if he was willing to do it himself. He was a bigger idiot than Cole had realized.

"But I will ensure that all those who help me take control and stand by my side are rewarded. That includes all of *you*. There is much wealth in Dragonia and many realms available for you all to rule."

They all practically salivated as they exchanged looks before nodding. Cole didn't know who was dumber, Alston for thinking Lexi would be easy pickings, especially after the destruction she helped rain down on the Lord, or these morons for thinking Alston would reward them with anything.

The last Lord had gone insane and nearly destroyed all the realms, his enemies, and his allies. Some immortals never learned there were things they shouldn't mess with. One of those things was the arach throne.

"You can all go to Dragonia too when I go," Alston said. "If they're looking for peace, they'll welcome us all. And then, they'll die."

"When do we leave?" the vamp asked.

"We'll go tomorrow at sunset," Alston said.

"I think this will work," one of the other dark fae said.

Cole smiled as he released the shadows cloaking him. "I don't."

As the traitors cried out and stumbled away from him, he focused on Alston. "First, you offer up your son for certain death, and now you plan to attack *my* mate and *my* brothers. I am your *fucking* king, yet you plot against me and mine. Your son didn't survive the trials, and I should have killed you after them; I won't replicate that mistake today."

Alston started stammering excuses. "Milord, I would never.... You misunderstood.... We only mean to... to...."

His words trailed off as Cole glided closer, carried by the shadows swarming around him. When some of the others tried to run, the shadows cut them off as they snapped in their faces while propelling them back.

Alston fell to his knees and clasped his hands before him as Cole loomed over him. "We only meant to offer them assistance!"

"Liar!" The voice that issued from Cole was a mixture of his and the shadows. "Do you think we can't hear? Do you think we are not *everywhere*?"

Alston started to sob as the shadows laughed. Their maniacal sound echoed around the room as Cole released the shadows. They'd been good so far; it was time for them to play.

They slid across the floor, dropped from the ceiling, and twined around their victims. Screams filled the air, blood splattered the walls, and scattered pieces littered the ground.

Alston's sobs grew louder, and his face became deathly pale. "Please! You're mistaken, milord. I was… I was…." When blood splattered his face, he released a muffled cry before blubbering. "I was trying to lure out your enemies. I swear, I planned to turn them all over to your brothers tomorrow."

"That's the worst lie I've ever heard anyone utter."

Alston's head bowed, and his shoulders shook as he wept. Cole rested his hand on the man's head before sliding his thumb down to wipe away some of his tears.

"Your son showed more courage in death than you, but that's not surprising. No more crying; it's humiliating."

Alston cried so hard his teeth chattered and snot rolled down his face. Disgusted, Cole returned his hand to the top of Alston's head.

"I meant to make this last, but I can't take this shit anymore," Cole snarled. "You're a coward."

The shadows were allowed to have the others, but Alston was his, and Cole broke his neck with a swift jerk. Ligaments tore as he twisted the head further before ripping it free.

Alston made a few more sounds, and his mouth opened and closed before going still. His lips remained partly open, tear marks stained his cheeks, and muscles and spine dangled from his severed head.

Cole tucked it under his arm. He still had work to do.

CHAPTER NINE

"She's down there," Alina stated.

Lexi gazed down at the river a thousand feet below. She looked back to the swiftly running water from the bridge she stood on with Alina, Orin, her dad, and Brokk. Then, over her shoulder where two other dragons stood at the end of the bridge.

Each of them flanked where Gibborim stood, waiting for them just off the end of the bridge. More dragons circled overhead, but she had no idea how to react to this revelation or what it meant.

Is the queen beneath the river?

"What do you mean she's 'down there'?" Orin inquired of Alina. "Do you mean she's *below* the water?"

"I do."

"Shit," her dad muttered. "How is that possible?"

"The river runs deep."

Lexi lifted an eyebrow at this obvious statement. If it was hiding a giant, then it definitely ran deep, but Alina thought they should all understand how the Lord could bury a giant *in a river* in the first place.

"How was she restrained?" Lexi asked. "How did he manage to get her under the water?"

"He poisoned her husband's drink and food and cut off his head. He drugged her drink and food with a potion that put her to sleep. The Lord's men encased her in chains afterward, and the Lord ordered the dragons to place her in the water. It was not a command we enjoyed."

Lexi rested her hand on Alina's neck and rubbed her scales as she remained focused on the water. "I'm sorry for that."

"We will not be ordered to do such heinous things again... I hope."

"You won't," Lexi vowed.

"What if the current has already carried her away?" Brokk asked. "It's pretty rough down there."

"The Lord's men weighed her down before placing her there," Alina answered. "As far as I know, she remains. The Lord enjoyed the reminder he got of her presence below whenever he crossed this bridge."

"How do you know that?" Orin asked.

"He said so."

Lexi shuddered. "He was a monster."

"Yes," Alina agreed.

"How do we get down there?"

"What is it?" Gibborim called to them. "Why are we stopped here?"

"She's in the water," Lexi shouted back.

Gibborim swore vehemently, and Lexi cringed a little. She would prefer not to go to war with the giants again, but would they blame her and the dragons if they couldn't rescue their queen? And if they saved their queen, would she *still* blame them? The dragons did aid in her imprisonment; she could be determined to exact revenge on them.

It was a catch-22 either way, but Lexi couldn't leave anyone to suffer such a hideous fate, even if she might have to kill that someone in the future. No matter how much she understood why the giants sided with the Lord, she would destroy them to keep control of Dragonia and safeguard the tentative peace they'd established.

"There's a pathway under the bridge, but the giant won't be able to traverse it. He'll have to follow the walkway down the mountain to the valley below. Then he'll walk beside the river until it becomes too narrow. From there, he'll have to traverse through the waters."

"Sounds simple enough," Brokk replied.

Apparently, Alina didn't get sarcasm as she replied, "Yes."

Brokk and Orin both shot her identical looks of incredulity that, despite the circumstances, made Lexi chuckle. The brothers weren't often on the same page about things, but they clearly considered Alina insane.

"Some of you can go with him," Alina continued.

Lexi's eyes widened as she studied the fast-moving current. They could traverse the river with a boat, but it didn't look like fun, and she was sure more than a few had dashed against the river's cliffs.

"I'll take Lexi down with me," Alina stated.

Lexi's amusement over Brokk and Orin's reaction to Alina vanished. "Wait... *what?*"

"You can fly down on me. The giant queen is not directly beneath us; she's a little further down the river, closer to the other side of the palace. The river widens there; that is where they'll locate the queen."

Lexi gawked at her as she tried to absorb this "fly down" on her statement.

"Maybe setting her free isn't such a good idea," Orin said.

"Maybe not," Lexi agreed, "but either way, we risk a war with the giants. Setting her free might be the only way to prevent it; keeping her imprisoned guarantees it."

"She's right," her dad said. "We have no choice. We can only hope that setting the queen free will make her happy enough to return home and not seek retribution on Dragonia and the dragons."

"We are not afraid of giants," Alina retorted.

Lexi ran her hand over Alina to soothe her. "Even so, we can't continue warring with other realms. This is supposed to be a time of peace and healing, not another period of more death. Now, let's get back to this whole 'I'll fly down on you' thing."

"I will allow you to ride down on me."

Lexi opened her mouth to reply before closing it. Beside her, Orin chuckled; she restrained herself from shoving him off the bridge.

"Go ahead, Kitten. Hop on board," Orin said.

Lexi grated her teeth as she glowered at him. "Call me that again, and I'll toss you in the dungeon with the others."

"I'll eat him for you, if you'd like," Alina offered.

When Lexi hesitated to ponder this, Orin rolled his eyes. "I know I'm an asshole, but I'm not annoying enough to be dragon shit."

"I think only *you* would agree with that," her dad retorted, and Brokk laughed.

"When Cole returns, he won't be happy to learn you let the dragons eat me."

Lexi focused on the river to keep her tears hidden. "That's *if* he returns."

Brokk rested his hand on her shoulder. "He will."

Lexi wanted to believe those words, but she didn't think Brokk was entirely convinced of them either.

"If we're going to do this before nightfall, we should go," her dad said.

CHAPTER TEN

Oh shit. Oh no. Why did I agree to this? I'm going to die. I don't want to die.

Lexi had no idea why she agreed to this... okay, that wasn't entirely true. She said yes because, if Alina offered, then her ancestors must have flown on the dragons too, which meant it was one more thing she would have to master.

Plus, there was a time when she dreamed of riding dragons and soaring high on their backs. Of course, she'd been an idiot kid who wasn't *actually* clinging to a dragon's back as it plunged from the sky at alarming speeds that whipped her hair around, plastered her clothes to her body, and caused her stomach to somersault.

Why is the ground so far away? If she fell off now, she'd splat all over the place, and she wasn't sure an immortal could come back from breaking every bone and organ in their body.

Closing her eyes again, she pressed closer to Alina's back as she tried not to think about her friends having to scrape her from the earth. She'd probably leave a dent in the dirt too.

Lexi dared to crack an eye open again. When she did, she glimpsed rocky cliffs flying by before she closed it again.

Stop being such a coward. You're still alive, and your ancestors survived this.

They were born into this, not thrust into it.

You were born into it; you just weren't raised in it.

She couldn't argue with that reasoning, no matter how badly she wanted to. Still, her eyes remained shut as the wind battered her.

As time passed and she didn't fall off, she slowly relaxed. Her death grip on Alina's spikes didn't ease, but she grew a little more confident she wouldn't become a part of the landscape.

As she relaxed, the open air suddenly offered a sense of abandon instead of dread. Up here, there were no wars, blood, or pressures on her shoulders. There was no Cole and no heartache. It was simply her, this wonderful dragon, and freedom.

She cracked her eye open again when Alina went lower. The dragon turned to the side; as she did so, her wing tip skimmed the water.

Lexi smiled as drops of cool water dampened her face and clothes before Alina righted herself. It was beautiful on the back of this magnificent, powerful creature. Alina wouldn't allow her to fall.

Gradually, she eased up, so she wasn't completely flat against Alina's back. When she did, the wind caught her more fully but didn't knock her off.

Lexi kept her hands around two of Alina's spikes as she savored the fresh air. Land and water whipped past in a blur as Alina banked to the right and swooped around a mountain cliff before entering a more spacious section.

In this area, the cliffs remained high, but they sat further back from the river. A rocky shoreline ran alongside the rushing water through here.

Or at least, on one side, there was a shoreline. On the other side, the river ran against the palace wall. In that wall, windows faced out across the water, but what lay below?

A sick feeling settled in Lexi's stomach while she contemplated this.

With a rustle of wings, Alina settled onto the shore before dipping her neck for Lexi to climb off. Lexi's legs trembled as she moved, but she managed to swing them over and slide down Alina's supple scales.

"Are there windows under the water too?" Lexi asked.

"I don't know," Alina replied. "I cannot enter that area of the palace, but with the Lord's penchant for misery, I'm sure they are."

A balcony jutted out of the palace a couple of floors up from the water. She pointed to it as she spoke. "It will be a while before the others arrive; can you take me up there?"

"Of course."

Lexi scrambled back onto Alina and held on as her wings flapped and she took flight. When they arrived at the balcony, Lexi took a deep breath and refused to look down as she slid off Alina and over the balcony railing.

Grasping the door handle, she pulled on it but wasn't shocked to find it locked. Unlike the palace in the Gloaming, this arach home didn't have a mind of its own. Or maybe it did and it was simply waiting to see if she was worth sharing its secrets with, but Lexi doubted it.

Lexi turned her head away as she used her elbow to smash out one of the glass panes next to the handle. Glass was still tinkling as it hit the ground when she reached inside to unlock the door.

"I'll be back soon," Lexi said over her shoulder. "If they arrive before I return, let the others know where I went."

"I will."

CHAPTER ELEVEN

Lexi pushed open the door to reveal the sheer, white curtains hanging on the other side. Glass crunched beneath her boots as she stepped onto the gray, plush carpet of the large bedroom.

A pink covering hung over the top of the white canopy bed. Baby dragons decorated the white walls, and stuffed animals crowded the wooden toy box pushed against the far wall. Small dresses in assorted colors hung in the open, walk-in closet.

Lexi's heart sank as she took in the child's room. She'd never considered that when the arach destroyed each other, they also destroyed their most vulnerable and those who required the most protection.

While they warred against each other, they wiped out their babies, children, and future. Lexi's hand instinctively went to her belly; there was no child nestled within, of that she was certain, but if she ever had a baby, she would do everything in her power to ensure it survived.

She would *not* allow hers or anyone else's stupid, stubborn pride, to destroy her child. And she couldn't understand how they had allowed such a thing.

Sometimes, she felt incredibly close to her ancestors. She'd never known them, but she could sense them here, moving like ghosts through the barren halls.

At other times, she felt so distant from them that it was as if they had nothing in common, not even blood and abilities. This was one of those times.

By the end of their time in this realm and this palace, they were as monstrous as the Lord. They'd been too determined to be right and to rule that they hadn't cared who they slaughtered in the process.

She bet the little girl who once occupied this room cared. Or maybe she was too young to understand what was happening when those meant to protect her turned against her.

Feeling sick and fighting back tears, Lexi started across the carpet again. No matter what happened, she wouldn't let the mistakes of her ancestors' past replay in the future. With or without Cole, she would repair the realms and bring the peace and security to them that *all* the children deserved.

When Lexi reached the door, she pulled it open and poked her head into the hallway. She tried to figure out where she was, but she'd never been to this area of the palace. She'd barely seen any of it yet, a fact she would have to remedy at some point.

Lexi stepped into the hall and glanced both ways. The open doorway and window at the end were the only sources of illumination. At the end of the hall, to her left, was a staircase.

Her footsteps didn't make a sound against the plush, white carpet lining the hall. The brass sconces on the walls shone in the dim light; the Lord's servants hadn't missed a speck of dust, but she could imagine how he would react if they did.

Gold embossed wainscoting covered the bottom half of the walls while the top was painted a pretty pink. *Did this whole wing belong to the little girl?*

The possibility intrigued her, but she didn't open any of the doors she passed to confirm her suspicion. Her heart still ached from what she'd seen in the bedroom; she couldn't take any more of that.

But she also couldn't imagine having a whole palace wing to herself. What was it like to grow up here, running down this hall and in and out of these rooms with their countless wonders behind them?

Maybe, if the arach hadn't been so horrible, she would know the answer, but she didn't. And she wouldn't have traded her childhood for anything.

The manor where she grew up was a beautiful, large home, but this place made it look tiny in comparison. Yet, this place was nowhere near as homey and welcoming as her now gone home.

Love filled her manor. A day didn't go by where she wasn't certain of that; she hoped the little girl who roamed these halls felt the same before it all fell, but for some reason, Lexi doubted it.

Her mother wasn't allowed to love her father because he was considered lesser in this society. Such thinking didn't usually signal a loving community. Lexi wished she could have known her parents but was glad she didn't grow up here.

And at the end of the hall, the spiraling stairs went up and down. Light from windows above illuminated the beautiful stairs as they spiraled up through at least six stories, but she wasn't going up.

When she glanced down, she saw about fifteen feet of the stairs before the darkness swallowed them. She had no idea what lay below, besides no windows, but she had to go.

CHAPTER TWELVE

Grasping the glistening, mahogany railing, she descended. With each floor, the air grew cooler, and moisture hung thickly in the air. She had to be beneath or at least even with the river.

The stairs finally ended in a barren hall with a rock floor and stone walls. If there were cell doors, she would have believed she'd descended into the dungeons, but there weren't any.

It was a long stretch of rocky corridor with a dim, bluish light a hundred yards ahead. That light came from around a bend in the hall.

Resting her fingertips against the cool wall, Lexi trailed them across the damp rocks as she made her way toward the blue glow. The hall smelled of water and fish, but her muted footfalls were the only sounds.

When she rounded the corner, she came to an abrupt halt. Ice ran through her veins as she gazed at the underwater scene.

Beautiful fish darted in and out of the rocks and multicolored weeds. The fish were colorful and exotic; some were two or three feet long, while others were smaller than minnows.

A big pool of weeds danced in the water. No... not weeds. It took her a few seconds to realize it was brown hair.

Long, brown hair that was attached to the queen of the giants. Lexi's hand went to her mouth as the woman's head turned toward her. The queen's brown, bulging eyes were so bloodshot the whites had turned completely red.

Her skin had taken on the bluish-green hue of death, but this woman wouldn't die; she would remain trapped in this hell as she repeatedly drowned. Lexi had no idea what the queen looked like before this, but she doubted the woman was this bloated and misshapen.

The time that passed since the Lord trapped the queen beneath this water hadn't been kind to her. And, of course, it wouldn't be.

Lexi approached the glass and rested her fingertips against it. When the queen opened her mouth, fury etched her features.

Lexi understood her rage; not only was this woman enveloped in chains laden with weights, but she'd also lost her husband. And there was no way to know how often the Lord came to torment her. Lexi suspected it was often.

Then, to her horror, she realized this scene was *far* worse than she'd realized. Her jaw fell as she shifted her attention from the queen to what lay on *top* of her.

After being removed, the Lord had the king's head mounted on a wall in his private solar. She hadn't seen it, but Cole had told her about the awful thing. It remained there for now.

Though his head was in the palace, chains bound his body to the queen's. The woman was trapped here with the decomposing body of her husband. Alina had failed to mention that part, but Lexi understood why; this wasn't something the dragons cared to remember.

Lexi swallowed back her bile when a fish darted in to pick away some of the king's remains. It wasn't the only one, as dozens of them feasted on the carcass.

The fish had removed much of the king's flesh. No bones were visible yet, but they'd be exposed soon.

If someone had done this to her with Cole.... She shut the possibility down. They'd be lucky if the queen didn't smash the palace to pieces once they freed her.

And Lexi would free her. It didn't matter if the queen turned on them or not; she couldn't leave her to this fate.

She shifted her attention back to the woman glaring at her and held the queen's gaze while she vowed, "We're going to get you out of here."

Please don't kill us when we do.

CHAPTER THIRTEEN

WHEN LEXI EMERGED from the palace, Gibborim and the others had arrived. Sahira, Kaylia, Varo, some dark fae, and lycans had joined them.

They floated in four separate boats a few feet from where Gibborim stood in the water. He would step on his sister and brother-in-law if he walked twenty feet forward.

"Don't go any closer," Lexi told him from the balcony, "or you'll step on them."

"Them?" Gibborim inquired.

Lexi took a deep breath before revealing the worst. "Your king is down there too… or what remains of him. They're bound together."

Gibborim paled as his jaw went slack. "How do you know that?"

"There's a hall beneath the water. The Lord would go to watch them."

Gibborim's lips compressed into a thin, flat line. "I see."

"She's going to come up fighting; can you keep her from trying to destroy us? If not…" She didn't want to say this, not after everything the queen and giants had endured, but she had to. "We'll have to kill her. We can't have her attacking the realm."

Gibborim closed his eye and bowed his head as sorrow emanated from him. "I can keep her restrained. I'm sure she's been weakened by her ordeal and probably hasn't eaten in months."

"We'll keep her in chains until you're out of Dragonia."

"That would be for the best."

"Then let's begin."

Alina took Lexi back to the shoreline as the work to remove the king started. It took dozens of dragons to lift the king's body from the river enough for more dragons to heat the chains until they broke apart.

Lexi couldn't see the queen anymore, but she imagined the queen half rising from the water only to fall again. Being severed from her husband was probably driving her more insane and enraging her further, but they couldn't lift them both from the water at once.

Gibborim couldn't take her back to Colossal while still bound to her husband; he wasn't *that* strong. And if they took them both out at once, the queen might become too infuriated to make separating them possible.

The dragons set the king's body on the shore a hundred feet from where Lexi stood with the others. Lexi gulped, and her nose wrinkled, but she resisted sticking her finger under it to block the smell. It didn't seem like a queenly action.

Orin's nose wrinkled in distaste. "Lovely."

Lexi struggled not to show her revulsion while Sahira weaved a spell to block the smell from them. When Kaylia created another one, the scent of lavender filled the air around them.

Less than half an hour later, they freed the queen from the river. Her enormous body hung in the air by dozens of dragons as Gibborim stepped closer and rested his hand on his sister's chest.

"You're free now," he whispered, but it was loud enough they could all hear it.

The queen tried to speak, but water spewed from her mouth. She coughed, hacked, and shook so much, the dragons nearly lost their hold on her. Lexi eyed the chains; Gibborim could easily snap them if he chose to do so.

"I think it's time for you to leave!" Lexi called to Gibborim. "I'll open a portal for you."

With that, Lexi imagined the big, beautiful land of Colossal and the magnificent, floating castle there. Large enough for the giants and dragons to go through, a portal opened in the middle of the river.

"I'll make sure she knows of your kindness," Gibborim promised Lexi.

"After what I saw down there, it might not matter, but make sure she knows we don't want to war with the giants, and nothing like this will *ever* happen again."

"I promise she'll know. I'd like to take our king with me."

"Of course."

"And his head."

"You can have it, but it's in the Lord's solar."

"Do you know where that is?"

"No," Lexi admitted.

"I'll return for it. For now, I think it's best to take my sister home."

"Of course." Lexi shifted her attention to the dragons. "Please carry her through before returning."

"We will," Alina said.

Water poured from the king's body when Gibborim lifted him from the ground. Lexi swallowed the bile in her throat when the king's flesh sloshed and water poured out of the hole in his neck.

She wasn't built for this.

"Thank you," Gibborim said.

With his brother-in-law slung over his shoulder, Gibborim strode proudly through the portal with his queen at his side. Once the dragons were safely back in Dragonia, Lexi closed the portal.

"We have to find his head," Lexi said, though none of them had time to search the palace. "Then we'll send word for Gibborim to retrieve it."

"Let's hope his head keeps them satisfied, and they don't try to kill us," Orin said.

"Their queen lives," Varo said. "They might take that good news and help us start a new world with it."

Only a couple of days had passed, but Varo had lost weight since the war with the Lord, his mother's death, and Cole's loss. Dark circles rimmed his white-blue eyes; judging by their size, Lexi didn't think he'd slept.

His shoulders were hunched forward as if he was trying to disappear. Uncertain of how to draw him out, when she was barely surviving herself, Lexi rested her hand on his arm. She hoped it gave him a small measure of comfort.

A small, sad smile twitched at the corners of Varo's mouth as his fingers found hers. It wasn't much, but it gave her some hope they would both be okay.

"I have some good news for you." When they all looked at him, her dad smiled. "He's in rough shape, but Maverick is alive."

For a second, Lexi wasn't sure she heard him right, but then Kaylia and Sahira laughed, and Brokk released a whoop of laughter. Joy burst through Lexi as what he'd said sank in.

"Take me to him."

CHAPTER FOURTEEN

Lexi knelt beside Maverick's badly burned body in the infirmary. Multiple beds took up space in the vast room located in a separate wing of the first floor.

There weren't as many here as she would have liked, but they'd retrieved a few dozen survivors from the battlefield. Some had already healed enough to leave, but most remained as crones, witches, and light fae cared for them.

Some witches and light fae were already placing healing compresses over Maverick. She barely recognized Cole's uncle; every part of him was burnt, blistered, and blackened.

Beneath his badly burned eyelids, the whites of his chestnut-colored eyes were all she could see. Then his eyes rolled down, and agony radiated from them before they were gone again.

"Maverick," she breathed.

She went to rest a hand on his arm but was scared she'd hurt him more if she did as a rough, moaning gurgle issued from his throat. The sound was one of death and suffering.

"Oh, Maverick."

Behind her, his pack shifted uneasily, and one of them

growled. They were worse than caged wolves as they sought to protect their alpha.

"Watch it," Orin warned. "None of us did this to him. We're all trying to help, but she is *the* queen, and if you lose control in here, we'll kill you."

"Do you think you could, dark fae?" one sneered.

"I *know* I could."

"That's enough!" Lexi snapped. "I won't tolerate any fighting here. This is the infirmary; there are *many* injured here, and nothing will hurt them again. If you're going to fight, then leave."

"We're not leaving our alpha unprotected," another lycan said.

"No one here is trying to hurt him; we're all helping."

The lycan shifted his eyes to Orin. "The dark fae *never* help."

"We *all* worked together to reclaim this realm, and we will continue to do so," Lexi said. "After what we've all been through, I won't tolerate *any* fighting between us. Now, it's time for all of you to leave. He has to rest, and we'll help him heal."

"I'm not going anywhere," another lycan said.

Lexi rose to stare up at the mountain of a man. "I am the queen of the Shadow Realms; I have given you an order, and you *will* obey it. Get out of this room. You can stay in the hall, but I won't have volatile lycans in this room. Get. Out."

With those last two words, flames rose from Lexi's fingertips to her wrists. Outside, the dragons bellowed; a shadow fell across the room when one landed against the side of the palace. Its head poked through the large window.

Besides letting in a lot of light, Lexi now understood why the palace's windows were so big. The dragon's talons bit into the palace's walls as his golden eyes narrowed on the lycans.

Another shadow fell across the room before a blue dragon landed on another windowsill. A green dragon soon occupied the third window. It was small enough to get most of its upper body through the window.

The green dragon leaned its head in so far, his nose nearly touched a lycan. A puff of smoke twisted from its nostrils as it bared its mouthful of flesh-rendering teeth.

Lexi had no doubt the dragons would tear the windows apart and be in this room if a lycan moved toward her. And they were strong enough and fast enough to do it in seconds.

Ever since claiming the arach throne, Lexi had felt a connection to all the dragons; apparently, they felt one to her too. They must have sensed a shift in her mood, and they'd come to her.

Lexi smiled as she rested her hand on the green dragon's neck, but she didn't tell it to back down. Orin smirked as the lycans paled.

No one else in the room dared to move or breathe while they waited to see what the shapeshifters would do.

One of the lycans finally took a step back. "We'll be *right outside,* in the hall. If anything goes wrong, we'll return."

"We'll keep you updated on his condition and do *everything* we can to save him," Lexi vowed.

When the lycans retreated, she looked to Orin, Brokk, and her dad. "It's probably best if you leave too. Having healers in here alone with Maverick is bad enough for them. Having you here is making it worse. The three of you can't help with this."

She didn't include Varo as he was half light fae and could help here. Plus, she believed he needed something to do, some way to help. She hoped it would help him heal.

Her dad kissed her forehead. "We'll be right outside."

The three of them left the room. When the door shut behind them, Lexi turned off the fire crackling along her arms and turned to the dragons.

"Thank you," Lexi said, "but you can go now too."

They chuffed, and the green one nudged her with his head before they all took flight.

CHAPTER FIFTEEN

ORIN LEANED against the wall and kept his head bowed as he propped his foot on the wall behind him. Despite his casual posture, he was acutely aware of the lycan pacing across from him and the others hovering around the door.

He disliked the lumbering beasts and the tension they emanated. He never understood why beings such as these allowed their emotions to rule them. The idiots would one day die because of it.

A step in the hall drew his attention as another lycan rounded the corner and stalked toward him. Except, this wasn't a member of Maverick's pack; Daphne had lived with him in the prison realm.

When she spotted the other lycans, she stopped and waved him over to her. Orin pushed himself away from the wall and strode down to meet her.

"What is it?"

She glanced past him as she spoke in a whisper. "Your brother has been spotted."

He forgot his irritation with the lycans as he stiffened. He still had three living brothers, but she could only be talking about one of them. He'd sent out word that he'd reward all who came to him with valid information on Cole.

"Where?" he demanded.

"Aurora."

Orin's eyebrows shot up at this revelation. He wouldn't have been surprised to find any other dark fae or immortal there, but *not* Cole, not even in his vengeful, shadow-enshrouded state.

He sure as shit didn't want to experience it, but he'd seen the love his brother possessed for Lexi. There weren't enough shadows in *all* the realms to make Cole stray from her.

But maybe he *could* be wrong on occasion. *Nah, not possible.*

"Are you sure it was Cole?" he asked.

"Yes, they're saying he left a massacre in his wake."

"So, he wasn't there for sex?"

The woman frowned at him. "How would I know?"

"You know about this."

"Only because the talk of it is spreading throughout the realms. Whatever he did in Aurora was bad enough to scare the immortals there. They're terrified of him, and that fear is spreading through the realms."

Orin rubbed his chin. "They should be, and it should."

Turning, Orin studied Brokk and Del while he pondered her words. He preferred to work alone, but he couldn't keep this from them. They would only hear about it soon enough anyway.

When he waved them over, they stepped away from the door and strode down the hall to join him. Orin wiggled his fingers at them when the lycans turned to watch. They scowled in return.

"What is it?" Brokk asked as they stopped before him.

"Cole has made an appearance," Orin said.

"Where?" Del demanded.

Orin hesitated; he wasn't sure how the vamp would take hearing that his future son-in-law was at one of the most notorious sex palaces in the realms, but if he didn't tell Del, someone else would.

They might be able to keep it from Lexi, at least for a little bit, but Del knew too many immortals. He would hear about it soon enough.

"At Aurora," Orin said.

Brokk's mouth parted, and Del scowled. "What was he doing *there*?"

"Apparently, scaring the shit out of everyone."

"They say he tore them apart," Daphne whispered.

Orin gave a dismissive wave of his hand. "Been there, seen that. It's his new favorite pastime. We all need a hobby."

Brokk rolled his eyes while Del swore, and Daphne chuckled uneasily.

"We have to go to Aurora," Del said.

Orin wasn't sure if the vamp wanted to go because he intended to see the wreckage Cole left behind, to find his future son-in-law, or to learn if that son-in-law had cheated on his fiancée.

Nothing astonished him anymore, but he'd be *stunned* if Cole cheated on Lexi while there. His brother was completely out of his mind and ruled more by shadows than himself, but he was a faithful lunatic.

Orin couldn't see Cole turning to anyone other than Lexi. Not only was she his mate, and lycans *never* strayed from their mates, but she was also the love of his life. However, if by some miracle he happened to be wrong, things could get ugly with Del.

He couldn't order Del to stay here, but he could give him a reason to. "The lycans are still outside the door; wouldn't you prefer to stay with Lexi?"

"The dragons have that under control," Del replied. "We should go now so we can return before Lexi finishes with Maverick."

Orin wouldn't argue with him, but they couldn't leave the door unprotected with those hairy beasts pacing about. He had no doubt Brokk was coming too; nothing would stop him from tracking down Cole, so he turned to Daphne.

"Are there any other immortals from the prison nearby?"

"Yes."

"Go and get them and come right back."

Daphne bent her head before hurrying away to find some of the others who had followed him in the prison realm.

CHAPTER SIXTEEN

Half an hour later, they stood outside Aurora with their heads tipped back to gaze at the top of an eight-foot dildo. *A dick that size must be meant for giants,* Orin decided.

However, there were plenty of immortals with some unusual talents. But still… he tilted his head to examine the penis before deciding it was definitely a giant's play toy.

No one had *that* unusual a talent with dildos. He would have found them and bedded them by now if they did.

Once he confirmed that in his mind, he examined the metal piercing at the top of the fake cock. Part of the piercing protruded through Alston's eye socket. His black eye, which popped out when Cole shoved the piercing through it, lay in front of the penis. The dead fae's mouth hung ajar.

In front of the dildo, written in Alston's blood, Cole had scrawled, *Traitors will die*, on the stones.

Simple but effective, Orin decided.

"Well, now," Orin drawled with a chuckle. "You don't see that every day."

"It's not funny," Brokk said.

"Oh, yes, it is. Alston was always a dickhead; now he's literally one, which makes it more funny."

A smile tugged at the corners of Brokk's mouth before he suppressed it.

"Let's find out what else Cole did while he was here," Del said.

"I think you can relax; I don't think it was any women. He may not be the Cole we all knew anymore, but I bet he came here because of Lexi. The shadows whisper to him and tell him things none of us could ever know. Alston always wanted power; I bet he assumed Lexi was weaker without Cole and would be easy pickings."

Del didn't reply or look back as he made his way into Aurora. None of the dancers were on the balconies or roof. To Orin's disappointment, no one threw pasties at him when they entered the building.

Some of the shadow kissed and assorted sex workers were still in the building, but they wore more clothes than normal. Considering death and destruction were everyday events for immortals, especially during the Lord's reign, it was strange how abnormally subdued they were.

"What happened here?" Brokk inquired.

"Something really scared them," Orin replied.

He'd stated the obvious, but felt he had to say something to fill the silence enshrouding a room normally reverberating with moans and hedonistic calls of pleasure. This unnerved him more than nearly being killed by a wendigo.

Del walked straight over to a shadow kissed human. "What happened here?"

The woman's lower lip quivered. "I didn't see him; I didn't know he was there, and suddenly, he was beside me... with a *head*. And the shadows...." Her eyes darted around as if the shadows were still there. "They were everywhere. They hissed.

They… they….." She leaned closer to Del and lowered her voice. "They *whispered* things."

"What did they whisper?"

"That traitors will perish, and we would be next if we continue to harbor them. I've never been so scared in my life."

Del leaned back as he surveyed the room. Orin didn't bother to look around him; if it was possible, and his brother could leave shadows behind to monitor things, Cole already knew they were there.

He tried not to reveal his uneasiness over the possibility. But if Cole had known Alston was here, plotting, then he could use the shadows to monitor the realms. Which meant he most likely had shadows in Dragonia too.

"Did any of you see him?" Brokk asked.

"I did," another woman said.

Orin studied the shadow kissed woman as she rose from a table and took a couple of tentative steps toward Del. Her face was so pale it was nearly translucent; her hands clenched at her sides.

"I saw him when he came in. He wasn't the Cole I knew. Not the one who… who made me feel so good. And then, he vanished. One second, he was there, and the next, he'd vanished down the hall. Screams soon followed from the back room."

Despite her words, some of the tension eased from Del, and his shoulders relaxed as he gave a brisk nod; Cole hadn't come here to cheat on his daughter. He turned back to Orin and Brokk before jerking his head toward the hall.

"Thank you," Del said to the woman before striding past her.

No one spoke as they walked down the hall and passed the closed doors that harbored abnormally hushed rooms on the other side. The last door was broken and open to the back room beyond. They moved deeper into the room before finding what they had come for.

Before entering the Lord's throne room after the war, the

sight that greeted them would have shocked Orin. While his stomach turned a little, he felt nothing else as he surveyed the blood-splattered walls and mutilated carcasses.

What his brother now did to immortals was something he'd never seen before, but it was effective. No one survived the wrath of Cole… or, he should say, the shadows.

"We have to get him back," Orin said.

"Before he destroys the realms?" Brokk asked.

"He won't destroy the realms unless Lexi dies, and none of us will let that happen, but this"—Orin waved a hand around the room—"this isn't Cole. This is the shadows *ruling* him. He sacrificed himself for the realms. We *have* to get him back."

"You won't hear any arguments from me," Del said.

"How do we do that when we have no idea where he is or where he'll strike next?" Brokk asked.

Orin kicked aside a shoe with a foot still inside it as he stepped into the room. "I'll find him. You two should return to Dragonia and protect Lexi; I'll search for him. If it's the last thing I do, I'll bring him home."

CHAPTER SEVENTEEN

Lexi trudged through the halls with her dad and Brokk at her sides. She wanted to tell them to go to sleep, she would be fine, but it would be pointless.

There was no way they would let her wander this place alone, especially after what they'd revealed about Cole and why he'd slaughtered a member of the dark fae council. It didn't astonish her to learn Alston had plotted against her; there were probably numerous other immortals out there scheming to bring her down.

She was young, she didn't have a large army, and she'd never ruled anywhere or been taught to rule anything. She didn't blame her dad and Sahira for this; they did their best.

Her family sought to keep her protected and alive, and so they did. There was no way they could have foreseen that she might, one day, have the ability to help bring down the Lord. They never could have anticipated Cole entering her life and giving her the ability to forge an army and rebellion.

But now, the other immortals saw her as weak, especially without Cole. Many of those immortals would fear and respect him, even if they considered her an easy target.

She *would* prove them wrong, but they would have to attack for her to do that. And if they attacked, there would be more fighting and death, the two things she'd hoped to avoid by taking the throne.

Eventually, those who plotted against her would learn she wasn't a weakling and be too afraid to attack, but immortals were stubborn and prideful. By the time that happened, more lives would be lost.

Lexi tried not to let the idea this had all been pointless niggle at the back of her mind. Yes, the realms would be more stable and safer without a madman on the throne, but if some immortals continued to attack, they would constantly undermine that stability.

They would constantly undermine *her*, and she wouldn't allow that. Fisting her hands, she kept her chin high.

If they continued to attack, she'd make them regret coming for her, and so would Cole, but where was he? What was his state of mind? And could he ever come back from all of this?

She sure hoped so, but the more he gave in to the shadows' darker impulses, the harder it would be for him. Lexi wished she could see him; there had to be something she could do to help, if he'd give her a chance, but she suspected the shadows were working to keep him from her.

So, she had to focus on a problem she could solve—making sure her enemies didn't succeed in taking the throne from her. The dragons would protect her, and she did have a small army of those who remained after the war.

She wasn't sure how much she could trust them all, but Lexi had to have faith in them, or she'd become a paranoid psycho like the Lord. With the death of Alston, Cole had made it clear he was still destroying any who were a danger to her, so that might make some back off.

Lexi doubted he could get them all, but he would find some of them, and she would take down any who entered Dragonia.

Until they eradicated all threats and firmly established her rule in Dragonia, they would insist she always had a guard at her side.

And the dragons would also be there to protect her. Shadows crossed the windows and fell across the stony floor as the dragons followed them through the halls.

While they were a *big* deterrent to any who might try to harm her, they wouldn't keep everyone at bay. Enough of them would think they could get past the dragons and to her.

Lexi had known taking over the rule of Dragonia would be challenging, but she was tired of this endless battle. *When* would it all stop?

It might never stop.

That sad truth whispered through her mind. One endless threat after another and one enemy after another could be how she spent the rest of her life.

Lexi closed her eyes, took a deep breath, and tried to focus on the good in her life right now. Maverick looked a lot better by the time she left him.

He'd settled into a deep sleep; his skin, while not healed, was a deep red color instead of that crispy, burnt awfulness it was before she and the others started working on him. It would take time before he fully healed, but he'd survive.

Her healing ability had done wonders on him. However, the damage was so extensive that unlike Morgan, the little witch whose life she'd saved, she couldn't heal him completely.

They'd also uncovered Niall's sword. It wasn't exactly great news, but it was something. They had nothing else of the man left except a bloody footprint in the ground; they could at least bury his sword.

Varo had already taken it back to the Gloaming, where they would inter it with others who the dark fae held in high esteem. When the time came, he would get a hero's burial.

Tears pricked her eyes, and the lump in her throat made breathing difficult. She missed her friend.

"We have to build what remains of our army faster," her dad said.

"How do we do that?" Lexi asked.

"Money. The Lord amassed a lot of it; we'll have to pay well."

"Money doesn't buy loyalty," Brokk said.

"No, that will come when they see how great Lexi is as queen. But money will keep them happy, and it's a start," her dad said.

Lexi was glad he had so much faith in her because she sure didn't. She was doing this because she had to, but she was far from great and didn't know if she ever would be.

"Money is a start," Lexi agreed. "I guess we should find where the Lord kept it."

"Varo and I will look for it tomorrow," Brokk said.

When they passed the gardens, Lexi stopped to look at the dead world beyond the arched doorways. Cole had told her about the hideous fountain in the garden's center.

She couldn't see it from here, but at least, with no new blood to fuel it, the fountain had stopped running. It would never run again.

Even if blood never flowed through its pipes again, she would always know what it once held and represented. One day, when she had more time and fewer death threats, she would help return the garden to its former glory. She would also have that fountain ripped out.

Lexi turned away from the garden and continued toward her room. She missed her manor, cozy room, and the warmth of her home.

This place was all cold stone. No portraits or decorations broke the barren space. Only the sparsely placed golden statues remained in any of the halls.

The Lord had commanded the removal of the things that had probably made this space more inviting. He'd kept the things worth money, which only made the place feel colder to her.

With its vast size, Lexi doubted this place could ever feel cozy. But it didn't matter because it was *her* home now, and she would make it feel like one... when she had the time, if there was ever time again.

No matter what, she would turn it into a home where she could relax and feel comfortable. She would make it a place where her children—

Lexi abruptly cut off those musings. Without Cole, there would be no children, and she wasn't sure Cole would ever be at her side again.

She hoped that one day he would regain control of the shadows and come back to her, but after everything he'd experienced, he wouldn't return the same. But she wasn't the same either, and she never would be.

Lexi reached the stairs leading to her room. It wasn't the royal suite; she'd never sleep anywhere the Lord once rested his head. Besides, she craved something smaller that she could one day make her own.

When they arrived at the second floor, she left the stairwell and strode down the hall with its gray stone floor and white, barren walls. This section of the palace had all the warmth of a tomb, but she was so exhausted her first night here that she couldn't bring herself to climb more than one flight of stairs.

Now, she didn't have the energy to locate another room she might like better. She didn't care as long as she had a place to sleep that didn't remind her of the Lord.

When she arrived at the first door, she kissed her dad on the cheek. "I love you. Good night."

"I love you too," he said gruffly. "Sleep well."

They both knew that wouldn't happen, but she turned to Brokk and squeezed his arm. "Good night."

"Good night."

Lexi entered the room and closed the door behind her. The lights in the sconces on the walls danced like flames, but some other energy fueled the light source.

She didn't know what that energy was, probably some form of arach magic. Lexi had no idea how to create that magic or bring it forth, but she felt it running throughout Dragonia. She'd tapped into it when she ascended the throne and sealed her connection to the dragons.

Her room was small, but unlike most of this palace, it felt cozy. A yellow blanket covered the bed, the walls were a pale shade of rose, and the windows across the way looked upon Dragonia's valleys and mountains.

Bones from the dragons' feeding once littered those mountaintops, but the war with the Lord had knocked many of them free. Craggy, rocky peaks stretched high into the sky, lit by stars and moon. Some mountains still had bones on them, but Lexi couldn't see them from here.

A small bathroom decorated in sage green was to her right. As the dragons called to each other and a piece of her soul, Lexi padded into the bathroom. All she wanted was a shower and bed.

CHAPTER EIGHTEEN

STANDING in the corner of her room, Cole watched Lexi while she slept. He shouldn't have come here; it was the last thing he'd planned on doing tonight, but he hungered for her so badly it had become a physical pain.

Over the past two weeks, he'd driven himself mad as he resisted seeing her. And tonight, the thin thread of control he'd maintained over his restraint broke.

She was safe; the shadows reported that to him all the time, but it had stopped being enough to keep him away. He *had* to see her; not even the shadows, or the knowledge of how bad this idea was, could stop him.

Two weeks had passed since he left her behind. Every day, the dark fae and lycan part of him became increasingly louder as they clamored for her. The lycan sought its mate, the dark fae was ravenous, and the man's heart ached to hold the one he loved.

The shadows were the only part of him against coming here. They ranted against it, but as the days passed, their protests were buried further beneath the needs of the fae and lycan.

He kept himself cloaked in shadows as he drank in her magnificent auburn hair sprawled across her pillow. The deep red strands stood out vividly in the moonlight streaming through her open windows.

He wanted to run the silken strands of her hair through his fingers and inhale her strawberry aroma. Over the past two weeks, he spent hours recalling every detail of her, what she felt like against him, beneath him, and on top of him.

The vivid, hunter green of her eyes, with their vibrant emerald flecks, haunted his dreams. No matter how much the shadows tried, they couldn't bury those memories.

Those memories didn't do the woman justice. Her beauty and sensuality were far more alluring in person.

He lifted his hands to examine his palms. Blood didn't stain them anymore; he'd scrubbed himself before coming here, but he couldn't erase the countless lives he'd taken.

And he didn't regret any of them. He'd slaughter everyone in all the realms, if it meant keeping her safe, even if every death pushed him closer and closer to becoming one of the shadows.

The shadows bobbed enthusiastically up and down while they rejoiced over his conviction. Tonight, he'd destroyed a group of warlocks, but their thirst for blood never eased. They'd mistakenly plotted to kill Lexi and take the throne from her.

The shadows laughed throughout the slaughter, and Cole smirked as he watched the men fall. Together, they'd eradicated this new menace, but countless others remained. He would find and destroy them all.

But he was becoming more of a monster than a man. His love for her, and a few others, were the only things keeping any piece of his humanity intact.

Cole's head turned toward the door, and shadows slithered beneath it as the guards outside spoke in low murmurs before falling silent again. They didn't know he was here, and they never would.

His attention shifted to the windows; the shadows had carried him up to them. Some dragons circling the palace might have seen him enter, but they wouldn't interfere.

No matter how much the shadows craved killing, the Shadow Reaver wasn't dangerous to them, and especially not to her. She was the one they sought to protect, though they worried she could take him from them.

When his attention shifted back to Lexi, a force he couldn't resist pulled him toward her. She was the sun, and he was the earth, moon, and every other thing caught in her gravitational pull.

He simply wanted to touch her before leaving.

Cole stopped beside her bed and gazed at her before lifting the silken strands of her hair. As it slid through his fingers, it was as comforting and familiar as he remembered.

When the shadows encompassed her, he tried to pull them away. Cole didn't like them touching her, but they were also drawn to her.

Finally, he reeled them back, and his jaw clenched as he restrained them from her. These murderous things wouldn't touch her. He was certain they'd never harm her, but their darkness would never know the feel of her flesh.

Cole retracted the shadows further before retreating to the corner of the room. They enveloped him while they whispered their demands for her.

Outside, a dragon roared. Cole's head turned to the window, and his senses went on high alert as the shadows slid toward the sound. They probed the night as Lexi stirred.

Cole froze when Lexi blinked; the dragon roared again, and she sat up. Her attention shifted to the window, and her heart beat so loud he could hear it. In response, the shadows turned toward her.

Cole ached to comfort and assure her it would be all right,

but he didn't move. If he moved, he didn't think he could maintain control.

Everything in him screamed for her. The dark fae was starving, and the lycan had been denied its mate for too long. It didn't help that the full moon's pull only increased the lycan's need for its mate.

Outside, the dragon quieted, and when no others picked up its cry, the night grew hushed again. Lexi threw aside her blanket and sheets, swung her legs out of bed, and rose.

The green tunic she wore caused his breath to hitch. It was *his*.

Despite the fact she looked ethereal, beautiful, and oh-so-tempting in his too-big shirt, that wasn't the reason air stopped entering his lungs. He stopped breathing because he realized how much she hurt, how much *he* hurt her.

She slept in his things because she missed him, and he couldn't be with her.

He'd washed away the blood that so recently stained his hands, but the memory of it burned into his flesh. It served as a reminder of what he'd become.

The shadows that incessantly whispered of death were muted around her, but they were always there, always talking, and *always* demanding more. They would never be satisfied or quenched, and he couldn't let them near her.

When she turned away from the window, her eyes landed on the corner where he stood. Her beautiful green eyes were luminous in the night; the moon bathed her in its silver radiance, but her shield remained in place, so she didn't glow.

"Cole?" she whispered.

At first, he didn't move. She wasn't sure he was here; he'd heard the uncertainty in her voice.

He could slip away from here, and she'd never know, but it would be cowardly. No matter what he was now, and he was *many* things, he wasn't a coward.

Besides, he had to warn her about the threats to her life. Lexi had to know that until he eradicated all of them, she could only be with those she trusted completely.

Slowly, he unraveled the shadows to reveal himself to her.

CHAPTER NINETEEN

Lexi's hand flew to her mouth as the shadowed corner of her room unfolded like some alien plant opening to reveal what lay within. One minute there was nothing, and the next, Cole stood there.

Except, it was a Cole she didn't recognize. The dark beard he'd always kept neatly trimmed was scruffier. The tips of his pointed ears poked through hair that had grown longer and shaggier.

His nudity revealed all the ciphers he allowed to remain visible to the public eye. The black markings ran from his fingertips, up his arms, and across his shoulders. The ends of a few of the flame-like markings also touched his chin.

Though she couldn't see them, she knew from tracing them countless times more ciphers ran across his shoulder blades, down his back, and stopped at his waist. The ciphers covered him from head to toe when he wasn't keeping some of them cloaked.

He was thinner than when she last saw him. Not too much more, but on his broad, powerful frame, the weight loss was noticeable.

He's not feeding, she realized.

Perhaps he was still eating, but the dark fae part of him hadn't fed since they were last together. The possibility he might go to another woman to ease the hunger of the dark fae had never occurred to her.

It simply wouldn't happen.

No matter how hungry he became and how much he lost himself to the shadows, a part of *her* Cole would always remain. That part would never stray from her, but it was taking a toll on him, as evidenced by his thinner cheeks and silver eyes.

The shadows may hold the most control over him, but the dark fae and lycan struggled to the forefront. The full moon wouldn't help him control his wolf.

There was so much she had to know and tell him, but the words froze in her throat. A million thoughts and desires raced through her mind as she stared at him.

Like the last time she saw him, shadows slithered across his skin. The ones blackening the whites of his eyes made the silver of them impossibly vivid.

The shadows creeping like tendrils of fog across his skin terrified her. They vanished only to be replaced by more. They were trying to take him over, but they hadn't succeeded… at least not yet.

And she couldn't let them win. This was Cole, the man she loved. He was suffering, and he was doing so because he'd sacrificed himself for all of them.

"Cole," she breathed.

When she stepped toward him, the shadows rose like the dragons when they were defending her. Like the dragons, these things were his protectors and hers, but whereas she had some command over the dragons who guarded this realm, Cole ceded most of his control to the shadows when he welcomed them into him.

And once again, she felt as distant from her arach ancestors as she did from the sun. Those horrible predecessors did this to him when they created the Shadow Reaver magic.

But he hadn't lost complete control; some of *him* remained, or he wouldn't be here. Which meant she still had a chance to save him.

"They're plotting against you," he said.

She barely recognized his voice. It had come out in that horrible, guttural way it did when they stood on the cliff overlooking Dragonia.

"I know, but we always knew there would be those who would. The throne might never be completely secure, but it's mine and will remain that way while I live."

"I won't let anything happen to you."

"I know, but you should come back. We work better together; we always have."

"We can't come back."

Lexi winced when he said "*we*." The shadows, those hideous things, *refused* to let him go, and now they were making sure she knew it.

There had to be some way to break through and loosen their hold on him. The lycan and dark fae were warring for control, but they'd always warred against each other.

She suspected those two pieces of him despised the shadows. The dark fae thrived on emotion, control, and power, the lycans were never submissive, but the shadows sought to control them.

And, if there was one thing *both* parts of him wanted... it was *her*. And she could give him that.

CHAPTER TWENTY

FEELING A LITTLE LIKE A SACRIFICIAL LAMB, she grasped the bottom of his tunic and pulled it over her head. With a soft rustle, it fell to the floor.

Lexi thrust back her shoulders as she stood naked before him. Cole's breath sucked in; she hadn't believed it possible, but the silver of his eyes burned brighter in the moonlight.

The shadows danced and swayed around him; some of them floated toward her before he reeled them back in. And *that* was when she realized the *shadows* wanted her too.

She had no idea what those things would do to her, but they also sought her out. She suppressed a shudder at the thought of those things touching her, but it didn't matter; she would let them if it saved him.

What if there's no way to ever separate them? What if this is what he is from now on?

Lexi tried to shove aside the possibility, but it refused to relent. She'd believed she would find a way to bring him back, but she might not be able to.

There was a chance this was who Cole was now, who he would always be.

And she would love him anyway. But she didn't think that would happen.

He'd come here tonight, something he couldn't do a week ago. He now stood before her, looking as if he would devour her as his gaze raked her body.

His hands clenched and unclenched, and bones popped as claws extended before retracting again. The lycan was seeking to dominate the shadows, and she hoped it won.

"You have no idea what you're playing with," the shadows hissed.

"Am I playing with fire?"

"Yes."

"Fire doesn't burn me."

The shadows wanted her, but they also feared her; she saw that when they recoiled from her words. If there was something to fear from her, the shadows could be defeated... or maybe brought under control a little more.

"Lexi," Cole breathed.

Tears pricked her eyes and burned her throat as his much-loved voice broke through the shadows. She'd longed to hear that voice for the past two weeks and *yearned* to see him again.

He was a dream in the sea of nightmares that had plagued her since the end of the war. She often woke, covered in sweat, and unable to catch her breath as she found herself back in the Lord's throne room over and over again, except, this time, he defeated them.

In some of her dreams, she watched Cole and all those she loved die. In others, she ran through endless halls covered in blood, searching for Cole, her dad, and Sahira, and unable to find them.

But the dreams that haunted her waking moments were the ones where countless immortals pointed at her and booed. She stood before them in the arach crown as they called her a failure, a pretender, and blamed her for failing them.

And she woke with the knowledge that, while the Lord was dead and couldn't torment anyone again, she could fail. One wrong move and she could let down every immortal in all the realms.

The Lord never worried about that, but she did. The weight of it was beating her down, but here, with Cole, she didn't feel as battered. She felt hopeful, happy, and *loved*.

"You have no idea the things I've done," he said.

"The things we've *all* done. I've killed too." And those deaths also plagued her at night.

"We *enjoy* it," the shadows murmured.

Lexi closed her eyes at this admission; he'd always been a killer, always done his duty, but when she first met him, those deaths haunted him. They didn't seem to anymore.

Would that change if the shadows relinquished their fight for control over him? Or had they forever altered him?

"I love you no matter what," she told him.

"You shouldn't love a monster."

"If you're the monster you believe yourself to be, then you wouldn't hesitate. I can see how hungry the dark fae is, and it's impossible to hide a lycan's desire for its mate. If you were truly a monster, you would already be on me, taking me as I'm offering myself to you."

When the shadows released an angry, guttural sound, Lexi realized she'd struck a nerve. The dark entities slid closer to her but didn't touch as they hovered around her body.

They were so close she wouldn't have to move an inch to touch one, but they didn't connect with her. Instead, they became a darkness swirling beside her.

Anger etched Cole's features as he strode toward her, and his joints continued to pop and crack. His fangs lengthened until they were outlined against his compressed lips.

"You don't think I'm a monster? I'll prove it to you," he said, and his voice mingled with the shadows again.

His hands grasped her biceps, and his eyes burned as the black slithered faster beneath his skin. The lycan sought to break free as his claws grazed her flesh.

He was a terrifying sight to behold; anyone else would have run screaming from him, but she didn't flinch. He didn't scare her, and he never would.

Lifting her chin, Lexi stared defiantly back at him. "Then prove it."

CHAPTER TWENTY-ONE

When Cole first grabbed her, he'd meant to make her understand. He'd meant to *show* her how volatile and broken he was.

The second his skin connected with hers, the vengeance and bloodlust driving him since he welcomed the shadows into his body, calmed. She didn't completely quiet the storm but turned a tumultuous hurricane into a windy day.

He could almost breathe again without feeling like the shadows would tear him apart and unleash devastation upon the realms.

He still wasn't entirely in control, the lycan, dark fae, and shadows continued to war against each other as each sought to claim something from her.

He knew what the dark fae and lycan sought; he had no idea what the shadows sought. Whatever it was, they wouldn't get it. If it was the last thing he did, he would ensure that.

As he held her, Lexi stared defiantly up at him, her chin raised and her magnificent green eyes blazing with determination and love. She shouldn't have so much faith in him when he didn't have it for himself.

When he clasped her throat, she didn't flinch, and her eyes didn't waver. She was beautiful, everything about her was magnificent, and she'd become the queen the Shadow Realms deserved.

He should push her away; instead, he pulled her closer. Given what he was, what she'd seen him do, and how he held her, she should show some alarm. She didn't.

Cole didn't know if that made him love or fear for her more.

He wanted to make her pull away, hate him, and seek to start a new life without him. She should forget him and go on to live a wonderful life in this world.

It would be difficult at first; she loved him, but she was young and would learn to move on. Maybe, though it was unlikely, she could love another again.

The idea of it happening tore his heart in two, and his claws extended but didn't mark her skin. It was selfish of him, but *no one* else would ever touch or know her as he did.

And that made him more of a monster than the shadows. He could never give her the life she should have; he should set her free, but he wouldn't.

"When are you going to prove it?" she taunted.

The shadows hissed at her words, and Cole pulled her closer. He claimed her mouth in a punishing kiss that should have made her recoil from his brutality, but this valiant woman didn't.

Instead, she gripped his arms, rose on her toes, and kissed him back. She didn't try to soften or change the kiss; her kiss was as harsh, demanding, and unrelenting as his.

When her fangs sliced his lip and drew blood, his erection swelled to the point of pain. His hand tightened a little more on her throat, but she didn't push him away or lessen her kiss.

Her fangs sank into his lip and set his skin on fire. With his hand on her throat, he guided her back until her heels hit the wall.

Releasing his arms, she slid her hands around his neck and

melted against him. He could *never* forget what it was like to have her in his arms, but over the past two weeks, blood and body parts had dampened the memory.

Now, how amazingly right she felt came screaming back to him. She was the missing piece of him, and he'd *finally* found her again.

The shadows slid further away as he released her throat, grasped her wrists, and drew them over her head. He slammed them into the wall harder than he meant to, but she still arched into him.

She wouldn't be frightened away, and he didn't want her to be… even if he was on the verge of losing it. The dark fae had gone too long between feedings, and the lycan had been denied its mate for two weeks.

They both clamored to be satisfied, and she was the only one who could sate them. When he lifted her off the ground, her legs encircled his waist. Her fingers dug into his nape as she released her bite and her tongue found his.

Her hips moved, and she ground against him until he was on the edge of coming. She was already so wet as she slid against his cock, and her scent intensified on the air.

When his hands entwined in her hair, he pulled her head back to expose her throat. The pale column of it glistened in the moonlight, revealing that his last mark on her had healed and vanished.

The lycan sank his fangs into her shoulder, claiming her as his again. The serum lycans' possessed to mark their mate entered her.

Feeling more content, the lycan's bite placated some of its demand, but it wouldn't be caged again. It also wanted more.

She slid over him once more, and he grasped her hips with one hand to position her. With one thrust, he sank into her as his heart went wild.

When her tight, wet sheath clenched around his dick, he

groaned as everything suddenly felt right again, and the shadows calmed. As she moved, the energy of their joining increased, and the dark fae feasted.

Power surged through him as she eased all his needs and took as much as she gave while fucking him with abandon. They were *one* again and inseparable as ecstasy built between them.

When she came, he muffled her loud cry with his hand so they didn't attract the attention of her guards. As her head fell back, he came, but he wasn't done with her.

As soon as his shaft stopped pulsing, he turned and carried her to the bed. He was still hungry, and she was happy to let him feast again.

CHAPTER TWENTY-TWO

With whispered words of treachery, the shadows pulled Cole from sleep before the sun rose. Sometime during the night, while they slept, the shadows had reclaimed their hold on him.

Slithering beneath the surface, they whispered of death and blood as he climbed from bed and padded over to the window. He rested his hands against the cool stone sill while studying the night.

Across the land, shadows shifted and swayed beneath the moon's glow. Those shadows crept beneath his skin as they curled into his mind.

For a little while, Lexi chased them away, but they wouldn't remain at bay—not when they whispered of another danger to her. Even the dark fae and lycan halves of him wouldn't fight the shadows if it meant protecting her.

When he glanced at her, she remained sleeping soundly. His warrior, his fiancée, his love, his everything... and someone was out there plotting against her again.

But if he left here now, it would only make things worse for her. Closing his eyes, his fingers bit into the stone as he struggled to retain control of the shadows and his growing impulse to kill whoever threatened her.

For a while, as he held her, he'd believed it was over and she would keep the shadows at bay. And she had for a bit.

The shadows, while not soundless, had calmed while they were together. They raged again now, and what they whispered also infuriated the dark fae and lycan.

They sought blood, destruction, and death to the point Lexi couldn't soothe them. Someone plotted against her, and it couldn't be allowed.

Cole stepped toward her to tell her he was leaving, but the shadows dug their tendrils into his brain. He couldn't think or feel beyond the call of the mayhem he would unleash upon those who sought to take her from him.

A touch of gray gathered at the edges of the black sky as he pulled the shadows around him. He cloaked himself in their insidious embrace as they carried him out the window.

While the shadows lowered him to the ground, the heads of the nearby dragons turned toward him. He didn't know if they could see or sense him, but they didn't try to stop him when he headed for the portals of Dragonia.

Excitement pulsed through his veins, and the shadows urged him faster as he slipped into a portal and on toward the human realm. Whoever the shadows led him toward wouldn't survive to see the sunrise.

CHAPTER TWENTY-THREE

When Lexi woke, she instinctively stretched her hand out to where she last saw Cole. As her hand moved, she knew he was gone before her fingers found the cool spot beside her.

She felt his absence like she would a missing tooth. She continued to prod at the emptiness while her mind screamed at her to stop, but she couldn't fully believe he was gone.

He'd left her... again.

Her eyes squeezed closed as she struggled to suppress the tears burning her throat and eyes. If it wasn't for the pleasant soreness between her legs, and his lingering scent on the air, she might have believed she'd dreamed last night, but she knew the truth.

Besides, she didn't have such pleasant dreams anymore. They'd died beneath the bloodbath of the Lord's war and the pressure of becoming a queen.

While Cole was here, she didn't have any nightmares either. By the time they finished with each other, she was too exhausted to do anything but sleep.

Which was why she didn't notice when he slipped away.

She didn't bother to hope this was a return to when they first got together and he'd sleep somewhere else because he was afraid he'd hurt her. Then, she'd always been able to sense him nearby.

Now, emptiness filled the room.

Frustration tore through her as she shoved herself up to take in the room. As she'd known it would, emptiness greeted her. No sign of him remained.

She didn't know when he'd left, but judging by the coolness of the bed beside her and the absence of his allspice scent, it was hours ago, which only made the emptiness of the room somehow more profound.

Lexi swung her feet out of bed and sat for a minute before rising to stalk over to the window. Judging by the sun's position, she'd slept later than normal.

Dragons flew around Dragonia as she took in the vast, beautiful kingdom, the towering mountains, and the residents who hurried about their business. Even as she searched for Cole, she knew it was pointless; he was gone.

She'd mistakenly believed she'd gotten through to him last night, that she'd chased away the shadows and he would stay. She'd been wrong, and it killed her.

Lifting her face to the ceiling, Lexi blinked rapidly as tears streaked her cheeks, and she wiped them away. She would *not* cry. This wasn't over.

However, she had no idea how to save him from the shadows' nefarious clutches. She had no idea what pulled him away from her, but it had to be something major. It wouldn't surprise her to learn he'd unleashed a lot of destruction on the realms after he left.

She jumped when a knock sounded on her door and spun away from the window. She rushed to the bathroom and called, "Hold on a second."

Stepping into the small room, she turned on the water and splashed her face before leaving it behind. She opened the drawers on the sage-colored dresser with delicate legs and elegant, leaf-shaped handles.

Not caring what she wore, she removed a green, fae tunic and a pair of supple, brown pants. She'd taken to wearing the dark fae's clothes; they were comfortable and easy to move in.

Besides, she didn't have many options. All her clothes burned when the dragons set her manor on fire. They followed the Lord's orders at the time, but she still lost all her possessions.

She also pulled on a lightweight cloak and buttoned it at her throat. When she finished, she walked over to the full-length mirror in the corner. Tilting it toward her, she carefully examined her reflection to ensure the cloak hid Cole's marks.

Lexi wasn't ashamed of those marks and never would be, but she wasn't ready to explain what happened last night. And if anyone started questioning her about them, she'd end up in tears.

She refused to let that happen.

CHAPTER TWENTY-FOUR

WALKING OVER TO THE DOOR, she checked to make sure no sign of Cole remained before unlocking the door. She opened it to reveal Amaris on the other side, as well as two of her lycan guards and Brokk.

There was a chance those lycans could still smell Cole and sex, even if she couldn't, but neither of them did anything to indicate they did. If the lycan and Brokk hadn't sensed anything different last night, she should be fine now.

"Good morning," she greeted Amaris.

The pretty, dark fae woman smiled at her as she breezed into the room with a dress over her arm. Lexi frowned at the dress, but her attention was pulled from it when Kaylia strolled into the room.

"Did you forget Cela and Yamala are coming today?" the beautiful crone asked.

Lexi almost closed her eyes and groaned at the reminder of the two sirens arriving this morning. They were bringing their followers who survived the final battle with the Lord.

The sirens had helped them defeat the Lord. In return, they expected her to treat them as equals among immortals.

Lexi didn't think anything was wrong with that, which was why she and Cole agreed to the condition in return for the sirens' aid. However, many immortals saw the sirens as nothing more than vultures who couldn't handle more difficult prey and therefore focused on mortals.

That was about to change as Lexi would do everything she could to include the sirens from here on out. The women had helped them defeat the Lord and proven themselves more trustworthy and courageous than many other immortals.

Since the Lord destroyed Aerie, the realm of the sirens, before the final war, the sirens had remained in Dragonia. They resided in a little section of land high in the mountains.

Occasionally, she spotted them flying overhead, but Lexi hadn't seen much of them since the war had ended. A few days ago, Yamala sent a messenger to request an audience with her in the palace.

Lexi would have preferred not to do it; they still had so much work to do in the palace, so many things to organize and learn. She had an endless list of things to complete, but they wouldn't have defeated the Lord without the sirens' help, and she'd given her word to treat them as equals.

She couldn't say no, but she dreaded this encounter. What happened with Cole last night would only make it worse, as her nerves and emotions were so raw the air felt uncomfortable against her skin.

She didn't mind Yamala, the leader of the sirens, but she wasn't a fan of the other, more heartless women who had slaughtered countless mortals over the years. But it didn't matter who she did or didn't like; she'd entered the game of politics when she claimed the arach throne.

She would win the game.

"I did forget," she admitted to Kaylia.

When she first met the sometimes abrasive, almost always serious, and powerful woman, she never would have believed it possible that Kaylia would become a good friend, but she had. Lexi now counted the crone as one of her most trusted allies.

Kaylia stopped before the window and gazed at the land before turning to face Lexi. The sunlight streaming over her emphasized her long, silvery blonde hair.

Kaylia had separated it into two French braids that started near her temples before twisting into a bun at her nape. With her hair pulled back, Kaylia's oval face, slender nose, and pink lips were more visible. The hairstyle emphasized her beauty, the slight cleft in her chin, and the pewter of her translucent, gray eyes.

"That's okay; we've still got an hour before they arrive," Kaylia said.

"Which is plenty of time," her aunt, Sahira, said as she breezed into the room.

Sahira didn't look back as she kicked the door shut. Before it closed, Lexi glimpsed Brokk rolling his eyes before turning to one of the lycans.

The last thing Lexi wanted was to be surrounded by these three women. She truly wanted to sink into a hot bath, drop beneath the surface, and watch the world through a watery abyss.

She didn't crave death; it was the last thing she sought. She just wanted a few minutes of peace.

She wouldn't get them, and she certainly wouldn't get them if these women saw the marks on her neck, which was why she lightly slapped her aunt's hand away when she reached for the button on Lexi's cloak.

"I'll do it. Besides, I still have to shower. I'll take the dress with me and put it on afterward."

Amaris's black eyes studied Lexi in confusion. Amaris usually helped her with the dresses, or at least one of them did, as Lexi often couldn't get all the buttons on her own.

Thankfully, she'd chosen a far simpler outfit for this meeting.

It was one Amaris showed to her soon after she approved her appointment with the sirens.

"Well, go on then," Sahira urged. "Time is wasting."

Her aunt's amber eyes were questioning as Lexi took the dress from Amaris, but she didn't ask any questions. It had been a rough couple of weeks, and they understood this.

They would never know how incredibly grateful she was for that. Feeling vulnerable and on the verge of tears again, Lexi hung the dress over her arm and walked over to her aunt.

Though it was in its customary bun, a few strands of Sahira's mahogany hair had straggled free to frame her beautiful face. They tickled Lexi's face when she kissed her aunt's cheek.

"I won't be long," Lexi promised before leaving the room.

CHAPTER TWENTY-FIVE

ORIN HAD SEEN MANY, *many* things in his lengthy lifetime. Some were good, others were average, and many were horrific.

This was definitely in the upper realms of the horrific. Cole had been in an especially foul mood when he arrived here.

Orin didn't know what to say or how to react to the carnage before him. A quaint, human home on the outskirts of a city devastated by the Lord was now the site of a massacre.

It was amazing the home had survived the Lord's war, but no one would ever reside there again. And it wasn't uninhabitable because dragons or war damaged the structure; it was because all the cheery, yellow walls were drenched in blood, bones, and brains as the grayish goop slid down the wall.

Orin's eyes rebelled against everything here, but he couldn't tear them away from the massacre.

"What happened here?" Maverick muttered.

Orin glanced at the six-foot-nine lycan with broad shoulders and hands that could crush a skull. Cole's uncle had healed well since his close encounter with fire and was back on his feet.

It was too bad this was his first experience out of Dragonia and back into the realms. But it was best if the man saw how much Cole had unraveled, especially if *he* had to see it too.

Things didn't often rattle Maverick, but his chestnut brown eyes were full of revulsion. It was an odd look considering his eyelashes and eyebrows hadn't grown back from the fire yet.

Also burned off by the fire, faint stubble had replaced his dark, wavy brown hair. He'd mostly healed, but his skin still held a pinkish tint.

Orin shifted his attention back to the room as Brokk started to step forward but halted before his foot came down again. His mouth hung half open as he stared in disbelief at the room.

They all knew what happened here; they preferred not to believe it.

Orin was incredibly glad Varo hadn't been around when he learned of this newest sighting of Cole. He'd returned to Dragonia to tell Brokk about it; his brother was with Maverick then.

He shouldn't have gone back for his younger brother. He should have come here on his own.

Orin had known this was going to be bad, as the voice of the pixie who whispered about it trembled when he spoke of Cole. Orin understood why now, but at the time, he'd blown it off because the man was a pixie, and he considered them weaklings.

Brokk would want to know about this, and while Orin preferred to work alone, he wouldn't keep this from him, so he'd returned for his brother. Now he regretted it, and he rarely regretted anything.

When he put out word through the realms that he was searching for his brother and would reward anyone who reported sighting Cole, he'd expected many to come to him and a lot of false leads. But if this kept up, they'd all be too petrified to say anything.

He didn't care how much carisle he offered them to talk; they'd all run at any sign of Cole. And they wouldn't report seeing him if they were afraid of becoming the next victim.

Though to be fair, Cole only slaughtered those who were a danger to Lexi, but that could change. And looking at this mess, it might change soon; his brother was becoming more barbaric.

There was a time when Orin would have sworn Cole could never do anything like this. That time had come and gone.

"Why did he do this?" Brokk muttered.

"They must have presented a risk to Lexi," Orin answered.

"But did he have to do *this*?"

Orin was wondering the same thing. His brother had left a lot of destruction behind since embracing the shadows; this was beyond anything he'd unleashed before.

He couldn't look too closely at the wreckage, but he was pretty sure a spine and rib cage still sat in what was once a light gray chair. But that could be more brain matter sticking to the upholstery.

Orin retreated out the door. There was nothing more to learn here; Cole was gone, and whoever had been foolish enough to plot against Lexi was gone too.

CHAPTER TWENTY-SIX

MAVERICK AND BROKK followed him outside. They inhaled the crisp air, but the stench of blood lingered in Orin's nostrils.

Fall had arrived, as was evidenced by the maple leaves already turning orange and yellow. The sun streaming through the branches illuminated the fallen leaves littering the ground and swirling in the breeze.

Down the hill and dozens of miles away, the city's ruins lay in a tumbled heap. He couldn't make out many details, other than the smoke spiraling lazily into the air.

For a while, that smoke came from the still smoldering remains of the humans' lives. Now, it was from something else. Most likely, the fires of the humans trying to stay warm.

He didn't know why anyone stayed in that forsaken place, but some humans were determined to forge new lives there. *Idiots.*

But someone else could also be hiding there. "Do you think Cole would hide in one of the decimated human cities?"

No one would expect to find him there. It's the last place *he* would ever think to see Cole, and therefore a good hiding spot.

Brokk's brow furrowed as he studied the distant

metropolitan. "No. I think he's still in Dragonia. He can't be around Lexi or any of us right now, but he won't go far from her."

"He's taking out her enemies," Maverick said.

"Even with them gone, he's still her main protector; he won't go far from her. I've been thinking about this a lot, and I can almost guarantee he's found a place to hide *in* Dragonia."

Orin tapped his chin while he pondered this. With his inability to open portals in and out of the realm, it would be more foolish and difficult for Cole to remain in Dragonia, and his brother was far from stupid.

However, Orin wasn't thinking like an idiot in love because he would *never* be one. He was thinking like a killer, which was something he would *always* be. His brother was a killer too, but love dominated his motivations now.

"He can use the shadows to cloak his movements," Orin said.

"Exactly. He could slip right past the guards at the Dragonian portals without them ever knowing he'd been there. Once out of Dragonia, he can travel anywhere the shadows direct him to," Brokk replied.

"Where in Dragonia?" Maverick asked.

"Fuck if I know," Brokk said. "That realm is huge. I don't think he'd go far from Lexi, but there are countless caves, mountains, valleys, and who knows what else near the palace. He could be anywhere there."

"How do we draw him out?"

Orin shrugged. "Threaten Lexi's life."

"Orin," Brokk said as he glanced around. "Don't joke about that. Cole didn't have much of a sense of humor before; I'm pretty sure he has *less* of one now."

"The remains of those behind us would agree," Maverick said.

Orin ran a hand through his hair as he tugged at the ends of it. "So, how *do* we draw him out?"

Brokk shook his head. "I think you may have said the one way we could do it, but he might kill us in the process."

"So, let's put that option on hold," Maverick said.

Orin couldn't help but agree. Threatening Lexi could end up being their only option, but it would be their last resort.

"What do you think pissed him off so much about this group?" Orin asked. "I've seen a lot of what he's done recently; none of it's as bad as what happened in there. He didn't brutalize the Lord this badly."

"Hell if I know," Brokk said, "but if someone else is in his way or on his list, I almost feel sorry for them."

"So do I," Maverick murmured.

Orin didn't, but he was glad he wasn't one of them.

CHAPTER TWENTY-SEVEN

"Your Highness," Yamala greeted as she gave a small bow to Lexi.

Lexi smiled back at the woman and her entourage of sirens. Unlike the first time she met them, none of the women were in their half human/half bird form and they all wore clothes as they stood in her scrubbed throne room.

The scent of lemons permeated the room, but she could still detect the coppery tang of blood beneath it. And no amount of scrubbing could take away the scorch marks on the floor.

Sahira offered to cast a glamour over the room to cover the marks, but Lexi refused. They would forever remain a testament to the lives lost here.

Yamala's ruby red hair glistened in the rays of sun filtering through the opening in the ceiling. A dozen dragons perched on the edge of the roof. Behind Lexi, Alina curled around the throne while Astarot, Belindo, and Nithe yipped while playing at Lexi's feet.

Lexi suppressed a laugh when Nithe attempted to fly and face-planted instead. Her ass went up, and her chubby hind legs kicked in the air before Astarot grabbed her tail and pulled her down.

Alina shooed them away before settling behind the throne again. Lexi couldn't see them anymore, but they continued to yip while they played.

Standing to Lexi's right, her dad shifted and looked over his shoulder. On her other side, Varo stood ramrod straight. He exuded an aura of strength she hadn't seen from him since the war, but she suspected most of it was pretense.

He could pretend strength, but inside, like her, he was a mess.

Sahira stood beside Lexi's dad, and Kaylia stood next to Varo. It was a strong, united front, but Lexi was acutely aware of those who weren't there.

"How are you, Yamala?" Lexi inquired.

As she spoke, Nithe leapt onto the arm of her throne. The small, red dragon settled like a cat on a couch; her tail even twitched while she watched the sirens.

Behind Yamala and her brethren, Maverick's pack of lycans had spread out to line the walls. She didn't know where Maverick was, but he'd ordered his men to watch over her while he was gone.

Mixed in with the lycans were assorted witches, crones, and dwarves. Over the past two weeks, all these factions had sworn fealty to her and the throne.

She trusted them and believed they would remain loyal to her... or at least she wanted to. Words could often be empty, pretty promises.

However, everyone in this room had fought to put her on the throne. So far, none had done anything to make her distrust them. But there were few she trusted completely anymore, and most were on the dais with her.

"We are well, Your Highness," Yamala replied.

Her daughter, Cela, strode forward to stand beside her

mother. Outside of the sirens, only she and Cole knew Cela was also the Lord's daughter.

Even if she never did anything wrong, many immortals would gladly see Cela dead because of her heritage. Because of that, Lexi would take the secret to her grave... unless the sirens did something to disrupt the peace or tried to kill her; that would certainly change her perspective on things.

Her father wanted her to ask the sirens to pledge fealty to her while they were there. Lexi planned to feel them out first; an imposed vow of loyalty was almost useless.

Resting her hand on Nithe's head, Lexi ran it down the dragon's smooth scales. She preened beneath Lexi's touch.

"How are you enjoying Dragonia?" Lexi asked.

"It is a beautiful realm, my queen," Yamala replied. "We are grateful and lucky to have been invited to stay while we try to find another home. That's why we've come today."

When Lexi's hand stilled on Nithe, two puffs of smoke escaped her nose. She huffed before lying on the arm of the throne. Lexi started petting the small creature again, and the baby dragon smiled as her eyes closed.

Yamala's attention briefly shifted to the dragon before focusing on Lexi again. "We would like to return to Aerie."

Lexi's fingers stilled on Nithe. "The Lord destroyed Aerie."

Technically, the dragons under the Lord's command devastated the realm, but there was no reason to remind the sirens of that.

"It was, my queen, but we will rebuild it. Dragonia is beautiful, but it's not our home. We miss the mountains and the sea. Aerie is in ruins, but we can make it ours again."

What they missed most about the sea was luring mostly mortal, unsuspecting sailors to their deaths. Lexi disapproved of their lethal instincts, but she'd promised not to judge them and would uphold her promise.

"Aerie is your home; you're free to return to it if you choose," Lexi said.

Her father rested his hand on the arm of her throne and leaned closer to whisper in her ear. "They're acknowledging they're not free. This is their way of saying they recognize you as their ruler; they're asking your permission."

Lexi didn't look at her dad as he rose and resumed his ramrod position with his hands clasped behind his back. Lexi studied Yamala, but she knew what she had to do.

It wasn't a forced vow of fealty if the sirens came here expecting to make it. She suspected they'd done exactly that.

"You're free to go... if you swear fealty to Dragonia and me," she said.

Yamala bowed her head. "Of course, Your Highness."

Lexi's fingers curled into the arms of the throne while she kept her face impassive; she hated this part. It was degrading to her, but this vow was taken millennia before the Lord ruled here and would continue for years to come.

All the realms obeyed Dragonia; that was simply the way of things. She could change it, and she did plan on changing many things, but this was one of the things she couldn't take away.

These vows of fealty would also show a stronger, united front to all who plotted to take her down. It might not be much of a deterrent to them, but it was something.

When Yamala, Cela, and the other sirens finished swearing their loyalty to her, Lexi rose and descended the steps of the dais. Her feet were noiseless against the stone floor as she walked out to Yamala and stopped before the tall, slender woman.

She knew this wasn't how things were done, but this would be one of her changes, at least this time. The sirens helped her win the war; she owed them something too.

Extending her hand, she waited until Yamala clasped it. When she did, Lexi enfolded the siren's hand in both of hers.

"Thank you for your help against the Lord," Lexi said. "If

there is something we can do to help you rebuild Aerie, please let me know."

Yamala stared at their joined hands before resting her other palm on Lexi's. "Thank you, Your Highness. Your kindness is greatly appreciated."

"Do not mistake kindness for weakness."

Yamala smiled as her eyes met Lexi's once more. "All those who do will perish."

Lexi smiled back.

CHAPTER TWENTY-EIGHT

"So, things went well with the sirens today," Orin said as they all gathered in the small dining room to eat dinner.

"Yes," Lexi replied. "They returned to Aerie, and I'm sure they'll continue to be allies."

"That's the best one can hope for," Varo said.

Lexi focused on her dinner as she cut the chicken into small strips. Things had gone well with the sirens, but she still felt sick with anxiety and hoped Cole would return tonight.

For some reason, she didn't think he would. Whatever drew him away would keep him there... at least, for a little while.

When he grew hungry again and the lycan sought his mate, he would return. *But will he?*

And is that what I want? To be the one he comes to when he's desperate and starving?

It wasn't what she wanted, but it was either that or none of him. She wasn't sure which was worse, but at least none of him wouldn't eradicate her self-esteem the way the other option would.

With a sigh, she admitted eating was pointless and set her fork and knife down. She lifted her golden goblet of wine and sipped from the heavy cup while she gazed out the windows to her left and the deadened gardens.

At one time, this must have been a beautiful place to eat dinner, but the view left much to be desired now.

To her right, the windows looked on rolling hills leading to the bailey and the outer wall below. She couldn't hear them, but from here, she saw the merchants who had returned to selling their wares.

Those merchants remained far more hushed than she was used to, but they would eventually find their voices again. Not living in constant fear of the Lord would help them do so. Once they realized she wouldn't kill them on a whim, their apprehension would diminish.

As the sun set on the land, it cast myriad colors across the sky. All of them were beautiful and inspiring, but whereas such a spectacle would have awed her before, she experienced only sadness now.

"The dwarves have found caves in Dragonia that we would like to make into our new home," Skog said with the slightly English accent all dwarves had. "With your permission, of course, Your Highness."

His words drew Lexi back to the conversation. "If someone or something else doesn't already reside there, I don't see anything wrong with it."

"So far, we haven't found anything else living there. They're on the ground, so the dragons don't want them, and those beasts probably scared off anything else that might have lived there."

"But the dragons won't scare off the dwarves?" Sahira asked.

Skog huffed and tapped the end of his battle sword against the stone floor. He ran his hand over the length of his thick, grayish-brown beard as he puffed out his chest. "Dwarves fear nothing."

Lexi couldn't help but smile as she set her goblet on the table and twisted the stem between her fingers. Much to Orin's displeasure, Skog had become a regular face at the dinner table. Often, during the day, he was with the other dwarves, doing whatever they did, but at night he returned to the palace and them.

Lexi suspected he returned to keep an eye on her. He was looking for her to start showing signs of craziness, like those who sat on the throne before her.

But she wasn't one of those imposter Lords; she was an arach, the last rightful ruler of Dragonia. Her grandmother was once queen here, her mother a princess, and that throne was hers.

Sitting on the throne wouldn't make her insane, it wouldn't turn her into a monster, and she *would* do right by all those who helped her claim Dragonia. She didn't blame others for being diligent in their search for signs she might crack.

They would be foolish not to make sure she was okay after everything the previous Lords, especially the last one, unleashed on the realms. Their insanity had nearly destroyed them all.

Besides, the arach hadn't shown good judgment when they destroyed each other. It was smart to distrust her, but she still felt perfectly sane, as well as exhausted and heartbroken.

"When you're ready, I'd like to visit your new home," Lexi said.

"I shall inform my peers." Approval and pride shimmered in Skog's hazel eyes. "I think we will be ready for visitors within a week or two."

Lexi bit her lip to keep from laughing over the seriousness of the dwarf's words. Skog was often grumpy and never pulled his punches, but she liked the nearly five-foot-tall dwarf who was bigger than most of his brethren by about six inches. His brown skin and bald head reflected the colors of the fading sun.

"I look forward to it," she said honestly.

They all returned to eating and idle chitchat while Lexi studied the darkening night. If Cole was going to return, it would be at night, but she couldn't bring herself to rise.

She yearned for him to return but suspected it wouldn't be tonight. Once she left here, she would sit in her room, awake and waiting, only to be disappointed. So instead, she stayed and tried to focus on the conversation.

Maverick and Brokk were unusually quiet, and she'd become accustomed to Varo's silence. Sahira, Kaylia, Skog, and her dad made up for it as they discussed the growing Dragonian army.

"Lexi has decided to give much of the carisle back to the realms the Lord overtaxed, but we still have plenty enough to pay a decent salary," her dad said.

"Money can buy loyalty," Orin murmured.

"Not always," Sahira said. "If someone comes along who offers more money, they'll happily turn on Lexi."

"There aren't many who *could* offer more money, and a larger army will cut down on some of the threats against her life."

Lexi felt all their eyes shift to her, but she didn't acknowledge them. She was aware there was a giant bullseye on her back.

Instead, she rose and walked over to the window. She leaned against the wall and stared at the valley bathed in silver moonlight.

She rested her fingers on the ledge as she inhaled deeply. The air still held the hint of fire and blood from the war, but the natural aromas of grass, flowers, the deepening fall, and the crisp freshness of mountain air had started to return.

"What is that?" Orin demanded.

Lexi turned to see what he was talking about. Her stomach plummeted when she saw his eyes were riveted on her... as was everyone else's.

And they were all motionless.

CHAPTER TWENTY-NINE

"What is what?" Lexi asked in confusion.

When he rose, Orin's chair skittered across the stone floor before toppling with a bang. Lexi winced as the sound rebounded off the walls.

Anger clouded Orin's features as he stomped across the room toward her. Lexi almost backed away from him, but there was nowhere for her to go, and this was *her* home. She wouldn't be intimidated by a pissy dark fae with a bee up his ass.

"Orin," Maverick said as he rose, "careful."

Orin didn't acknowledge him as he snarled, "What is on your neck?"

Lexi's blood ran cold. She still wore the cloak to hide Cole's marks on her, but in the moonlight, they would glow silver. The cloak didn't hide the radiance of his bite.

Throwing her shoulders back, Lexi lifted her chin as Orin loomed over her. He wasn't as tall as Cole, but he was still a good eight inches over her five-seven height. Still, she refused to be intimidated by him.

She had enough shit to deal with without adding his crap to the mix.

"Who did you *fuck*?" Orin exploded.

Lexi recoiled as if he'd slapped her.

"Was it one of your lycan guards? Did you invite one of them into your room last night? Is *that* why my brother was so pissed?"

Orin fired the questions at her as his hands fisted, and he leaned further over her. At first, she was too stunned to reply, but as that wore off, fury rose to replace it.

"Lycan's only mark their mates; no casual fling would do such a thing," Maverick said.

These words didn't seem to sink in as Orin's face remained thunderous. "He's only been gone a couple of weeks, and you've already thrown Cole aside to bang someone else. *Who* did you cheat on my brother with?"

Her teeth ground together as she slapped him so hard his head flew to the side and spittle shot out of his mouth. The sound of the slap lingered in the room as silence descended. Then, her dad, Brokk, Skog, and Varo jumped to their feet to join Maverick as he started around the table.

"Stay back!" Lexi shouted and pointed her finger at them. "This is between *us*."

Orin's nostrils flared, and his cheek was already turning red when his eyes returned to hers. He was taller, but she was more powerful.

"I'm only going to tell you this once, and you better listen carefully because I will set your ass on fire if you don't; do you understand me?" she demanded.

Orin didn't respond, and she hadn't expected him to.

"*Cole* came here last night; I believed...." Lexi broke off as her sorrow swelled, but she wouldn't give in to the emotion. "I believed he would stay. I was wrong. When I woke this morning, he was gone."

The fact Orin had forced her to reveal what she'd started to consider a little humiliating in front of *everyone* made her blood boil. Since first meeting Cole's younger brother, she often contemplated murdering him, but none so much as now.

Some of the color drained from Orin's face as she spoke, and she thought he might feel bad about what he'd said and done, but it was impossible for this asshole to feel bad about anything.

"*Your brother* left me. Twice, now. So, not that it's any of your business, but if I decide to be with someone else, it will *not* be cheating."

"He sacrificed himself for *you*."

So much for thinking this dickwad might be a little repentant. Lexi stepped into him, and to her amazement, Orin gave way a little as she poked him.

"He sacrificed himself for *all* of us, and I doubt you've been abstinent since then. And since you're so eager to discuss my sex life, let's also discuss yours. Have you slept with anyone in the past two weeks? Have you forsaken everything you enjoyed to honor Cole for his sacrifice?"

Orin didn't respond, but when he went to grab her finger, fire sparked to life on the tip of it. Before, she always had to focus on love to get her fire to blaze to life, but she was getting better at calling on her powers.

Orin jerked his hand back when his skin sizzled. His face darkened again, but he wasn't a fool; he had to know that Cole's brother or not, she'd had enough of him and would torch him.

"Now, let me make this clear, if I decide to fuck *all* of Dragonia, you will have *no* say in it. And it would *not* be cheating on your brother if he's the one who's decided *not* to be with *me*."

"He still wants to be with you," Varo said.

Lexi didn't tear her gaze away from Orin's as she spoke. "We don't know what Cole does and doesn't want. We don't know what he's doing, where he's been, or what's going through his mind. He came to me last night and was gone again before I woke. Am I supposed to spend the rest of my life hoping for him to come back every couple of weeks? Is that really a life?"

Something changed in Orin's face as it softened a little.

"I don't want anyone else, there will never *be* anyone else for me, but no matter how much I love him, I can't spend the rest of my life like that," she continued.

Saying it out loud made the loneliness and heartbreak of possibly waiting centuries for him more real. She loved Cole with everything she was, but that life would destroy her.

"He sacrificed himself for *us,* but I won't have pieces of him. I won't repeatedly continue to put myself through that heartbreak over and over. And you"—she extinguished her fire before poking Orin's chest again—"have *no* right to judge me for my choices. I'm going to do everything I can to save Cole, I won't ever give up on him, but if I can't help him, I'll also have to let him go."

Orin glanced at her finger but was wise enough not to grab it again.

"And you *will* treat me with respect." She stabbed her finger into his chest again. "You will *not* stomp across a room while swearing at me. I'm no longer the girl you bullied into harboring refugees in my tunnels, and I'm *not* a kitten.

"I am *your* queen, and if you don't start treating me with more respect, you won't be welcome here. Do you understand?"

No one breathed as she and Orin glowered at each other. For a second, she didn't think he would back down, and she'd have to toss his ass out of Dragonia.

Eventually, he raised his hands and stepped back. "Whatever you say, Your Highness."

She didn't want that either, but she didn't say it. If she gave Orin a fraction of an inch, he would try to turn it into a mile, and she refused to let him run all over her.

"Now, what did you mean when you said, 'is that why my

brother was so pissed'? How do you know he was pissed about anything? And when did you see him?" she asked.

When Maverick, Brokk, and Orin exchanged a look, Lexi inwardly groaned when she realized they'd been keeping something from her. And whatever it was, she wasn't going to like it.

CHAPTER THIRTY

Lexi kept her hood up and the cloak covering as much of her hair as possible while she stood in what would have been a cheerful room. It was now the scene of a massacre.

Her dad's breath sucked in before he composed himself enough to keep his reactions hidden. However, his body remained rigid against hers.

Lexi clasped her hands together to hide the tremble in them before she turned away from the house. Orin, Maverick, and Brokk stood a few feet away, gazing toward the city as the stars shone down and the moon rose higher.

If it wasn't for the occasional song of the peeper, the night would be completely hushed. Then, somewhere in the distance, a coyote howled; dozens of others picked up the eerie sound until it came from all around them.

And inwardly, Lexi screamed.

Cole left her last night and came here to do *this*. She hadn't seen Cole's other kills, but Orin's reaction to her earlier, his words, and the apprehension oozing from Maverick, her dad, and Brokk now told her this was different.

This was something far worse than she ever could have imagined. Cole crawled out of her bed and came here to do *this*.

While he was with her, the lycan and dark fae part of him were more in control. She'd seen and experienced it, but the shadows made him pay for suppressing them. And they made the immortals in that house pay more.

She didn't doubt those immortals had been plotting something awful, but no one deserved to die like that. The shadows ruthlessly slaughtered them because part of *her* Cole had returned for a little bit. It was gone again.

Before he drew the shadows into him, he'd told her: *"There is one who will always have the power to destroy me. Shadows can't thrive in the light."*

At the time, she'd refused to believe it would ever come to that or that she'd ever be capable of doing such a thing. He was far too powerful, and she loved him too much to destroy him.

But what if that's what has to happen? What if this is only the beginning? What if he loses complete control and starts slaughtering immortals who don't deserve it?

Eventually, he would run out of traitorous immortals to kill. They would either stop plotting publicly, figure out spells to keep themselves hidden, or, as improbable as it sounded, he'd eradicate them all.

Then what?

What if he turned on the realms? The realms *she* was meant to protect.

She loved Cole with every fiber of her being. Her need for him had become a physical ache in her chest. She couldn't picture her life without him, but she couldn't let him become a monster worse than the Lord.

The Cole who existed before he fully embraced the Shadow Reaver would never want such a thing. He would have rather died than become a monster.

And she couldn't let countless immortals and mortals suffer

because of her love for a man who was gradually ceasing to exist.

Standing there, listening to the coyotes howl as the wind blew the cloak around her ankles, it hit her that she might have to kill him. Or maybe, they would kill each other.

Tears didn't come with the realization; she was beyond tears now. There was only a vast, hollow emptiness inside her and the awful knowledge the future might be bleaker than she'd ever suspected.

With a rustle of wings, the three dragons who accompanied her here settled on the ground. They became as still as stone while they studied the night.

"Were you going to tell me about this?" she asked.

"Yes," Brokk said.

"When?"

"After dinner. You were already eating when we arrived, and we decided not to interrupt."

If Orin had revealed this, she would have believed he was lying and never planned to tell her, but Brokk wouldn't lie to her. Lexi rubbed her arms against the chill in the air and her body.

"What if I *do* have to destroy him?" she whispered.

Orin winced, and Maverick bowed his head while her dad closed his eyes and rubbed the bridge of his nose. Brokk remained stone-faced.

"That stupid prophecy says he'll destroy the realms," she continued.

"Only if the last light falls, and since we're going to keep you protected, that won't happen," Orin said.

"But you all keep saying prophecies are garbage and get things wrong. What if it doesn't matter if I fall or not? What if the prophecy got that wrong?"

No one answered her.

"He believed I could destroy him," she continued. "Before

drawing the shadows into him, he put that responsibility on my shoulders if it became necessary."

"It won't be necessary," Orin stated.

"It won't?"

"No. Cole *will* regain control of himself. Besides, those fuckers in there got what they deserved." Orin waved a hand at the house, but no one glanced at it. The smell and sight were forever ingrained in their memories. None of them required a reminder of what lay behind them.

"No one deserves that," Lexi whispered.

"They were plotting to kill *you*."

"I'm well aware, but *no* one deserves to die like that."

"What do we do?" Maverick asked.

"He's losing control," Brokk said. "I don't like admitting it, but what happened in there is a sign of that."

"He's not losing control," Lexi said. "Or at least… I'm not sure how to describe it or if you would call it control. I feel like this was a way for the shadows to exert their dominance because, while he was with me, the dark fae and lycan were more in control than the shadows. Once the shadows caught wind of what was happening here and drew Cole away from me, they could unleash their anger over that on these immortals."

They all stared at her, but she kept her eyes on the distant city. "Parts of Cole return; I've seen it, but I don't know how to break the shadows' control over him."

"The lycan will exert its dominance again," Maverick said. "The wolf can't go long without its mate."

"So will the dark fae," Orin said. "We are not dominated by anything."

"It's not a competition," Lexi muttered.

"Everything's a competition," Orin said.

"Oh good, the dark fae and lycan can both be winners when I kick him out of my room the next time he decides to stop by."

Her dad muttered something she didn't catch before rubbing

his nose again. As if sensing her increasingly foul mood, one of the dragons turned its head toward her. Puffs of smoke billowed from the nostrils of the others.

Lexi reined in her temper while she contemplated this mess. Even if there did come a time when Cole had to be destroyed to save the realms, she still had no idea how to do it.

Yes, she had powerful abilities, but the shadows were ruthless, and the dragons wouldn't stand against the Shadow Reaver. Her fire could chase away the shadows, but could she unleash her flames on the man she loved so much?

Everything in her screamed against it. She'd rather watch all the realms burn than hurt Cole, but she couldn't let all those immortals, mortals, and creatures die because it would destroy her to kill him.

And it *would* destroy her. She would, in the end, do whatever was necessary, but she wouldn't survive it either. Of that, she was certain.

Maybe, she would continue breathing and functioning, but it would be a miserable existence.

"So, what do we do now?" her dad asked.

"We find him and help him," Orin stated.

Lexi squeezed her hands together as the coyotes stopped howling. The ensuing quiet was unnerving. "We have no idea where he is or how to track him."

"We believe he's still in Dragonia," Maverick said.

"He wouldn't go far from you," Brokk said. "And, with the shadows' help, he could slip past the guards protecting the portals in Dragonia without them noticing. I have no idea how to locate him in Dragonia; maybe the witches can help us."

"They said they couldn't track him before," Del reminded him.

"That was when we didn't think Cole was in Dragonia. Things might be different if he's closer."

"Maybe Sahira could take her tracking spell off me while they're at it," Orin muttered.

Feeling the first tiny bit of hope for the first time in weeks, Lexi agreed with them. "Okay, let's see what Kaylia and Sahira can do."

CHAPTER THIRTY-ONE

BEFORE SHE COULD OPEN a portal for them to leave to see Kaylia and her aunt, a portal opened in the sky and Alina swept through it. The beautiful red dragon soared over their heads before banking to the right and coming back toward them.

When Alina landed, earth skidded up beneath her feet, and she ran for a few feet before finally settling to a stop. Lexi had never seen the speaker make such an ungraceful landing before and knew something was wrong before Alina spoke.

"Wendigos are invading Dragonia," Alina said with more urgency than Lexi had ever heard her use before.

Her heart leapt into her throat at this revelation and the idea of those monsters entering *her* realm again. They'd just gotten some semblance of normalcy back, and now they were trying to destroy it.

"We have to stop them," Lexi breathed.

Without thinking, she sprinted away from the others and raced toward the speaker. Before she could reach the dragon, a hand gripped her wrist and pulled her back.

She yanked on her wrist but couldn't get it free as she spun to face Brokk. From behind him, the others rushed forward to join them.

"Let us handle this!" Brokk shouted. "You should return to the palace and stay somewhere safe."

"Let me go!"

Brokk glanced around before reluctantly releasing her. She realized he feared that Cole, or his shadows, lurked nearby. And if they decided Brokk was a threat to her, they would destroy him.

"I'm not going to argue about this," Lexi stated. "I am the queen of Dragonia and all of the realms; I won't hide while lives are in jeopardy, and I *will* fight to keep everyone safe."

"And if you die, they'll all suffer when some new asshole claims the throne."

"Then destroy the throne before they can claim it."

"That's not possible," Alina murmured. "It's protected by powerful magics and cannot be eradicated."

"Of course it can't." Lexi sighed. "But it doesn't matter; I won't be like the Lord. I will not hide while others die for me."

"You can stay with me. You'll be safe then."

"I'm not staying out of this battle," Lexi retorted.

"I would never suggest such a thing, my queen," Alina said. "Nor would I ever sit out a battle. But if you are on me and in the air, you'll be part of the battle and watch as the wendigos die."

"That's not a bad idea," her dad said.

Lexi pondered this before nodding. She wasn't thrilled with the idea of climbing back on a dragon, but it would be nice to have a front-row seat to the death of those things.

"Then let's go," she said.

She spun away from the others and closed the distance between her and the speaker. When Alina bent her neck down, Lexi scrambled up her leg, grabbed one of the spikes running along her neck, and hoisted herself onto the dragon's back.

When she settled into position, she looked down at Brokk, Orin, Maverick, and her dad. "Stay safe."

"You too," her dad called back.

Alina rose into the sky as the four of them turned and ran for the portal one of the other dragons opened on the ground. Lexi closed her eyes against the uneasiness in her stomach and tried not to think about the distance separating her from the earth as Alina opened a portal and plunged into it.

I won't fall. I'm safe.

It was true, as she had a death grip on Alina's spikes and nestled securely on her back. However, no matter how much her brain repeated this, her stomach continued to somersault.

Screams greeted them as soon as they exited into Dragonia. The strength of those screams wasn't as bad as the Lord's war—she didn't think anything could ever be that bad again—but they threw her back into the war, with all its blood and violence.

They'd lost so many because of the unquenchable appetite of the wendigos the Lord unleashed on Dragonia. Now, they would lose more before this was over.

The numbers wouldn't be as high if they didn't have as many fighters down there this time, but one life lost was too many, especially when there was *no* reason for this continued fighting. Although, to some, greed and power far outweighed the value of life, but not to her.

From the open portals into Dragonia, the wendigos were already spreading across the recent battlefield. The awful creatures were emerging from the portal that once opened into the dwarf realm of Drumbledon.

She hadn't considered it necessary before, but since the dwarves weren't returning to their old realm, Lexi would shut the portal down. She wasn't close enough to close it now.

Most of the residents of Dragonia had retreated from the open portals or already returned home for the night. Only the guards remained to stand against the wendigos. There weren't enough of them to stop the monstrous creatures from flooding out of the portal.

The wendigos' hands dragged across the ground; their foot-long claws left gouges in the earth as they walked. Their arms were nearly as tall as the seven-foot beasts, with distorted black faces consisting more of ligaments than flesh.

Made mostly of bone, the wendigos' ribs protruded from their bodies, and their sunken stomachs almost touched their spines. They were repugnant creatures that could never be satisfied, no matter how much they killed and ate.

Lexi had hoped never to see them again, but something had driven them here, and she suspected it wasn't their idea. Someone had unleashed a new plot against her. They'd managed to slip past Cole's shadows, and now they were here.

Some other idiot was out there, pulling strings and foolish enough to think they could somehow control these monsters. But the wendigos ate anything in their way and would turn on their puppet masters soon enough. They had no loyalties to anything other than their unquenchable needs.

CHAPTER THIRTY-TWO

Lexi leaned closer to Alina's neck as Alina arced to the side. The other dragons took up her call as from behind the wendigos, dark fae, lycans, berserkers, and vampires emerged from the portal.

As she'd suspected, the wendigos weren't doing this alone. Someone was pulling the strings.

She'd like to think only one, big enemy remained out there, and once eradicated, they'd all be safe, but she wasn't foolish enough to do so. Her enemies were like the hydra; as soon as they cut one down, two more emerged.

Countless others plotted against her; these just slipped past Cole's shadows. They'd also been foolish enough to bring another battle to Dragonia.

For that, she would show no mercy.

She was tired of killing, screams, blood, and nightmares, but if one of these invaders survived to grace her dungeon, others would see it as a weakness. When they tried to exploit that supposed weakness, more would die, and she wouldn't allow that.

"Torch them!" Lexi shouted to be heard over the wind

rushing around her. "But before you do, let me tell our troops it's coming!"

Alina didn't respond, but when she dropped to soar only ten feet above her army trying to hold back the horde, Lexi knew the dragon heard her when she didn't unleash fire on them.

"Fall back!" Lexi commanded. "The dragons will take care of them! *Fall back!*"

The tip of Alina's wing skimmed the ground as she banked away from the battle. As the guards retreated, a blue dragon filled the space Alina vacated. The blue dragon unleashed its wrath on their enemies in a wave of red and orange.

The fire ripping across the earth scorched the wendigos and drove back any others trying to enter through the portal. Another dragon fell in behind it, and then another, and another until fire blazed across the earth.

Most of those who entered behind the wendigos perished or were repelled. Some of them eluded the dragons' fire and continued to rush the guards, but they had to know they wouldn't survive. She was sure panic was what propelled them.

Lexi spotted her dad, Brokk, Maverick, and Orin below. They charged into the battle with swords raised as they joined the guards. The clash of steel against steel rang across the land as the crackle of the flames increased in intensity.

When Alina swept close to the earth again, her fire scorched through more wendigos and lycans. The heat of those flames, billowing back over the dragon, warmed Lexi's skin but didn't burn her.

She barely felt the chunks of earth and debris flying up to pepper her flesh as she leaned low over Alina's neck. Her apprehension vanished as a sense of strength flooded her. She was one with these powerful creatures, and she loved it.

As Alina banked to circle back, shadows enveloped a wendigo who had survived the fires. The shadow swiftly wrapped around the wendigo's neck and squeezed until the creature's head popped off like the top of a dandelion.

Lexi's heart lurched as she searched the area, but she couldn't see him amidst the flames, shadows, and bodies littering the ground. That didn't mean he wasn't there.

He could have sent the shadows ahead of him and would be arriving soon—because he would most definitely come—or he could be cloaking himself in shadows to remain hidden. But what would keep the dragons from accidentally killing him if she couldn't see him and neither could the others?

A lump lodged in her throat as her heart raced. She wanted to jump off Alina, run onto the field, and scream for him.

She remained where she was. Doing something that foolish was a good way to get herself, and anyone trying to protect her, killed.

Though everything in her screamed to go to him, she turned away from the shadows. Cole was good at taking care of himself, and he would have to do that… if he was down there.

When Alina swooped low over the battlefield again, her next blast of fire eradicated the last of the wendigos. Maverick and her father took down a lycan and berserker while Brokk, Orin, and the guards destroyed what remained of the army trying to invade their home.

"Take me down," Lexi commanded.

Alina dropped from the sky and settled gracefully on the ground. Lexi stroked Alina's neck and thanked her as the dragon lowered her head for her to scramble off.

Ignoring the fresh bodies strewn across the earth, Lexi strode across the bloody ground, through the still raging fires, and on toward the portal once leading to Drumbledon. Shadows shifted around her, and some rose to her fingers before abruptly pulling away.

Fire crackled around her as she stopped before the open portal. The wind its flames created billowed around her and caused her hair to sway around her face. She felt its heat, but it didn't bother or burn her.

With a wave of her hand, she permanently closed the portal. The ones who planned this whole thing might still be on the other side; she could send guards after them, but they didn't have enough guards for that, and she would only be putting the ones who remained at risk.

Besides, the immortals behind this could already be dead. She never believed she'd hope for someone's death, but she hoped for theirs. It meant one less enemy out there.

Lexi glanced at the other open portals; some led to realms that were also no longer inhabited. She shut them down too.

If any of those immortals decided to rebuild their realms, she would reopen the portals. Until then, they were a danger to her and everyone else in this realm.

From now on, anyone who entered Dragonia must come through an intact realm. She'd have to rely on the immortals from that realm trying, and succeeding, in giving them some warning about an impending attack.

There was no guarantee that could or would happen, but it was something. Plus, with fewer options for portals, there was less chance of a mass invasion from different realms, like the one they unleashed on the Lord, happening.

She contemplated shutting them all down and only leaving one open, but it would have to be the one in the human realm, as many of the different immortal species didn't like each other. It could cause fights if they were forced to go through an inhabited realm to enter Dragonia.

However, she didn't want them all going to the human realm either. The mortals had been through enough without having a possible horde of invaders funneled into their realm.

For now, she could only hope no one would be stupid enough to invade an occupied realm before coming for her. They risked more than her wrath if they did.

Lexi turned away from the portals and strode back through the flames. None of the shadows reached for her this time; she looked for Cole but didn't see him or any unusually shifting shadows.

With a sinking heart, she realized he'd either left already or retreated, taking the shadows with him. She searched the mountainsides but didn't sense him anywhere.

Carefully, she stepped over a wendigo's body before joining the others. Some guards were already tossing dead bodies onto the fires before they died. Lexi would have to ensure a couple of dragons kept the fires going until only ashes remained.

"How many did we lose?" she asked tiredly.

"Two," her dad replied.

Lexi realized the fire had burned away all her clothes when Maverick pulled off his shirt and handed it to her. She barely acknowledged her nudity as she tugged it on.

When she finished, she turned to Joffrey, a lycan from Maverick's pack and the head guard on duty tonight. "I'll send more to help clean this up and stand watch with you for the rest of the night. I've shut down the portals leading to uninhabited realms, so hopefully, this won't happen again."

"We will be ready if there is another attack," he vowed.

"Do any of the enemy still live?"

"They're all dead."

"Good."

They probably could have questioned some of them and tried to get answers as to who was behind this, but she doubted there would be any. She focused on her dad, Brokk, Orin, and Maverick.

"I'm going to clean up and get dressed. I'll meet you in the witches' room in half an hour. Hopefully, Sahira and Kaylia are still there."

It was where they spent a good deal of their time now, but the battle had probably pulled them away.

"If not, I'll find them," Brokk offered.

"Thank you."

"This can wait until morning," her dad said.

Oh, how she wished it could. Maybe, by some miracle, her exhausted body would finally get a decent night of rest after all this, but… "No, it can't."

CHAPTER THIRTY-THREE

"There's nothing we can do to track Cole," her aunt said.

Sahira stirred her cauldron over the fire in the hearth. Her familiar, a black cat named Shade, sat at her feet. She and Kaylia were the only two witches in what Lexi had dubbed the "magic room," as that's what it had become.

The battle had drawn their attention and pulled them from the room, but once they learned there weren't any injured to tend to, they returned to bolster their supply of healing potions. They didn't require them now, but they would in the future.

"Believe me, we've tried, even after we said we couldn't do anything." Kaylia tossed some lavender into the pot. "We knew it was a long shot, but we gathered a coven and tried to track him through scrying and throwing bones. We didn't detect him anywhere or come up with a lead."

"How come you didn't tell me this?" Lexi asked.

"We were afraid to get your hopes up and then dashed," Sahira said. "If it worked, great. If it didn't, then no harm done."

"I'm tired of everyone keeping things from me. I'm not going to break. I've made it this far without falling apart, and I'll make it further."

Sahira squeezed Lexi's shoulder. "We all know that, but we didn't think it was necessary to tell you when you already have so much to deal with."

"It wasn't. I'm done with all of the secrets and unknowns."

She shot a look at Orin, who purposefully ignored her.

"We can't do a tracking spell because we need *him* for it, and we can't do a locator spell because it's just not working," Sahira said as she returned to stirring.

Kaylia tossed some more herbs into the cauldron. "We think the shadows are somehow blocking it or, more likely, the arach magic is too powerful and is blocking ours."

Despite how horrible all this was, Lexi couldn't help but smile as she watched the two of them working together. When they first met Kaylia, she wanted nothing to do with Sahira or Brokk.

Their half vampire status had put them on her hate list, but she'd learned to work with them, and somewhere along the way, she and Sahira became friends. The other witches still weren't thrilled about having to work with a vampire, even one who was half witch.

Sahira's witch mother left Dragonia shortly after the war and refused to return. That only made Lexi despise the stupid, stubborn, hateful woman more, but she kept it hidden from her aunt. Sahira had enough animosity toward her absentee mother without Lexi fueling the fire.

Despite all that, the women had gone from reluctant allies to friends. It warmed Lexi's heart to see her aunt with someone she could trust, who wasn't related to her.

Kaylia plucked a feather from the phoenix perched on her shoulder. It gave her a disgruntled look and ruffled its feathers before settling back into place. A puff of smoke billowed from the cauldron when the feather landed in the brew.

"We're assuming the shadows or, more likely, the arach

magic that created the Shadow Reaver is blocking ours," Kaylia said.

Lexi frowned as she clasped her hands together and gazed around the large, airy room the witches had filled with potions, cauldrons, and other assorted magical supplies. Located on the first floor, Lexi understood why they'd claimed this room as its French doors opened onto beautiful rolling hills. Its floor-to-ceiling windows flooded the room with light.

Dainty red couches, a white marble floor, and barren walls made up the room, but the witches filled it with their things. If any arach items once decorated the room, the Lord destroyed them because that's what he did best.

The floor-to-ceiling windows surrounding them allowed the silver radiance of the moonlight to pour into the room. Judging by its location in the sky, midnight was approaching.

"Speaking of tracking spells," Orin said as he pinned Sahira with his ebony gaze. "I think it's time you took off the one you have on me."

Sahira didn't look at him as she continued to stir with a pensive expression. Finally, she lifted her head and smiled at him. "I don't think so. Cole asked me to put that spell on you; I'll take it off when he decides it's time."

Orin scowled at her as Sahira smirked and returned to stirring her potion.

"He would want it off," Orin growled.

"Then he can tell me that. Until then, it stays."

"Is there anything else you can do to locate Cole?" Brokk interjected and shot Orin a warning look.

When Kaylia tossed in another herb, sparks shot out of the cauldron. "Not unless we catch him or get some of his blood."

"The blood might be an option if he gets injured during a fight," Maverick said.

"The chances of that are small," Brokk said. "Plus, how

would we tell his blood from the copious amounts he spills from others?"

Lexi's nose wrinkled at the reminder, but he was right.

"We have no chance of catching him," her dad said.

"He'll come back for Lexi," Maverick stated.

Great, now she was also bait. Like she didn't have enough going on in her life, but she *was* the only thing they could count on to draw him forth. So, that meant it was a waiting game until he decided to bless her with his presence again.

Lexi crossed her arms over her chest and watched as the dragons' shadows swept over the land. Some were outside the room, looking in from the ground. Her connection to them told her they were there but hidden by shadows; no one else would know they were there, watching, waiting, and protecting her.

And now she was waiting too, and she hated it. There had to be something more she could do. Well, there was plenty more she could do power-wise, but she still didn't know all of it.

There was so much untapped potential inside her; maybe some of it could help her find Cole. She needed to learn more about her heritage and what she could do.

She'd learned a lot about her abilities since first discovering she was an arach, but there was so much more to learn. Unfortunately, she didn't think there was anyone left who could help her.

Kaylia, Alina, and Elfie had done their best, but Kaylia and Alina didn't know anything more. Elfie perished during the war.

Lexi now lived in the home of her ancestors; there *had* to be answers here. She'd been so swamped since taking the throne that she hadn't explored this place, but it was time to start.

The Lord could have destroyed any answers that might have resided here.

The possibility was real, but not one she was willing to entertain. She kept running into depressing dead ends. She needed this olive branch of hope.

"I have to go," she announced.

Before anyone could say anything or protest, she turned and left the room as a small pop sounded from the cauldron.

CHAPTER THIRTY-FOUR

THE SHADOWS COILED and slithered as they dug deeper into the host. They would *not* let go. They would *not* lose their hold over him.

They'd finally gotten their freedom and wouldn't relinquish it, but the host kept fighting them. The host sought revenge; it wanted its enemies dead, but it also wanted the woman.

Those *things* had attacked her in *her* realm, and the host seethed with the knowledge of it. The damn wolf and dark fae pieces of the host wouldn't relinquish their hold when it would be so much simpler if they would let the shadows seek their vengeance.

It's not like those two halves of the man weren't looking to kill too. They were as eager to eradicate any threat to the woman, and they were good at it. But no matter how hard the shadows battled for control, they wouldn't let go.

The shadows hated them; they wanted them dead, but they couldn't get rid of those pieces. Those two sides of the man were a part of the host and, therefore, a part of *them*.

The shadows seethed. They wanted to be *free*, to kill any

who got in their way whether they deserved it or not and to make those who threatened the host pay.

The woman rattled the shadows' control of the host, but they had to protect her. However, they wouldn't let her win or break their hold over the host.

He was *theirs*.

And there was a new threat out there.

"They're plotting against us," the shadows hissed to the host. "Your brothers, the arach, the witches, the lycan, and the vampire are plotting to capture and take you from us. They are the enemy. We *must* stop them."

～

THE LYCAN PART of Cole tried to shift as it sought to take control over the shadows. It wanted its mate *now*.

She'd been in danger tonight, and he'd missed the impending attack. The shadows, though powerful, *couldn't* know everything.

They'd missed this plot to come after Lexi, and because of that, the enemy breached Dragonia. They sent *wendigos* after her! Those monsters, with their unending hunger, had entered Dragonia to kill her.

And I missed the ones who planned it!

It could happen again, and if he wasn't at her side....

Cole couldn't think about what might happen then. He had to be with her but couldn't go to her like this. He was falling apart; the shadows were tearing him down, trying to take over, and whispering of vengeance.

And he so badly wanted that revenge. He yearned to go after all who posed a risk to Lexi and tear them apart. He'd hunt them across all the realms, but that meant leaving her.

The shadows had gotten him to the battle quickly tonight, he'd beaten Lexi to the fight, but he should have been at her side, not skulking like a fox through the night. But he had to leave; the shadows sought to keep killing after their enemies were all dead.

He had to take them away before they started slaughtering those who didn't deserve it. He allowed a couple to remain to watch as she left the battlefield and returned to the safety of the palace, but he took the majority with him and buried them in the darkness.

And now they were trying to bury him too.

A guttural roar tore from him. His back bowed as his hands clawed at his bare chest, and his face elongated into a snout. But as the lycan sought to break free, the dark fae also sought to take control.

It didn't happen often, but a dark fae could fall in love.

And once a dark fae loved, they loved deeply.

Cole's head bent as his shoulders hunched, and he tried not to scream as war raged inside him. He battered his hands against his forehead and temples.

FUCK!

His nostrils flared, and his lungs burned. He couldn't breathe; his chest was too constricted from the fury and longing tearing him apart. Bones and joints cracked and popped as he started to shift.

"They are the enemy," the shadows said. "We can't kill the woman, but we can eradicate the others."

"No!" Cole snarled.

He knew what his loved ones wanted to do, and he didn't blame them, but it infuriated the shadows. There was no way to separate him from the shadows, he was becoming increasingly certain of that, but his family and friends wouldn't give up.

At least not yet. Eventually, they would come to see the truth as Cole had and concede defeat, but they would do everything they could to save him until then.

He wouldn't let the shadows hurt them because of it. His control over them was spiraling; with every passing day, their madness seeped deeper and deeper into his soul, but he would keep those he loved safe from them.

There was no other choice.

His hands hit the ground, and claws scoured rocks as they shifted into paws. The wolf almost broke free before the shadows exerted their dominance again.

The lycan part railed against their control. *No* lycan could stand to be dominated; only an alpha was ever allowed to do so.

As he shifted back toward his male form, the wolf's howl reverberated off the rocks while it battled the shadows and dark fae for control.

CHAPTER THIRTY-FIVE

OVER THE NEXT WEEK, Lexi spent every free second she had exploring the palace. Some of that time came in the day, but most of it was at night, when she couldn't sleep or when nightmares roused her from sleep.

She couldn't handle one more night of running through the palace and Dragonia with thousands of unseen faces booing as they called her a failure. Or one more night of bloodshed and death as she discovered herself back in the throne room, fighting the Lord.

The worst were her dreams of Cole, of being back in his arms and whispering words of love. Every time she woke to find herself without him, it was a devastating blow again, and she was tired of tears.

She averaged a few hours of sleep a night. Her body had adjusted to the lack of it, but she still missed it. Usually, she had her best sleep after exhausting herself, searching, and returning to her room.

Her forays in the palace were also a good way to avoid Cole if he returned. She intended to make it clear that she wouldn't be his occasional pit stop. She wouldn't accept small pieces of him; she selfishly wanted *all* of him.

Every day, she reminded herself of this resolve, but if she saw him, she would weaken. She missed him so much.

She also didn't kid herself into thinking he wouldn't find her in the palace when he returned for her. But at least there most likely wouldn't be a bed present when he did.

Instead of tossing and turning through any more nights, she climbed out her window, waved a dragon over, and rode it down to the ground. From there, she started her explorations of the palace without the hindrance of her guards.

Few were awake and about at this time of night, and she avoided them. She wasn't concerned about her safety as the dragons followed her around the palace.

Over her explorations, she encountered so many destroyed rooms she lost track of them. She opened the door to a musical room full of shattered instruments. For some reason, a lute, saxophone, and grand piano survived the devastation.

Lexi shut the door of the room without stepping foot inside it. One day, she would clean out the numerous destroyed rooms she encountered and make this place beautiful.

She would make it more welcoming to all those who lived here and their guests. It would be a day far in the future when things were much more stable, but she would erase all evidence the Lord ever resided here.

At least she hoped the future would come.

Most of the rooms were barren, or the things inside them were so demolished she sometimes couldn't tell what they were. A few, mostly the bedrooms, still had their furnishings intact.

She suspected that was so the Lord could entertain or, more appropriately, scare the shit out of immortals by inviting them here and making them stay. Lexi shuddered at the idea of being locked in this palace with him.

Most probably didn't survive to leave here again; Cole had, but his father didn't.

On the second day of her search, she came across the giant king's head in the Lord's private solar. Brokk, Maverick, Orin, and her dad helped her remove the head, the Lord's other trophies, and the hundreds of pixies nailed to the beams.

Cole had mercy killed one of those pixies, and as they worked to bury them in the woods, Lexi couldn't help pondering which it had been. She would never know, but Cole's act of mercy had caused the Lord to retaliate by killing hundreds of pixies; he had Malakai leave them at her doorstep.

The reminder only made her hate the man more.

She sent word to the giants that she had the head. The next day, a solemn Gibborim arrived to retrieve it. They didn't speak much, but he thanked her before leaving.

Lexi had the solar permanently sealed off —no one would enter that death room again— before resuming her exploration of the palace the following day. On the third floor, she opened the door to a beautiful, three-story-tall library.

The few windows in the room were on the opposite side of the bookshelves. The dark red, shredded drapes hung in tatters around the open window, and beyond the windows was a meadow with a river running through it.

The shutters that would have protected the room from storms were in the center of the room. Rain, and countless other debris from the changing seasons, had blown into the room.

However, it didn't matter, as no books were left to protect. What remained of the ones on the floor had their spines ripped in half, and their pages littered the ground. When a breeze wafted through the window, some of those pages fluttered.

On two of the walls, the shelves had been torn down. Their remains mingled with the pile on the floor.

Out of all the destroyed rooms, the library was the only one that made a lump form in her throat as she entered. There was once so much knowledge, entertainment, and countless years of enjoyment to discover in this room.

It was all ruined by a madman with a mind so rotten, he wrecked everything he touched.

Tears burned Lexi's eyes as she gazed around the room. She missed having the time to read; she missed being able to lose herself between the pages of a book and go on grand adventures.

She couldn't remember the last time she sat down to read. It was her favorite pastime before her life turned upside down and she became a queen. She couldn't wait for the day when she could do it again.

This room would have been her perfect retreat; now, it was nothing.

Before she could cry, Lexi shut the door and continued her exploration. Unlike the Gloaming's palace, there weren't any locked doors, and the building didn't shift around her, but it was so big and easy to get lost there.

More than a few times, she found herself exploring the same area for the second or third time. After a week, she finally made her way into the upper levels of the palace.

It was there that she encountered the Lord's bedroom. It was easily three times the size of the other bedrooms she discovered. Its bed was twice the size of a normal king bed, and the sprawling rooms making up the entire suite took up most of the floor.

Gold trimmed all the rooms. The color scheme was mostly burgundy though black and white were interjected into the furnishings too. The Lord's robe and slippers remained beside the bed, waiting for him.

The room smelled of spices, and while she expected it to also smell of blood and insanity, it didn't. After everything she'd seen in this palace, after everything the Lord had done, this small corner of organized, untouched sanity was more unnerving than all the destruction.

Lexi forced herself to search the Lord's closets, trunks, and drawers in case the man hid something away there. When she finished, she climbed up to the tower of the Lord's room.

With the wind ruffling her hair, she gazed out at the breathtaking realm with its purple sky and fluffy pink clouds. Dragonia was a lush, fertile land with high mountains and numerous caves.

After what Brokk had said about Cole not going far, she was certain it was true. He was in one of those caves, and she would find him.

Discovering nothing, Lexi retreated from the Lord's rooms, closed the door, and vowed to have this area sealed off. Those rooms most likely belonged to her ancestors, but they would *never* belong to anyone else.

The only other room on the floor was the document room she'd been looking for; as she'd feared, the Lord had demolished it. However, unlike all the other rooms, she couldn't retreat from this one.

She had to know if she could salvage something from here; this room could hold the answers she'd been seeking for months. Stepping inside, she surveyed the splintered wood fragments from the smashed trunks and the thousands of papers littering the floor. Many of them had been shredded and were probably beyond repair, but she had to try.

CHAPTER THIRTY-SIX

Paper and wood crunched beneath her as she crept through the debris. She made her way over to the metal shelves built into the wall on the other side. Each shelf was at least five feet wide and two feet high.

The drawers probably once contained numerous amounts of information, but when she pulled the first one open, she wasn't surprised to find it empty. She had no doubt the contents of all the others littered the floor too.

In some places, the debris was piled so high it caused her to stand two to three feet off the ground. She tried not to let hopelessness get the best of her; she'd spent all this time searching for answers in this place, and they might be here, but the Lord *ruined* them.

She had no idea how to fix any of this, but she had to try. Taking a deep breath, she set to work, trying to piece some of this together as she sorted it into piles.

The dragons' shadows passed across the windows while they flew around the room. During her search, Lexi uncovered pieces of the black drapes that must have once covered the windows.

As exhaustion crept in, she called off her mission, walked

over to a window, and waved down a dragon. Becoming used to riding them, she didn't hesitate before scrambling out the window and onto its back, but she still didn't look down as they descended to her room.

Lexi slept for a couple of hours before rising, dressing, and returning to the top floor with her guards in tow. They didn't ask where she was going or how she knew about this place; they simply remained outside while Lexi returned to work.

The sun had risen, and it was nearing lunch when Alina appeared in one of the windows. "The others are looking for you."

Lexi wiped the sweat from her brow as she turned to face the speaker. "Here I am."

"Perhaps you should tell them that; they're worried."

Lexi gazed around the room; although it seemed hopeless, she wasn't ready to give in yet. "Please let them know I'm here. I'm not leaving."

"Yes, my queen."

When Alina pushed away from the window, Belindo, Nithe, and Astarot landed on the sill she'd vacated. The dragons were getting bigger, and their wings had grown enough to support the weight of their plump bodies. Occasionally, little plumes of fire escaped them.

They hopped down to join Lexi in the mess. Belindo and Nithe toddled around while Astarot spread his wings and flew up to Lexi's shoulder.

She suppressed a grunt when his tiny body weighed down on her but smiled when he nuzzled her cheek. Pretty soon, he would be too big to do such a thing, so she enjoyed it while she could.

About ten minutes later, her dad, Sahira, and Kaylia arrived in the doorway. Their eyes widened at the mess before shifting to her.

"What is this?" Kaylia inquired.

Lexi gestured helplessly over the documents scattered around her. Some of them were scrolls, but most were broken. She'd spotted the word arach on some, but she had no idea what they were about.

"I think it's answers," she said and then admitted, "or maybe it was. I think it was once the arach history."

"Oh," Sahira breathed. "Okay then. You need help; thankfully, you have a couple of witches to give it."

"Your powers can help with this?"

"We might be able to piece some of this back together," Kaylia said. "First, we'll have to get the debris out of here."

The dragons helped by carrying off the shattered chairs, trunks, and cloth. As the day wore on, exhaustion battered Lexi, and her neck and shoulders ached.

When the sun set and night descended, she told the others to go to sleep, but they remained to help her. As the night wore on, Brokk, Varo, and Maverick joined to help them.

She had no idea where Orin was, but he'd been scarce lately. She suspected he was searching for Cole, but the one time she saw him over the week, she didn't ask. It was a much happier life when she didn't have to talk to him.

As the night started to spin toward day again, they finally declared a break, and Lexi agreed to retreat for some rest. She was too tired for nightmares.

She didn't sleep much, and when she woke, she returned to the room. All the debris had been cleared away, and remnants of the scrolls, papers, and parchment were sorted into different piles. More still littered the floor, and she got to work separating them.

A couple of hours later, the others had all rejoined her, and by the time lunch rolled around, the floor was clear.

"Okay," Kaylia said. "Let's see what we can do."

She and Sahira each grabbed a section of parchment and set it on the floor. They whispered a few words over their pieces, and the others watched as, in the piles, pieces of parchment started rattling.

Lexi held her breath as the piles shook before more pieces broke free. Those pieces flew across the room to the witches.

The two of them fit the pieces together before saying the words again. Over the next few hours, Sahira and Kaylia worked diligently together. Sometimes they found matching sections, and at others, nothing would happen, but over time, some things started coming together.

CHAPTER THIRTY-SEVEN

Over the next week, they worked to piece together what they could of the Lord's mess. As Sahira and Kaylia worked, the rest read through the restored writings.

When Sahira or Kaylia started to burn out, they would stop and help them with the reading or retreat to rest. Unfortunately, much of what they repaired was simply the arach history.

While some of it was fascinating, and Lexi enjoyed learning about her ancestors, it didn't help her learn more about her abilities or how to save Cole. Despair grew with every passing day, but she wouldn't quit until she'd read everything they managed to piece back together.

On the sixth day, slumped against the wall and looking like he hadn't changed, showered, or shaved in days, Brokk suddenly shot upright. "Here!"

Lexi lowered the parchment with the cramped, nearly indecipherable writing she'd been cursing for the past hour and scrambled over to him. "What is it?"

"It's about the Shadow Reaver."

Lexi's heart fell before crashing against her ribs. She

collapsed against the wall beside him and leaned over his shoulder to look at the parchment he held.

"Shit," he breathed through his teeth.

"What is it?" Lexi breathed.

When Brokk lifted his head and their eyes met, distress and something more radiated from them.... Was it anger? Confusion? Then an unseen fist hit her in the chest as she recognized what it was... resignation.

She didn't like that at all. What had he discovered?

And then, he held the piece of parchment out to her. Lexi steadied the small tremor in her hands before taking it from him.

The others gathered closer while she held Brokk's gaze a moment longer before turning her attention to the parchment. Beneath her fingers, the parchment was brittle, yellowed, and far older than anyone in this room, including Kaylia.

The words were small and in a neat, no-nonsense manner. Lexi blinked a few times to clear her vision before focusing on the writing.

> I don't have much time for this. They are approaching, I can hear them below, and when they arrive, they will kill me. I'm too weakened, and there are far too many.
>
> I cannot believe it has come to this: an arach hunted by other arach. Our great realm is in ruins, and death is rampaging through a realm once filled with life.
>
> I could not have foreseen this, but Carleah did. Not many believed her when she issued her prophecy of a time when only one arach would live.
>
> The realms were always ours for the taking; we

are the most powerful immortals, and we have the dragons. No other immortal could ever take those things from us, and no other immortal did.

We took it from ourselves.

But I digress. I am writing about a time more than fifty thousand years ago when Carleah issued her dire warning.

Carleah was one of the most powerful ones of us all, even back then. She would never say such a thing unless it could come true, but many didn't want to believe her.

We agreed to meet to discuss her warning, and it was there that Carleah declared we must do something to protect our future, and the only arach who will survive what is to come. Many thought she'd lost her mind, others agreed with her, and some were too frightened to believe her.

I was torn.

On the one hand, I knew how powerful Carleah was. On the other hand, I didn't see how anyone could take down the arach. It is simply impossible; the dragons would never allow such a thing.

However, I didn't see what harm it could do to protect a future that could never be. It appeased Carleah and those who believed her to take such action.

We agreed to continue discussions on what we

could do to protect our future, but at first, no one had any ideas until the dark fae came to us.

They requested our aid in deciding their future rulers. Their last ones were chosen by birth and completely inept.

The dimwitted species had finally realized birthright didn't always equal ruling rights. They wanted our help in creating trials for the future leaders to best.

We agreed to help, on the condition they pay us a lot of carisle and send warriors to join the Dragonian army. There was also a condition the dark fae didn't know about, as Carleah saw this as a chance to ensure the safety of the final arach.

Not all arach knew about what we did as some still didn't believe Carleah's prophecy and wouldn't approve. I was still uncertain but saw no harm in helping.

Carleah decided we would slip hidden magic into the trials. The dark fae are symbiotic with the shadows, and Carleah declared that one day, a dark fae would rise who could master the control of those shadows above all others of their species.

Our hidden magic won't unleash into a dark fae until this special one enters the trials. It hasn't happened yet, but knowing what I know now, I have no doubt it will happen.

Carleah revealed that the timeframe of this dark

fae's rise would coexist with the discovery of the last arach. With our magic infused into this dark fae, they will have dominion over the shadows in a way no other dark fae has before or ever will again. They will be powerful enough to keep the last arach alive.

Carleah has deemed this fae will be called the Shadow Reaver. A fae who can gather shadows from all corners of the realms and unleash them upon our enemies.

When asked what would happen if this Reaver turned against the arach, Carleah said we would word the spell to make it impossible. Our magic will bring the Reaver to life and keep it from turning against the arach.

The Reaver will be ours to control and destroy if it becomes necessary.

Lexi gulped at that sentence and tried not to give in to the panic clawing at her chest. It took her a minute to be calm enough to continue reading.

CHAPTER THIRTY-EIGHT

It wasn't long before the trials were in place and our hidden magic worked into them. If a dark fae manages to survive all the trials, in the end, they will enter a stretch of land where our unknown magic awaits them.

This magic is set to recognize and react to the amount of power that dark fae possesses. Only the most powerful to cross through there will trigger the spell.

When our magic is released, it will meld the shadows into the fae, making them one with the shadows in a way no other dark fae has ever experienced. It hasn't happened yet, and I will not survive to see it come to fruition, but it will come.

I no longer doubt that.

At the time, I still wasn't convinced Carleah was right, but I couldn't help feeling uncertain about everything. What we put into those trials was the most powerful brand of magic I've ever encountered; we were all drained from it, and that has never happened to me or the others before.

Even with our safety measures in place, and a way to control the Reaver, I couldn't help feeling as if we'd done something horribly wrong.

LEXI'S HEART raced as beads of sweat broke out across her forehead. *How do I control the Reaver?*

She yearned to scream this question at the parchment, this immortal in the past, and Carleah. The woman had seen the future; she'd known only one arach would survive, but she hadn't devised a way to ensure the last arach had access to *all* their powers and could help the Reaver?

This arach writer had called the dark fae dimwitted, but they were so arrogant they didn't realize how stupid *they* were.

They'd established a way to control the Reaver and help Cole, and she had no idea what it was. Glancing around the room, her heart sank as she recalled the countless shredded things here.

Maybe they *had* written it all down, and the Lord destroyed it. There was also no way of knowing how much he might have taken from this room, thrown out the windows, burnt, or demolished in other ways.

All the answers could have been here, and now they could all be gone. There was a chance they could still uncover them, but those chances dwindled with every passing piece of useless writing they pieced together... until this *one*.

Lexi finally focused on the parchment again.

And now war has broken out between the arachs in Dragonia. I never could have imagined a day such as this coming to our realms, but Carleah really did see it.

She knew, and she prepared for it. I have no idea if she foresaw our downfall would come from the arach turning on each other, and I cannot ask her as the war has already claimed her life.

Before the war started, we were the only two arach left from that long ago time when we set something in motion that we could not undo. Now, I am the only one still standing, but that won't last.

And for that, I am almost grateful, as whispers from the battlefield have reached me. Amongst the ruins of bodies and land, a new prophecy has risen.

I have no idea who issued it first, but it started with the peasants, amid those who knew naught of what we did.

They never could have known of our secret, but they speak of the Shadow Reaver on the battlefield, and a new prophecy revolves around its rise...

As the writing continued, the letters became shakier, and the pen dug into the parchment hard enough to leave holes in some spots.

They whisper of the Reaver and say that when the last light blooms, the Shadow Reaver shall rise. When the last light falls, the Shadow Reaver will destroy us all.

How can they know what we've done? How? And so many of them know as the prophecy has raced across the land and is whispered everywhere.

Lexi could almost feel the panic oozing from the pages as she read.

No one else knows what we did with the fae trials, but I know what that prophecy means. Oh, I know.

All I can do now is hope that whatever lies beyond this life has mercy on our souls for what we've done and that the final arach, the last light, is strong enough to destroy what we've set up to unleash upon the realms.

There is a way to control the Reaver or destroy it. To tame the shadows, the last arach must—

CHAPTER THIRTY-NINE

Lexi couldn't breathe as she read the final line. Her vision blurred, and her hands shook as the blood drained from her face when she saw only the ripped parchment and the missing piece.

"Where's the rest?" she whispered in a choked voice that sounded like a bullfrog was speaking from her throat.

Brokk looked helplessly at her and then around the rest of the room. Hundreds of remnants of paper remained to be sorted and matched; it could still be there. It *had* to be there!

There was a way to save Cole, and she had no idea what it was! When she first learned of her arach heritage, not getting her shield into place was frustrating and scary, but this made that look like a walk in the park.

"What does it say?" her dad asked.

Not trusting herself to read it to him, she handed the parchment back to Brokk. He stared at her for a few seconds before shifting his attention back to the words.

He started to read out loud but stopped when a sound in the hall alerted them to Orin's arrival before he stepped into the doorway. Unable to look anywhere else, Lexi kept her attention focused on Orin.

He was the only one in this room who wouldn't look at her with pity once Brokk finished reading. And she couldn't handle sympathy right now.

As Brokk read, the eyes of the others bored into her, but she kept her attention on Orin. When Brokk finished, Orin remained focused on the wall across the way before finally looking at her.

"So, there is a way for you to destroy him."

"I have no idea what it is, and I could also save him." Lexi looked down when tears welled in her eyes; she wiped one away before lifting her chin. "What if I accidentally do one instead of the other?"

No one had a response to that.

"We have more papers to go through; the answer could still be here... somewhere," Kaylia said. "If we've found that much of this parchment, there must be more."

Lexi's heart thundered in her chest as she tried not to get her hopes up too high. She was too scared of having them dashed to bits around her if she did.

"What if we only uncover how to destroy him?" she asked.

"Then we burn it," Orin said.

Varo bowed his head and rubbed at his temples. "We will require that knowledge... just in case."

His words hung heavily in the air as Sahira and Kaylia shifted uneasily.

"You're all a little too eager to find some way to kill my brother," Orin said.

"That's not what I want at all! I want him *back*, to save him and have him with me. I miss him so much it's almost impossible to breathe some days, but I also have to..." Lexi's words wavered and broke.

She steadied herself before continuing. "I also have to acknowledge that he might not be there anymore, and if there is a way for me to save him, I might never know it."

She couldn't imagine losing Cole and having to live with the knowledge she had some way to save him, but no idea how, every day for the rest of her life. It would *destroy* her.

She'd rather be dead than bear that burden.

"He hasn't returned to me. The lycan and dark fae must be seeking their mate and starving, but he *still* hasn't returned."

"Probably because the shadows told him you wouldn't welcome him again. You did say so, and they are watching over you. Why would he come back to be rejected?" Orin said in an accusatory tone.

Lexi recoiled before stopping herself; there was a chance he was right. Maybe the shadows had whispered her words to Cole, along with every other insidious thing they could think to tell him.

"I would never reject him," she whispered.

"You said you wouldn't have pieces of him and wouldn't go through that heartbreak anymore. Don't you—"

"Enough!" her father snapped. "Not another word from you."

"You're such a prick," Sahira spat. "Maybe instead of always being part of the problem, you could try to be part of the *solution*. It's obvious she doesn't want him dead; none of us do, but we also can't have a being in the realms who could destroy *everyone* if something happens to her. That's worse than anything the Lord did. Now, stop attacking her!"

Orin glowered at her as he folded his arms over his chest. "I'm trying to find him; that *is* the solution."

"And how do you plan to contain him once you find him?" Sahira demanded. "Throw a net over him? Bind him in chains like you did with the dragon? Do you think any of those things will stop him when he can tear your head off without touching you?"

"Cole wouldn't do that."

Sahira slapped her hand off the floor before she rose. "He's not Cole anymore! Or at least not entirely. He's also the Reaver and would gladly kill you to ensure his survival. We must find a way to protect ourselves, and catching him isn't the answer. He'd kill us."

"All except for Lexi," Maverick said. "I have no doubt my nephew loves me, and I'm just as certain the Reaver would kill me, but he'd never do anything to her. Not only would the arach magic prevent that, but the lycan part of him would *never* let something happen to its mate."

"And the dark fae side is in love and will do anything to protect her," Brokk said.

Lexi stared at the piles of ripped paper, parchment, and scrolls still waiting to be pieced together before shifting her attention to Orin again. He was such an asshole, but it came from a place of love. Like her, he wanted Cole back; he was just a lot more vicious about it.

"Have there been any new sightings of him?" she asked.

"No."

Lexi tried not to let despair get the best of her. "All right then. We'll finish going through this stuff. Maybe the answers are still here, or maybe they aren't, but we've come this far and we can't stop now. If there's something here that can help us, we have to know."

CHAPTER FORTY

They uncovered as many answers in the following pages as they did in the first ones. It took two more days to piece together the rest of the pages and read through them. Most of what remained was more history of her ancestors.

Whoever wrote about the Reaver and the magic that created it before hiding it within these historical tomes hadn't written anything more. The missing piece of the parchment never turned up.

Lexi didn't know if the Lord realized what he held when he destroyed it, or if it was just one more thing amongst the thousands he ruined. Despite knowing it was mostly history documents, Lexi read through it all.

She'd hoped to learn more about her ancestors, but most of it was accounts of the dragons, crops, architectural design, buildings, population, and detailed agricultural notes. There was some on the civil war, but not much.

They didn't discover any other prophecies, but then, prophecies weren't common, and Cole considered them garbage. But unfortunately, she'd come to believe not all of them were.

When they finished, hundreds of pieces of shredded documents remained, but none of them went together, and even though they'd read what was on them, there weren't any answers.

She didn't know if there was ever more than this here and the Lord ruined it or if it was always just these minute details. However, they'd finished, and she could leave this room for something more than a shower and sleep for the first time in weeks.

Rising, Lexi stretched her cramped legs and hobbled over to the window. Resting her hands on the sill, she leaned out to take in the scenery. She greedily inhaled the fresh air as the dragons swooped through the sky. As her growing army trained, the clash and scrape of steel sounded from the bailey.

Over the past couple of weeks, once they finished with the documents, they filed them back into the cabinets. Behind her, one of them clicked shut with an air of finality.

Despite not learning anything and being left with more questions when it came to Cole, some of her tension eased. She no longer had to worry there might be some answers *somewhere* in Dragonia that she was missing. There weren't.

She would have to continue stumbling through learning more about her abilities, just like she had up until now. At least she had friends and family to help her get through this.

She wished she still had Cole. But there was a way to save him, and like she learned to wield some of her abilities, she *would* discover how to help him control the shadows. She would have to be careful not to accidentally destroy him when she did.

"After we all get some rest, there's something else we have to discuss," her dad said.

Lexi turned away from the window and sat on the sill. Leaning forward, she clasped her hands before her. "What?"

"The prisoners in the dungeon."

The others in the room stopped what they were doing as Lexi

bowed her head. It had only been a matter of time before she had to deal with them; as much as she hated it, that time had come.

"Okay," Lexi said.

"But we can talk about it later."

"No, let's get it over with now."

He sighed before continuing. "They've been down there for weeks; it could become cruel to keep them there."

"Keep them there and let them suffer," Orin said. "They would have gladly seen us dead; why should we care if it's cruel?"

"Is that what you plan to do with the prisoners still in the prison realm?" Lexi asked. "You're going to keep them there and let them rot?"

"No, I had them all executed soon after the Lord fell, but they stewed in their poor choices before I did."

"Is that why you kept me there?" her dad asked. "So, I would stew in my *poor choices*?"

Orin shrugged. "I couldn't turn you free, Del, and you know that as well as I do. You were vital to the Lord's war and Cole. What was I going to do? Turn you loose and let you return to helping them?"

"You knew we were secretly plotting to take him down."

"And you failed to do so."

"And you failed to win the war!" her dad retorted. "You were nothing but a hunted loser after the war, and you would have been dead if my daughter didn't save your sorry ass."

"Stop it," Lexi interjected. "You hate each other; we get it. Orin's an insensitive asshole, but could we please stop with the bickering? Isn't there enough awfulness to deal with, without having the two of you at each other's throats every time there's a discussion?"

"That would be lovely," Brokk said.

"He started it," Orin muttered.

Lexi dropped her head into her hands. A shadow passed

behind her a second before a dragon landed on the sill next to her.

It stuck its head inside, and when its snout turned toward her, Lexi patted the creature as she assured it, "Everything's okay."

The dragon snorted but didn't fly away. Instead, it shifted its attention to the others. Orin closed his mouth as he wisely chose not to say anything more.

"I will have the prisoners executed," Lexi stated. "They shouldn't be made to sit and suffer when it's what has to happen."

The words felt like mud in her mouth, and her stomach churned with nausea. She almost put her head between her knees to breathe, but she couldn't let them know how badly this affected her.

The dragon rested its head across her lap. When it did, she placed her hand on its head and rubbed its soft, black scales. The beautiful beast's strength, flowing into her, hardened her resolve, even if she still wanted to throw up.

She'd just declared an end to hundreds of men and women. She wasn't sure how to live with herself after that, but she would find a way. They wouldn't be the first men and women she'd killed, and they wouldn't be the last.

When tears burned her eyes, another dragon landed on the sill behind her. Its talons brushed her back but didn't slice her or her clothing. Then it rested its head on her shoulder.

When she looked to the others again, sorrow etched their faces. They were trying to support her but also making it more difficult for her to keep her tears in. She took solace in their presence.

"You don't have to make this decision now," her dad said.

"Don't I? You're right; it is crueler to keep them locked away when we all know their eventual fate. None of them can live. The Lord might have forced some to fight against us, but not all.

There are many out there plotting to overthrow me; we can't turn loose more soldiers who might help them.

"And how do we decide who was willing and who was forced? Besides, if we don't kill them, it will be seen as a weakness on my part. If we do, it will only add fuel to their fire. They'll see me as weak and come after the throne even more. They'll come after *all* of us, and I can't allow that."

"It's the right decision," Maverick said. "I know it doesn't seem that way, and I know it's extremely difficult, but it is the right one."

"I hope so," Lexi murmured as a third dragon landed on the sill to her left and poked its head through.

The creature eyed the room before shifting its attention to her. Another one landed on the windowsill across the way. Kaylia jumped a little when Alina stuck her head inside and nearly bumped into the crone.

"My queen," Alina said. "The queen of the giants is here."

"Wonderful." Lexi patted the heads of the dragons closest to her before gently nudging them away and rising. "More fun times ahead."

CHAPTER FORTY-ONE

LEXI WALKED OUTSIDE to discover the queen of the giants standing in front of the portal to Colossal. Gibborim stood behind her with his head bowed.

Feeling like an ant before them, Lexi was acutely aware they could stomp on her and never know it. Overhead, dozens of dragons circled, and more landed to settle on the ground behind her.

They made it clear they'd attack at the first sign of a problem; Lexi hoped there wouldn't be an issue. She had enough to deal with right now.

The queen of the giants bent and rested one hand near Lexi; she kept it far enough away to make it seem like she wasn't a danger. Lexi wanted to believe that.

The woman looked far better than the last time Lexi saw her, but being able to breathe would add color to anyone's cheeks. Her brown hair lay in a knot against her nape; tendrils of it spiraled around her shoulders.

The red shirt and black pants she wore hugged her massive frame. Her brown eyes were still bloodshot and red-rimmed;

most might think it was a remnant from her time spent underwater, but Lexi knew it was from tears.

The queen had lost her love. She would never get over that.

"Your Highness," Banba greeted.

"Good day, Queen Banba," Lexi greeted. "What has brought you to Dragonia today?"

When Banba glanced at her dragons, Lexi stiffened a little, and a powerful wave of protective urges descended over her. She was connected to these dragons, cared for them, and wouldn't let anyone attack them, even if they did play a role in the demise of the giant king.

The dragons had only done what the Lord ordered them to do, but she could understand if the queen still possessed animosity for them. It would be nearly impossible for the woman not to hate the creatures that helped bring about the death of her husband and her own tortured imprisonment.

"They no longer obey the Lord's commands," Lexi said.

"Do they obey yours?"

"They do, but I would never order them to be unnecessarily cruel to others. The throne won't corrupt me like that. I'm sorry for your loss and can understand if you're angry with them, but they had no choice. They were as chained by the Lord as you."

Banba winced a little before bowing her head. "He was a good man and an outstanding husband." Then she met Lexi's gaze again. "You say the throne won't corrupt you like it did the others who ruled before you, but you don't know what power and the throne will do to you as the years pass."

"I am an arach; the throne won't make me crazy like it did those who didn't belong on it."

"But a thirst for power drove your ancestors to kill each other; isn't that a form of crazy?"

Lexi gave a small, humorless laugh. "I've thought the same thing about them and worried about it too, but I *won't* be like them. Of course, I can't guarantee anything in this world, and neither can you.

"I *can* promise always to do my best as a ruler, be fair, and I won't force the dragons to enslave, torture, and kill those who don't deserve it. They won't ever have to do anything they don't agree to again. I expect disagreements, and I hope others disagree with me, as long as they're peaceful about it and don't threaten my loved ones or me.

"I will listen to all those who disagree with me, and if I find they're right and I'm wrong, I'll acknowledge it. I won't terrorize or torture any who live in the realms; I *can* promise that."

"For now."

"For now and the foreseeable future."

"I hope you're correct. I hope these things *do* happen as you claim, but if they don't, you *will* have an enemy in the giants."

"I wouldn't expect anything else, but the same goes for you. If I discover that you're plotting to take over the throne and this realm, you'll have an enemy of the dragons and me."

"Agreed," Banba said. "And what of the Reaver?"

When Lexi stiffened a little, a couple of the dragons behind her crept closer. "What of him?"

"What do you plan to do about him?"

"Unlike the dragons, I have *no* control over the Reaver."

Well, she might, but she had no idea how to exert it. This wasn't the time to let herself fall down that rabbit hole of doubt.

"Do you plan to continue to let him wander free? He is taking out your enemies, but what if he turns on the realms like he's prophesized to do?"

"Only if I die, and I plan to be here for many more years."

"There is no guarantee of that, and after seeing what the Reaver can do, I believe he could kill us all if incensed enough. Your death would ensure it."

"Then, perhaps, you should help ensure I live."

The queen smiled as she bowed her head. "That would be a wise choice, Your Highness. And one the giants will take."

Lexi didn't reply as she studied the woman. The queen sounded sincere, but there were few she trusted anymore.

"Now that we've finished with the niceties, I thank you for allowing Gibborim to free me. You had no way of knowing if you would unleash an enemy upon your realm when you did so. I also came to speak with you and, if I liked what I heard, to swear fealty to you and Dragonia."

"Have you liked what you heard?"

"I approve of your actions and words. Only a fool would promise never to change and not become corrupted by time, circumstances, losses, and greed. You're not a fool… at least not yet."

"Doesn't age make you wiser?"

Banba snorted. "You have many eons to go, my queen. I'm sure many of them will entail foolish things."

Lexi smiled. "I'm sure you're right."

"Gibborim and I shall swear fealty now. I hope you'll accept it as coming from the rest of the giants too."

"I will."

While the giant queen and her brother swore to uphold Lexi as their queen and aid her in wars, more dragons landed to stand with Lexi's growing guard. When they finished, Queen Banba and Gibborim both bowed to her.

"Would you like to have dinner with us?" Lexi inquired. "It's a bit chilly, but the sun is warm, and it would be good to sit outside."

"I think so too," Queen Banba said, "and I would like to talk with you more."

"So would I."

CHAPTER FORTY-TWO

THE DARK FAE WAS STARVING, and the wolf had become half mad with its need for its mate, but as they battled to break free, the shadows fought them. And they gave in to the shadows because they also knew the truth…

They couldn't go to her. It wouldn't be good for her if they did.

They could *never* stay with her again, and if they continued to return to fulfill their needs, they would repeatedly break her heart. The dark fae and lycan couldn't allow such a thing to happen, but they yearned to see her again.

Though he remained deep beneath the earth, the shadows slithered around him. But wasn't that impossible?

It must be because shadows couldn't thrive in the dark; they required light to exist. He tried to reason this out, but there was little room for reasoning when they didn't shut the fuck up!

They whispered incessantly as they demanded death and blood over and over again. However, they didn't surround him; they couldn't down here. They were inside him.

During moments of clarity, he recalled he'd been the one to

welcome them, to draw them further into him, and give them control of his body. Which meant he should be able to fight them off.

He'd been so certain he could when he accepted so many inside him. He was the strongest dark fae ever to walk the realms, but the shadows refused to relinquish the tentacles they'd latched into him. Their hooks dug deeper into his flesh as they burrowed through his insides.

He would *never* be free of them.

His back bowed, and claws extended as knuckles popped and twisted. The lycan had stopped caring about anything other than getting to its mate.

His knees shifted into something more canine, but as the lycan sought to break free, the shadows whispered something new.

"There's a threat," the insidious things murmured.

Cole realized he'd spoken out loud, but it wasn't his voice and seemed to come from a different part of him.

"It is out there, plotting against her. We can hear them," the shadows murmured.

This calmed the wolf into ceasing its fight against the shadows, but didn't suppress the lycan as his body shifted into a new shape. Loping across the rocky floor, he wound his way toward the surface.

As soon as he crossed into the light, the shadows rejoiced as more surged toward him. Laughter filled the air as they realized they'd be allowed to play.

They coalesced over and around him as they concealed him from any who might see him. When he raced past the guards, they never noticed as he slipped into a portal and moved on to the human realm.

Once there, he opened a portal to the outer realm the shadows whispered about. Their excited words were malevolent as they anticipated the coming fight and death they would unleash. As the wolf ran, Cole sent more shadows to watch over Lexi.

He emerged into the outer realm and a rocky outcropping facing a bar. He'd never seen it before, but there were an unknown number of realms. No one could see them all, but the shadows had seen this one.

His claws ticked against the rocks as he prowled out of the shadows. The lycan part of him had been denied its mate for too long and was spoiling for a fight. If it couldn't claim her, at least it could kill.

The dark fae was more than happy to slaughter its enemies… and one of the enemies it sought to destroy was the shadows. The dark fae and lycan halves of himself often contrasted with each other. Lycans were dominant creatures by nature, but until Lexi entered his life, the dark fae was the more dominant part of himself.

Upon recognizing her as its mate, the lycan sought to dominate. The two sides of himself were often at odds with each other, but they'd still worked together because they both wanted *her*.

While determined to protect Lexi, the shadows didn't want any other part of him to exist. For now, while another enemy was present, the war inside himself calmed a little as *every* part of him focused on seeking out his foe and keeping Lexi safe.

Cole sniffed the air while he prowled around the outside of the bar. The familiar scents of immortals, alcohol, food, and smoke wafted out.

As he padded around to the back of the small, wooden structure, his ears flicked while he listened for any hint of treachery. Only the sounds of laughter, music, and chatter filled the night while the rest of the realm remained still, but the shadows whispered of something more here.

While he despised the things, they had yet to be wrong. Heading to the front door, Cole pushed it open with his snout and entered.

CHAPTER FORTY-THREE

THE PLACE WAS full of assorted immortals sitting at scarred wooden tables, teetering on uneven legs. Lanterns on each of the dozen tables were the only light source as no windows opened onto the night.

A small card table was shoved in the corner by the bar. Immortals sat around it, tossing cards onto the table and sipping from their mugs while bickering.

In the corner closest to the door, two pixies danced over the keys of a scratched and dented upright piano. They played a lively, upbeat number that didn't mesh with the sullen crowd.

Behind the bar, a vampire was pouring drinks. When he spotted Cole, he thrust a finger at the door. "No wolves allowed in here. You either enter in your true form or get out."

When Cole growled at the man, he thumped the glass down on the bar. "If we're going to have a problem, I've got a gun loaded with silver bullets."

Despite his dislike of the man, Cole chuffed a little. The man was a fool; silver bullets wouldn't destroy him, just as fae metal through his heart wouldn't kill him. They may often contrast with each other, but his dark fae and lycan halves made him stronger.

And now, the shadows made him nearly invincible.

Those same shadows itched for a fight, and the bartender's words caused them to skitter across the ground as his hackles rose and he bared his teeth. The bartender blanched a little, and his hand dropped behind the bar.

"You shouldn't do that," a melodious voice interjected. "First, he'll kill you before you get the gun out. Second, he's not your typical lycan; those bullets won't kill him."

Cole kept his attention on the bartender, but his ears flattened when he recognized the voice. *Becca.*

He hadn't seen his ex-lover and member of the dark fae council in a while. She didn't fight against the Lord, but she didn't fight for him either.

Movement on his left alerted him that she'd risen from her seat and started toward him. Cole suspected Becca was the one who kept running to the Lord to report what was going on between him and Lexi and inside the Gloaming. He'd never been able to confirm it, but his gums skimmed back more.

Was she the reason the shadows had drawn him here? Was she plotting how to bring down Lexi?

It wouldn't surprise him; she'd never kept her disdain for Lexi hidden. But if she was the reason he was here, her time left alive was ending.

However, the shadows whispered of something more sinister in this realm, and it wasn't in this room. He turned his head back toward the bartender and the door behind him.

"What are you doing here, Cole?" Becca inquired.

When he remained focused on the man behind the bar, Becca stepped in front of him. Her black corset pushed her lush breasts up; a short, black skirt emphasized her small waist and toned legs. Her black hair swayed around her chin as she tilted her head to study him from her assessing black eyes.

"I'd put your hands back on the bar," she said to the vampire.

The man's eyes narrowed, but before he could speak, a dwarf asked, "Cole? As in *King Colburn* of the dark fae?"

A murmur ran through the crowd, and the bartender carefully placed his palms back on the bar.

"That's the one," Becca murmured.

"Also known as the Reaver," someone else whispered.

When the shadows shifted, the sharp intake of breaths followed their movements. Cole ignored the call of those shadows as they whispered for him to follow them. The threat wasn't in this room; it was elsewhere.

"They're looking for you, Cole," Becca said. "Orin's put out a reward for any knowledge of you; your family and your fiancée are hunting you."

He growled, but it didn't dissuade her from speaking; she just did it faster.

"Your fiancée is leading the charge," Becca continued. "What do you think they'll do when they find you? Everyone has heard the legend of the Reaver; do you think they'll let you live? She cares more about power than *you* now."

The shadows shifted as her words caught their attention. Becca was trying to turn him against Lexi. He understood this; the shadows didn't.

"I can help keep you hidden from them," Becca continued.

When Cole shifted back into his normal form, he knelt with his fist on the floor while staring at her. Chairs scraped as immortals rose, and a few edged toward the door.

They stopped moving when the shadows swarmed over the door. The tension in the room ratcheted up as the occupants shifted uneasily, and the vamp behind the bar glowered at Becca.

"What are you doing?" the vamp demanded.

"I'm offering him help," Becca replied.

When Cole rose before her, Becca's eyes ran hungrily over

his naked form. Everyone else in this room realized their peril, but Becca licked her lips, stuck out a hip, and smiled.

He didn't return her smile. "Do you really think Lexi would try to kill me?"

"I think she'll do whatever's necessary to keep the throne, and you're the biggest threat to her."

"But I'm not. The shadows won't harm her, and neither will I; she knows that."

"*Maybe* she knows that, but it doesn't mean she'll take the risk; they might try to eradicate you. If the shadows do turn on her—"

"That will never happen."

"How does she know that? How do *you* know that?"

Becca glanced around as the shadows made a strange, almost tittering noise as they laughed.

"The shadows seek blood; they love to kill, but they can't hurt her." Cole leaned closer as if he were going to tell her a secret, and Becca swayed forward too. "The arach created them; they created what *I* have become. Because of that, they can't turn on her. They'll always protect her, and she knows it."

Becca's eyebrows rose as she swayed back on her heels. He could see the wheels in her mind spinning as she tried to devise a new way to turn him against Lexi.

As he studied her, he realized maybe Lexi was right about her. Perhaps Becca hadn't simply sought power when she pursued him; maybe she *was* in love with him.

If true, that made her more perilous.

"How often did you go back to the Lord to report on Lexi and me?" he asked.

Becca did a double take before she started sputtering. "What? I would *never* do such a thing!"

"You didn't tell him about Lexi? You didn't tell him she was my mate and my fiancée?"

"Of course not! I can't stand that bitch—"

"Watch it!"

The sharp bark of his words caused most of the room to jump. A nymph in the corner whimpered, and a lycan hunched as if about to transform.

When a shadow rose before her, the lycan relaxed a little, but her eyes remained riveted on the shadows.

"What are you doing?" one of the dwarves hissed at Becca. "Shut up."

Becca lifted her chin in a haughty gesture and threw back her shoulders to better show off her breasts. While the others feared him, she remained undeterred as the look she gave Cole made it clear what she sought from him.

Denied sustenance for too long, the dark fae was ravenous, but it recoiled from the idea of fucking this woman again. There was only one who could ease his hunger.

"I believe your fiancée is a poor match for you, but I would *never* betray you," Becca said. "I never told the Lord anything about you or her."

"You didn't fight against him either."

"I'm not a fighter, Cole. We both know that."

It was true; she wasn't a fighter. She most likely would have perished as soon as she stepped foot on the battlefield.

"No, you're not."

And he didn't have time to stand here and deal with her. If she had been the one who kept running back to the Lord, he would learn the truth, and she would die. Until then, others would soon meet their end.

He stepped to the side and started toward the bar, but her next words stopped him. "If your fiancée isn't worried about you because she thinks you'll take her throne, then what about because of the prophecy?"

While Cole didn't care what she had to say, her words piqued the shadows' curiosity. They swiveled toward her.

CHAPTER FORTY-FOUR

"If she's not concerned about herself, what about everyone else in the realms?" Becca taunted. "She comes across as a boring, always-do-good type; if she thinks you'll kill others, or there's a chance the Reaver *will* destroy the realms, what will she do to protect them?"

The shadows whispered to each other and him as they moved through the line for a report on Lexi. Cole knew what she uncovered in that palace room and what they discussed. The shadows didn't like it when his possible demise was a topic, but it would never come to that.

He couldn't fully control what he was now, but he would *never* destroy the realms. He'd kill himself before he ever allowed that to happen.

She's with the giant queen, the shadows whispered in his mind. *The giants could become allies in destroying us.*

Cole gritted his teeth against the shadows as they whispered louder. They were wrong; Lexi would never plot against him.

The whispers became louder and more incessant until they were shouting. When one of the dwarves ran for the door, the shadows raced after her.

They ensnared the woman's legs, ripped her off her feet, and lifted her into the air. The woman screamed as she flailed about, but her punches didn't connect with anything.

"No one leaves," the shadows hissed.

For the first time, the smug expression on Becca's face faded. She paled a little before glancing anxiously around.

"What have you done?" someone whispered.

"Someone here is plotting against Lexi," Cole said in a voice more his own, but one still corrupted by the shadows. "Where is the back room?"

"Back room?" Becca asked in a slightly tremulous voice.

"There are traitors here, and I want them. *Where. Are. They?*"

Everyone shifted their attention to the bartender with his hands on the bar and a deathly pale face. "We have a storage room."

Done with Becca, Cole stalked across the floor toward him. He didn't go after the man but followed the shadows toward the swinging door leading into the storage room. He shoved it open and stepped inside.

He didn't bother to look around the room full of liquor bottles, boxes, and other assorted supplies. Instead, he followed the shadows out the back door.

As he walked, he pulled the shadows away from the bar and freed the immortals inside. The retreating shadows watched the immortals scramble to get away.

Some of those who fled might report his whereabouts to his brother or Lexi, but he didn't care. He'd be away from here and their enemies dead by the time anyone arrived.

The only one who didn't run was Becca; she trailed him out the door. Halfway across the yard, he stopped before a door set into the earth.

Made of concrete, it had to weigh at least three hundred pounds. Not many shadows remained in the darkness, but there were enough to slip beneath the door to explore below.

The ones he sought were down there. He suspected those below believed the concrete would hide their conversation, but it was only a matter of time before the shadows found them.

Cole smiled as the shadows rejoiced at the bloodshed to come. Nothing could keep them out except for spells and light. Whoever was down there had made a fatal mistake, and they were an idiot.

He reached out to the ones still guarding Lexi, but she remained safe. And once he finished here, she would be safer.

Bending, Cole grasped the handle carved into the door and easily lifted it. Maybe it would help keep out those weaker than him, but it was nothing compared to a pissed-off lycan's strength.

He plucked the door from its hinges and tossed it aside. Cloaking himself in shadows, he descended into the dark depths and glided toward the light at the end of the stairs.

CHAPTER FORTY-FIVE

THE SUN HAD SET, and the moon was rising when Lexi parted ways with Queen Banba and Gibborim. Despite feeling minuscule compared to them, she enjoyed their dinner and company.

Banba was quiet and thoughtful, but Gibborim was funny. He had a quick wit, enjoyed laughing, and when he slapped his knee, the breeze he created blew the hair back from her face.

Once, he accidentally knocked her over with a slap to the grass. Grasping her by her shirt, he carefully plucked her off the ground and righted her as he chuckled.

Lexi couldn't stop laughing after that, though her dad, Brokk, Maverick, and the others weren't as amused. Muttering something, Orin walked away to do whatever Orin did while Sahira and Kaylia went to rest.

After a while, Varo also wandered off. The last Lexi saw of him, he'd strolled over the hills and toward the merchants hawking their wares.

Those merchants sounded more enthusiastic about the things they sold than they used to, but still not as much as those who resided in other realms. An overeager warlock thrust a bottle of something at Varo, who didn't acknowledge him as he continued.

Now, as she walked back to the palace, some of those merchants remained, but most had returned home. "My queen," one of them blurted before falling to a knee in front of her.

Uncomfortable with the gesture but knowing this was something she was supposed to accept, Lexi rested her hand on his shoulder. "Please rise."

The man staggered to his feet as she stopped to examine the satchels of herbs the man had on display. A pleasant aroma wafted up to her, but there were so many herbs she couldn't differentiate one from the other.

She tried to hide her awkwardness over his reaction to her and to engage him in conversation, but she had no idea what to say. "It's a beautiful night."

"It is," the man agreed and cringed when a dragon swooped overhead.

"They won't hurt you," Lexi assured him.

"Maybe not now."

Lexi lifted a satchel of lavender and rose. She could use some relaxation, and though Sahira would make her something like this if she asked, she felt compelled to buy something now that she'd stopped.

"How much is this?" she asked.

"For you? Nothing."

She smiled. "That's awfully kind of you, but I'm going to pay."

Lexi dipped a hand into her pocket and pulled out a few carisle. She set them onto the man's booth, thanked him, and walked away.

She'd probably paid too much, but she didn't like all the attention or fawning that came with her new position. Over time, she'd get used to it… maybe. But she certainly hadn't had enough time to adjust.

When they arrived at the palace gates, the guards outside them pushed one open for her and the others. Lexi studied the mountains as stars twinkled to life in the sky and the moon rose higher. It was only a half moon, but its radiance bathed the land.

Now that they'd finished going through all the papers, she had a new mission. Tomorrow, after they executed the prisoners, she would continue searching for Cole.

She'd hoped to be armed with the knowledge of how to save him when she found him, but that hadn't worked out. And now, she just wished to see him.

She had no idea where to start her search; it would be in Dragonia, but there were *so* many mountains and caves in this unfamiliar land that it could take her years to search them all. Alina would help her, or one of the other dragons, as Alina had her hands full with her offspring, but Lexi would figure out a way to find him.

He'd left her, and he hadn't returned, but she wouldn't abandon him. He was suffering, and she could ease it.

And every ounce of her missed him. It had been a month. One endless, *horrible* month without him by her side. She'd never felt so alone, broken, and lost.

She hooked her arm through her dad's and rested her head on his shoulder. She inhaled his familiar scent of the outdoors and mint; it was such a comforting aroma and it soothed a part of her ragged soul.

"You're doing a good job," he said as he patted her hand. "You're a great leader, Andi. It will take some time, but we'll get through this."

She smiled at his much-loved nickname for her. "I hope so."

He squeezed her hand as they arrived at her room. Two lycans stood outside the door, prepared to stand guard for the night. A feeling of suffocation descended over Lexi as she stared at the closed door.

She missed the freedom anonymity afforded her. With a sigh, she kissed her dad's cheek, opened the door, and disappeared inside.

Closing the door, she leaned against it and studied the moonlight spilling through the windows across from her. Feeling as if she were going to crawl out of her skin, she crossed to the window, rested her hands on the sill, and leaned out to inhale the crisp, fresh air.

She should start closing the shutters at night, but she loved the fresh air and couldn't shut Cole out. He could probably get past the shutters, but she wasn't taking the chance he couldn't.

A dragon dipped its wing toward her. In the moonlight, its orange scales shone like the sun as it swooped beneath the window.

Without hesitating, Lexi scrambled across the sill, onto the dragon's back, and up to its powerful neck. Her heart hammered and excitement pulsed through her body as its wings flapped and it pushed away from the building.

Lexi grasped two of the spikes on the back of its head as she flattened herself against its back. The wind ruffled her hair and tore at her clothes as the dragon soared across the land.

Below, the small, hut-like homes of many who resided in Dragonia looked like miniatures. Their domed, thatched roofs reminded Lexi of mushrooms, but these were much cuter than the fungus.

They flew over the mountain peaks and valleys. Dragonia was a fertile place full of lush, green grass, grain fields, and mountains touching the sky.

Houses and villages were nestled amid the fields and on the mountains. The torchlights flickering on the dirt roads below illuminated the darkness.

Lexi searched for some sign of Cole as they soared further over the land. If he was in Dragonia, he was most likely in the mountains or caves, but the realm was so vast, he could be anywhere.

At one point, they soared over the dwarves, gathered around a large bonfire as they laughed and waved their battle-axes in the air while dancing and laughing. Their happiness made Lexi smile before the dragon moved on.

She didn't know how long they flew across the land, but she saw no sign of Cole, and when she started to yawn, the dragon turned back toward the palace.

Exhausted but unwilling to crawl into her bed and let the nightmares take over, Lexi leaned forward to tell the dragon, "Take me to a different window."

The dragon lowered her to one of the first-floor windows, and Lexi scrambled off to climb inside. Once her feet were back on the ground, she rubbed the dragon's snout and kissed it.

In response, it nuzzled her before pushing away from the window and returning to the sky. The dragons followed her every move as she traversed the palace.

CHAPTER FORTY-SIX

AT THE END of the tunnel, Cole spotted a grouping of warlocks, vampires, dark fae, lycans, and other assorted immortals gathered. They must have bonded over their intent to kill Lexi; it wasn't often so many different immortals were seen together and getting along well.

They'd defeated the Lord because so many immortals had worked with them. And these assholes were gathering an army.

His fingers popped, and his joints cracked as the lycan tried to exert its dominance, but the shadows were in control here. It was almost time for them to play.

He was almost to the group, who remained unaware of his presence, when a gate crashed down in front of him. At first, Cole was too astounded to react before another gate slammed down behind him.

The shadows rose as he realized these assholes had tried to trap him. He roared as he charged the gate protecting his enemies from him.

When he crashed into it, sparks erupted around him, and a jolt of something quaked his body and stuttered his heart. His body spasmed before the magic flung him back.

He hit the ground and bounced across it before coming to a stop. His fingers involuntarily curled inward as the incantation they'd weaved over the gates continued to affect him.

"Easy, Cole," Becca coaxed from behind him. "We mean you no harm. We're trying to keep you alive and in power."

Regaining control of his body, Cole's head swiveled toward her. The second he saw her in the bar, he should have killed her, but she hadn't given him a reason to. He couldn't slaughter her without proof that she was running to the Lord.

Now, he had his proof, and she would die.

"Do you really think these bars can keep me caged?" the shadows snarled.

Becca gulped as she glanced behind him. The shuffling of feet alerted him the others were approaching the bars there.

Rocking onto his back, Cole threw his legs up and jumped into the air. He stood in the middle of the bars as his attention shifted to the other group.

"We ensorcelled the bars," a warlock said. "You can't break them."

Cole reached out to the shadows beyond the bars so they could tear these assholes to pieces, but his connection to them was gone. Frustration mounted as he realized their spell kept him from speaking with the shadows out there.

"Listen to me, Cole," Becca said. "You're the most powerful being in all the realms—"

"He's not so powerful now," one of the others muttered.

Cole's eyes narrowed on the vampire, who smirked at him. "You'll be the first one I kill," Cole vowed.

The vamp's smile grew.

"With your help, we can take Dragonia," Becca continued as if no one had spoken, "and eradicate the only enemy you have."

"Lexi is not my enemy," Cole growled.

"She'll destroy you, and we both know it. She'll take you out before you can destroy the realms or her. You have to strike first; if you do, she won't expect it."

"He's not going to turn on her," one of the warlocks said. "This was a mistake."

"Give him time to realize the only way to save himself... is to destroy *her*," Becca said.

Now that he knew what to expect from them, Cole crept closer to the bars nearest Becca and gripped them. Magic thrummed against his palms, bolts of electricity hammered his flesh, and pain radiated into his bones as the magic battered him.

He didn't release the bars while he smiled at her. Around him, the shadows screamed for blood as they danced through the air while seeking to break free of the bars, but they couldn't get past the spell either.

"He shouldn't be able to touch the bars," one of his enemies murmured.

"Don't worry, he still can't break them," another assured him.

Cole smiled at Becca as she warily eyed him. "You're wrong, Becca. I'd destroy myself before I ever hurt her."

She gulped before shaking her head. "Your survival instincts will kick in, and you'll see what has to be done."

"My survival instinct is perfectly fine. I became the Reaver to protect her and to see her on that throne—"

"The *shadows* don't want to die," Becca said.

"How do you know that?"

"I saw you in the bar. I saw your reaction to my words; maybe the lycan part of you seeks to protect its mate, but the rest wants to *live*."

Cole tilted his head to the side as he studied her. "The dark fae part of me loves her, as does the lycan. The shadows seek to protect her; that's why we're here."

"We can make you king!" Becca shouted.

"So can Lexi. All I have to do is marry her. Besides, I already have a kingdom in the Gloaming; a kingdom is not what I seek."

"What do you seek?" one of the others asked.

Cole didn't take his eyes off Becca as he replied, "Death."

Becca gulped, while behind him, the other's feet crunched against the dirt when they shifted uneasily.

"We can give that to you," someone said.

"I don't need you for that."

"You don't need her either," Becca said.

"And I need you?"

Becca's chin lifted as she replied, "I have power in the realms, allies, and an army I can give you."

"I don't want your army, and I especially don't want *you*."

Sadness flickered through Becca's eyes, and Cole gripped the bars harder. The muscles in his arms vibrated, and the cells inside him quivered as magic continued to pummel him.

"That's too bad," one of the women behind him said. "If you won't work with us, then you're against us, and we can't have that. Kill him."

Becca blanched a little. "No! He'll see we're right and that *she's* the enemy."

Cole smiled, but it was more a baring of his teeth. "You're all going to die."

∽

"Orin!" a voice shouted gruffly from behind him.

Orin jumped a little at the sudden intrusion of sound, and his feet dropped from the table where he'd been enjoying a drink after another pointless night of searching for Cole. The few other people in the palace's lounge turned toward him.

As Skog stormed toward him, he set his glass down and rolled his eyes. With every step, the bottom of the dwarf's battle-ax clinked against the rocky floor. The look on his face stopped Orin from cracking some wiseass retort.

"What is it?" Orin demanded.

Skog stopped in front of him and planted the end of his ax on the ground. "Cole has been spotted. I know where he is… or where he *was*."

Orin's chair skittered back as he rose. "Take me to him."

CHAPTER FORTY-SEVEN

Lexi admired the play of the moonlight filtering through the windows lining the hall. This was an outer hall; it didn't lead to the inner rooms. It circled the palace and gave those who traveled it a view of the outside while they walked.

She loved being out here where the cool air against her skin gave her a sense of freedom. On her left side, she passed by the base of the palace's towers, which blocked her view for about twenty steps before the stone wall opened up again.

The towers were spaced every fifty or so feet. On her right, it was mostly the palace's outer wall, although she passed an occasional door to the inside.

She ignored those doors as she savored the sounds of the night. They were different than what she was used to on Earth; peepers or crickets didn't sing, owls didn't hoot, and the occasional murmur of passing humans didn't pierce the quiet.

Here, the hush was broken by the occasional beat of a dragon's wings as they patrolled the land. When she turned a corner, the rush of the river drifted up from below.

Lexi poked her head over the side to gaze at the water a hundred feet beneath her. It was beautiful as it reflected the moonlight, but after what she witnessed in that underground room, it made her shudder.

Her footsteps were soundless against the stone as her attention shifted away. When it did, she caught an odd sway to the shadows.

Lexi's step faltered as she searched for something more from the shadows, but she didn't see it again. Frowning, she continued forward, but her eyes constantly roved over the walls and ground.

She was about to turn another corner when a flicker went through the shadows. Stopping, she glowered at the shadows surrounding her.

There weren't many of them, the night didn't allow for that, but she could tell some were off. And she knew why.

"If Cole can't be here himself, then you're not welcome. Tell him you can't be here without him."

Lexi released her shield to chase them away. There wasn't enough moonlight here to allow for much of a glow, and it certainly wasn't enough for her to chase away the shadows.

Frustrated and knowing they wouldn't obey her command over his, she turned and strode through the opening beside her. Only focused on getting away, she realized too late what she'd walked into.

The garden.

Her footsteps slowed but didn't stop. She hated this garden with all its barren bleakness and the awful fountain somewhere inside; she despised the shadows more.

She wouldn't give them the satisfaction of following her further. Unlike the outer walkways she'd left behind, the garden was wide open with no cover. The half-moon shone down on the dead plants with a radiance unequaled by that of the Earth's moon.

As she strode into the moon's light, her glow intensified to chase the shadows further away. Lifting her chin, Lexi smiled when a sound of annoyance issued from them.

When the shadows reported back to him, her actions would piss off Cole, but that was too bad. As she walked, bathed in luminescence, she felt something inside her stir.

Overhead, the beat of the dragons' wings increased as, drawn by her glow, more of them circled overhead. She couldn't quite put a finger on what it was and had no idea what it meant, but something inside her came to life as she moved through the deadened plants.

This wasn't the first time she'd lowered her shield while in Dragonia. She felt a connection to the land the last time she did too, and now something new vibrated to life within her.

Though she didn't want the shadows coming closer again, the increasing number of dragons overhead would alert someone that she was out. She stopped and resurrected her shield before calling out to them in a whisper they would hear.

"It's okay. I'm fine; you don't have to worry about me."

She'd put her shield back into place, but the vibration continued. The connection rose from her booted feet and spread to her fingertips before pulsing across her hairline.

Her connection to the earth... no, that wasn't right either.

To the gardens?

Walking over, she kept her shield in place in the hopes the remaining dragons would stay asleep, but more of them took to the sky. She stopped before a plant so dead she couldn't tell what it was.

But then, she might not know what it was even if it was alive. So many things in this realm differed from Earth.

When her fingers brushed over the plant, it twitched beneath her hand. Lexi almost jerked her fingers away, but the plant's unexpected reaction wasn't unpleasant.

It felt *right*. As she stroked the plant, she recalled how the luna flowers reacted to her and how they made her laugh while playing with her.

She'd always felt an affinity with nature on Earth, but nothing had ever reacted to her there. However, Sahira's potion had suppressed her powers at the time, so maybe things would have been different.

She lifted the plant to rub the brown and shriveled leaves. There must be some life left in it as the leaves hadn't fallen off completely.

Perhaps the plant had gone dormant beneath the rule of those who didn't belong on the throne. Lifting her head, she gazed around the garden. Maybe *all* the plants were dormant and not dead.

As she contemplated it, the stem twitched in her hand, and green spread across its leaves. Lexi gasped as she leaned closer to examine the plant as more green brightened its leaves and brown deepened its stem.

She had no idea why, but the urge to fall to her knees and weep hit her. Amidst all the death and destruction plaguing her for months, there was hope, and she badly needed it.

In this barren place, there was life and beauty. It was all seeking to break free, and *she* could be the one to do it.

The now green stalk brushed her fingers before rising to rub her cheek. Lexi gave the now colorful plant a final caress before turning her attention to the rest of the garden.

The whole place was a mess of death and decay, but it wouldn't stay that way. She would make sure of it.

Releasing her shield again, she used her glow to chase away the shadows. She didn't want those things here, amongst her hope.

Lexi smiled and laughed as she strolled through the garden, reawakening the lost plants.

CHAPTER FORTY-EIGHT

Cole turned as one of the warlocks unleashed a jagged bolt of something resembling lightning at him. He didn't know what the warlock's spell contained, but as it flew toward him, the shadows rose to bring it down.

The dark fae sought to use the power of the air; it gathered air around him but couldn't push it beyond the bars. As he tried, two other warlocks gathered fire in their hands.

Cole's muscles cracked as they bent and shifted into something else. His joints took on his wolf form as his jaw elongated.

Behind him, Becca screamed, "No! Don't hurt him!"

But her words didn't matter. These assholes had decided he would die, and they would do everything they could to make it happen.

A ball of fire hit Cole's shoulder. It seared across his hair and the muscle of his flank as he leapt at the bars.

Throwing the full power of his weight into it, he smashed against the bars with everything he had. He ignored the agony of his burnt shoulder and the magic continuously zapping him as he shoved his snout through the bars while snapping at the fuckers beyond.

They were so convinced their magic would keep him contained, they didn't move away from him. But though it didn't make any noise yet, he felt the metal giving way beneath his weight.

When they threw another ball of fire at him, the dark fae's power somehow rose and knocked it aside. Disbelief rippled through him at this new development.

Usually, when he was in wolf form, his dark fae abilities were suppressed, but now, the lycan and fae worked together to keep the wolf protected while it tried to break free. All around him, the shadows bobbed and weaved; if possible, they would have salivated at the idea of breaking free and unleashing terror on all who dared to trap them here.

Metal screeched as the wolf pressed into the bars. That thrumming, painful sensation intensified until it vibrated his ears, battered his bones, and shook his muscles, but he refused to give up.

The wolf stifled a whimper as the power racing through him amped up until every part of him quaked and zapping noises pulsed through his ears. The warlocks unleashed three more fireballs on him and more of those lightning bolts.

With its ability to control the elements, the dark fae part of him knocked aside the fire, but a lightning bolt slammed into his head. An explosion went off in his skull as lights erupted before his eyes; his body jerked and swayed as his claws tore into the stone.

Cole had no control over himself anymore and he'd lost his vision and some of his hearing, but his instincts told him to move, or die.

"Stop it!" Becca screamed. "I command you to *stop*!"

"We don't follow your commands," someone stated.

Fire singed his right shoulder, but most of the blow missed him as he rolled across the floor and bounded onto his paws. Still unable to see, his instincts guided him as the lycan charged into the bars again. He would see them all dead, but he had to *see* for it to happen.

Crashing into the bars, he shoved against them until they twisted with a screech before something finally gave way beneath his weight. Shaking his head, he couldn't stop a grunt when more lightning bolts blistered his flesh, but he didn't cease his efforts to break free.

These soon-to-be-dead fuckers had underestimated his strength, and they would pay for it. The bars sliced across his flesh; one bit into his shoulder but using his jaws, he ripped it free. He shoved himself the rest of the way through the bars.

When he emerged on the other side, the shadows surged as he regained control of them again. His vision started to clear and delicious screams filled his ears. He relished every one of those agonized screams as the shadows tore their victims to pieces.

With his paws thudding against the ground, the wolf barreled toward one of the warlocks. The man released another fireball that exploded in Cole's face.

The stench of burnt hair filled the tunnel, but as the fire burned him and his skin sizzled, his jaws clamped on the warlock's waist. Cole lifted him off the ground and bashed him into the rock.

The warlock's head burst like an overripe tomato. His arms and legs kicked against the floor, but Cole wasn't finished with him as his jaws sank onto the warlock's head, and he tore it free.

Swinging his head, he launched the skull at a vamp running deeper into the cave. The head crashed into the back of the man's knees. It knocked him off his feet as another warlock heaved a fireball at him.

Cole darted to the side in time to avoid the fireball as a dark fae gathered the power of the air and shoved it at him. The blast would have thrown him back if his dark fae powers hadn't blocked and pushed it back.

The air hit the dark fae and slammed her into the wall.

Before the fae could recover, the shadows ripped away her skin and plunged into her chest to tear out her heart.

When the rest of his enemies fell beneath his claws, teeth, and the shadows, Cole turned to where he last saw Becca, but she was gone. He didn't have time to deal with the bars on the other side of the cage, so he plunged deeper into the tunnel as he searched for another way out.

He would find her and make her pay.

CHAPTER FORTY-NINE

Brokk stepped from the portal into an outer realm with the female dwarf who'd come to get him. Cole had been spotted, and the dwarf knew where. Brokk could only hope his brother was still here.

As he searched the night, another portal opened, and Orin emerged with Skog at his side. Brokk didn't have time to acknowledge his brother before motion from the corner of his eye drew his attention. Becca sprinted across the grass as she raced toward a building and the portal opening before it.

What the fuck?

He didn't have time to intercept her and find out what was going on before the back door of the building burst open and a large, black wolf leapt out. He recognized the wolf as the one Cole transformed into.

He had no idea what was happening here, but it couldn't be good. Before Becca made it to the portal, the wolf lunged forward, grabbed her around the waist, and bashed her into the ground.

Becca's scream reverberated across the land as blood sprayed from her mouth. Brokk's jaw dropped when Cole violently shook Becca while she battered his head.

"Cole!" Orin shouted.

At the same time, he and Orin raced toward them. Brokk didn't care about Becca. The manipulative bitch wouldn't be missed, and the hierarchy of the dark fae had crumbled, but he had to know what she was doing here and what she'd done to enrage his brother so much.

Brokk was almost to them when a wall of shadows rose before him, blocking him from getting closer. He ducked when one of the shadows lashed out at him. When another tried to wrap around his wrist, he staggered back and nearly fell over his feet.

"Shit."

"Cole!" Orin yelled as two shadows encircled him. "Cole!"

Brokk threw himself to the ground and rolled toward the portal where he'd entered this realm. The female dwarf scrambled forward, seized his arm, and helped pull him to his feet.

Orin had shaken the shadows and retreated to stand with Skog as Cole planted his paw on Becca's chest. When his claws dug into her flesh, she screamed louder and beat him with fists that did nothing to dissuade Cole from planting his other paw on her head.

Brokk swore the wolf smiled as it pulled her head and body in two different directions. Becca's screams became high-pitched, broken shrieks as, much slower than necessary, Cole decapitated her.

After a minute, Becca's screams finally ceased when he succeeded in tearing her head away. As the shadows retracted into him, Cole transformed into a man again.

Blood covered him from head to toe; it dripped from his black hair to plop onto the rocks. Burns marked his shoulders, and more lacerations decorated his back, chest, and hands, but he seemed unfazed by the injuries.

"Cole." Brokk's voice sounded abnormally loud in the hush following Becca's death, but it didn't deter him. "Come back with us."

Cole's head swiveled toward him, but he didn't respond before walking into the portal Becca had opened.

"Fuck," Brokk muttered before plunging into the portal behind his brother.

"See what's down below!" Orin shouted to the dwarves before following them.

They tracked Cole into the human realm and, from there, into Dragonia. The guards jumped out of the way and yelped when Cole shifted into a wolf, wrapped the shadows around himself, and vanished.

"Paw prints," Orin said as he pointed at the ground, still wet from recent rain.

Cole could cloak himself in shadows, but he couldn't hide the bloody paw prints he left behind when he raced across the earth. He and Orin tracked those prints into the mountains.

CHAPTER FIFTY

BROKK WAS the one who remained behind to guard the cave Cole entered while Orin returned to the palace. Orin wasn't sure if Cole had known they were tracking him and didn't care, or—and he believed this was more likely—Cole was too lost in the madness gripping him to notice.

Before they ever reached the mountain, the bloody prints faded, but the words of Cole and the shadows didn't. Although they couldn't see him, they heard his muttered words and the hiss of the shadows as they battled each other.

Climbing up those rocks, following the words, Orin kept waiting to be greeted by shadows and shoved off the mountain or torn to pieces, but they never attacked. When they arrived at the cave, they weren't certain if Cole had entered until a bellow erupted from inside.

The shout, and the emotions within it, rattled the cave walls and rebounded off the rocks. Standing there, a chill crept down Orin's spine as Cole's words drifted further away until only silence remained.

He wanted to stand guard, but Brokk won the fight. It was less likely Cole would see Brokk as a danger should he emerge again; in his foul mood, he might kill Orin, who had always enjoyed being a thorn in his older brother's side.

It had taken him far more time to descend the mountain than he would have liked. The sun was high in the sky when he arrived at the palace.

Now, as his boots rang out across the rock while striding through the hallways in search of Lexi, he regretted the decision. He should have stayed, but it was too late to do anything about it. The sooner he found Lexi, the sooner they could return and make sure Brokk was okay.

The throne room was empty, as were the kitchens, the dining room, the parlor, tavern, and the room where they'd all searched through the documents. Though it was early afternoon, he went to her bedroom, but the guards were gone and no one was inside.

No one was *anywhere,* as far as he could tell. He'd yet to run across another soul in his search, which should have proved impossible by now. Someone should have to eat, or want a drink, or be standing in the hall.

"Where is everyone?" he muttered.

His heart raced, and his feet moved faster as he swept through the palace. Had something happened to them? Had he somehow missed a battle or a spell that did something to all of them?

They finally knew where Cole was, and he couldn't find the one woman who might be able to save him or *anyone* else. Outside, a dragon cast a shadow across the hall as it soared past the window. If they were still around, so was Lexi, but the palace remained eerily hushed.

He descended to the first floor and stood in the main entryway as he looked back and forth and tried to decide where they all could have gone. Another dragon soared across the windows, heading toward the center of the palace.

He followed it; if anyone or anything knew where to find

Lexi, it was the dragons. He lost sight of the dragon almost immediately but followed its trajectory.

Winding his way through the palace, Orin realized he was heading toward the gardens Lexi had stalwartly avoided since taking over here.

This can't be right.

But he'd checked everywhere else; he might as well check the place Lexi was least likely to be. Turning a corner, he stopped when he spotted the wall of immortals standing outside the garden, peering in.

They stood, crammed into every opening, sometimes two or three deep. Their shoulders pressed against each other as they spoke in low whispers, or not at all. The wall of their backs prevented him from entering the garden.

"Excuse me," he said.

No one moved or acknowledged him as they focused on whatever lay beyond. He'd tried being polite, something he rarely was, and now he was over it.

Lowering his shoulder, Orin drove it into their backs and sides as he shoved his way through them. They grunted and shot him nasty looks that he ignored as he pushed his way to the front.

Once there, he started to straighten his tunic but froze as his attention was captured by the scene before him. The gardens that were once so brown and dead now teemed with green and life. None of the plants had flowers, but he suspected that as the plants grew and flourished, flowers would follow.

"Shit," he breathed. "What happened here?"

No one bothered to answer him. He didn't know if it was because they had no idea, if they were too flabbergasted to respond, or because it was him. Either way, though he couldn't see her, he knew Lexi was responsible for this, and she was somewhere in the garden.

Orin stepped away from the crowd. When he did, he realized

why none of them had moved further into the garden. The dragon had been so still, he hadn't noticed it sitting there until its head turned toward him and its wings rippled.

Orin held up his hand placatingly as he edged away from the creature and deeper into the overflowing green of a garden he'd believed dead. He'd seen a lot of things over the years, but this verdant jungle was in the top ten most astonishing things of all.

He had no idea how Lexi had done any of this, but it felt *right* that she could. The dragon's eyes followed his every move, so he kept his hands up until he was certain the beast wouldn't eat him.

He lowered his hands again when he was out of view of the dragon. No one else tried to follow him, probably because they weren't crazy.

He spotted Sahira first amid the trees, now teeming with life. He had no idea what some of the trees were, but their mixture of green, red, orange, purple, and yellow reflected the sun streaming through them.

This breathtaking burst of color was so beautiful it caused his step to slow as he drank it in. Then, he reminded himself that he was here for a reason.

CHAPTER FIFTY-ONE

When his foot crunched a rock on the path, Sahira's head turned toward him. A radiant smile lit her face and amber eyes as the sun sparkled in them; that smile vanished when she spotted him.

He grinned as he stopped beside her. "Good morning, little witchy witch. It's a pleasure to see you too."

She rolled her eyes before shifting her attention away from him.

"Our queen has been busy," Orin said, "or at least I'm assuming this was her."

Sahira crossed her arms over her chest as her jaw tensed. "This was her."

The way she said it made it sound like talking to him was the equivalent of having her teeth pulled. It made him smile more.

"How interesting," Orin murmured. "Who knew she could bring things back to life."

"I don't think it's that, at least not completely. These plants were never dead, at least not fully. They were more in a state of dormancy."

"And she reawakened them?"

"Yes. I think we've discovered another arach talent."

"What's that? They're plant whisperers?"

"She definitely has a way with them. Lexi was always good with animals and loved being outside. She has an affinity with all living things."

"Interesting. Where is our little plant whisperer?"

Sahira thrust her chin forward, and through some ivy draped over a wall and spilling toward a bench, Lexi strode into view. Del and Maverick sat on the bench. Del sat forward with his elbows on his knees while Maverick stretched out his long legs and had his arm over the back of the seat.

Lexi stretched up and touched the brown limbs of a tree towering over the others. As her fingers stroked the branch, color seeped into it.

Orin blinked as he tried to process everything he was seeing. Seeing the garden had been a shock, but watching her reawaken these plants was…

Well, it was miraculous, and he wasn't one for miracles.

"Shit," he whispered.

From behind Lexi and in between some trees, Varo and Kaylia emerged. They stood in the shade of a tree with leaves so purple they rivaled the purest amethyst.

Orin resisted the sudden urge to sit down and watch as the rest of this unfolded, but he couldn't do that. Lexi had discovered some peace in the garden; her tranquil face and the small smile tugging at her mouth said as much. This garden had given the immortals of this realm a large measure of hope, and they *all* required it.

He gave her a hard time, but he admired his sister-in-law. She was strong, stubborn, and handling all she was thrown into amazingly well, considering everything she'd endured.

He didn't want to take Lexi from this, but she had to know, and if he had any chance of saving his brother, he needed her. And he wanted his brother back.

"We know where Cole is," Orin murmured.

His words didn't travel past Sahira, and they took some time to sink in as the witch remained staring at her niece with that radiant smile back on her face. Then, it vanished, and her head swiveled toward him.

"What? Where?" she demanded.

"In the mountains. Brokk and I tracked him there after a rather... eh... bloody night. Brokk remained at the cave to ensure we don't lose him if Cole emerges again."

Sahira paled while he spoke, and her arms fell limply to her sides. "Now what?"

Orin looked to Lexi as she moved on to a bush. "Now, I'll bring her to him to see if she can save him. If she can bring this place back to life, maybe she can do the same for him."

"And what if he doesn't want to be saved? What if we're offering her up for slaughter?"

"He'd never hurt her."

"Are you so sure?"

Orin recalled those shadows and how his brother muttered and fought with himself before vanishing into the cave. And then his bellow shook the earth.

Cole was completely out of control; every day, he spiraled further and further into madness, but if he knew one thing for sure in his life, it was that his brother cherished Lexi. He'd die before he ever harmed her.

"Yes."

The clink of a battle-ax against stone drew his attention as Skog rounded a big tree with heart-shaped, yellow leaves. At his side was the female dwarf who accompanied Brokk into the outer realm, where they discovered Cole.

The dwarves stared around the garden with their mouths ajar as they drank in the splendor of everything surrounding them. They were so focused on the garden that Skog nearly walked into him.

Orin sidestepped to avoid being plowed into by the dwarf. When his chest brushed Sahira's arm, she recoiled and edged away.

"Sorry, little witch," he murmured as he purposely caressed her arm with his finger.

She glowered at him as she moved further away. Finally realizing they were there, Skog abruptly stopped, but the woman took a few more steps before halting too.

The dwarves' arrival had drawn Lexi's attention. Since Orin hadn't talked to her yet, he knew he had to move. She should hear this from him and not the heavy-handed dwarves who had all the tact of a bomb.

"I'll talk to you later, sexy," he murmured in Sahira's ear.

He chuckled when she planted her hands on his chest and pushed him away. He thoroughly enjoyed getting the little witch all riled up.

"Did you go into the hole?" Orin asked Skog.

"Yes," the dwarf replied gruffly.

"What was down there?"

"The remains of a cage. They must have tried to trap Cole down there."

"And failed."

"They died, brutally, because of it."

The look on the dwarves' faces told Orin how brutal those deaths were.

"What is it?" Lexi inquired as she strolled toward them.

That small smile remained on her face, and joy sparkled in her green eyes as she approached. His brother wouldn't physically hurt her, but he could shred her heart.

Orin didn't have a choice. She had to know what they'd discovered.

When she stopped before him, he didn't hesitate before telling her, "We know where Cole is."

CHAPTER FIFTY-TWO

MADNESS CHURNED inside Cole as it bubbled to the surface. The shadows and insanity battered his brain, tore at his insides, and hammered him until he couldn't breathe.

He sank to his knees by the pool of icy water and dunked his head to calm his turmoil. When that didn't work, he crawled into the small pool that was only a couple of inches deep.

He'd been using the water that trickled from the cave's wall to bathe in, but now he wanted to lose himself to it and let it drown out the incessant chatter. But before he knew it, he'd traveled deeper into the cave.

Cole didn't recall leaving the water behind. He didn't realize he had until he bounced off the cave wall and spiraled into darkness.

The shadows clamored for more blood while the lycan raged for its mate, and the ravenous, famished, dark fae sought the woman it loved. All of them screamed for something different as he went to his knees before somehow rising again.

As the different parts of him screamed to be heard, something inside him snapped as he pummeled the walls. His fists battered the rocks around him until debris rose to encase his ankles.

Blood spilled from his broken flesh, down his arms, and splattered on the floor. Everything inside him spiraled completely out of control as the three parts of himself clashed for dominance.

And then, as they had in that underground pit, where those assholes tried to trap *him*, the dark fae and lycan shifted and came together. They each sought the same thing... *her*... and would do whatever it took to have her.

They banded together as their powers combined and something inside him clicked into place. The two parts of himself had come together earlier; they'd worked together in a way they never had before, and now they were declaring war against the shadows.

For the first time in his existence, the dark fae and lycan were one. They were united and wouldn't be defeated.

The shadows fought back as they refused to relinquish their hold over him. Their whispered words of death and vengeance churned throughout him.

It was too dark for the shadows to thrive down here, but the ones inside wouldn't relinquish their hold. After all these centuries, he'd finally found peace amongst the two warring factions he'd dealt with since birth... and now a new part was ripping him in two.

Cole roared as the shadows sought to bury what remained of him while he pummeled the walls.

∾

"Stop that. No! *Don't* do that. Oh no. Oh, *fuck me*. Stop it!"

Lexi stifled her laughter as she glanced back at where Orin clung to Alina's neck, his skin pale, his knuckles a bright white, and his eyes scrunched closed as he pressed his cheek into her back. Every time Alina shifted or flapped her wings, he cursed, told her to stop, and muttered something about never taking his feet off the ground again.

Lexi didn't offer any words of reassurance or tell him she'd ridden the dragons dozens of times without any problem. First, he didn't deserve them; secondly, no one knew about her late-night forays, and she planned to keep it that way.

As far as she was concerned, Orin deserved every second of this. Below, Brokk came into view as he waved to them. Orin groaned when Alina descended to the earth.

As soon as the dragon's feet touched the ground and she settled into place, Lexi slid to the side and hopped off to stand next to Brokk. Orin continued clinging to Alina with his eyes closed and his arms spread wide.

She wasn't sure if he realized they'd landed, and she didn't tell him. Instead, she turned to Brokk. "Where is he?"

Brokk pointed to the cave fifty feet away. "He's in rough shape, Lexi. I mean *really* bad. He was shouting not so long ago, and it sounded like he was punching the walls. There was a lot of banging and thuds. He's also… he's also…." Brokk's eyes flitted away before meeting hers again. "He's also talking to the shadows, and I think himself."

Lexi gulped as she looked at the cave. She knew Cole was in rough shape, but it sounded like he was completely spiraling out of control.

Her heart ached for the anguish he was enduring. He deserved better than this, and she would do everything she could to ensure he got it.

"I don't think it's a good idea for us to go down there right now," Brokk continued.

"I agree," Lexi said, "and that's why you won't be going with me."

"You're not going alone."

Orin finally cracked his eyes open. He blinked at them a

couple of times and groaned when Alina rose and flapped her wings before settling back into place. Lexi smiled at the dragon, who grinned back in return.

"Never again," Orin muttered as he carefully slid off Alina.

"Not a fan of heights?" Lexi taunted.

He gave her the finger as he staggered a little before righting himself. "I'm not a fan of heights that *move*."

Despite the awfulness of this situation and the tension still thrumming through her, Lexi chuckled. "You're a mess right now."

Orin scowled at her, but a thunderous crash from the cave cut off whatever he was about to say. Lexi forgot all about enjoying Orin's small comeuppance as she lurched toward the entrance.

Before she could get to the cave, Brokk grasped her arm and pulled her back. Turning, she almost swung at him but restrained herself in time to keep from hitting him.

"I have to go," she said.

"Not alone."

"I *have* to be alone, or it will be much worse for him and all of us."

"He's out of control."

"And I can help with that."

"Lexi—"

"This is my realm, and *I'm* in charge here." She softened her next words as she knew fear and love drove Brokk now, but he had to understand. "He needs me."

"I know, but I'm in charge of keeping you safe."

"Do you think it's necessary to keep me safe from Cole?"

"You didn't see him last night, Lexi, and you haven't heard him down there."

"No, but I saw what he did to those immortals in the human realm. I *know* what he's capable of, and he's struggling to retain control, but the shadows can't hurt me, and Cole *never* would. They *will* hurt you."

"Are you so sure about the shadows?" Orin asked. "I think they're starting to develop a mind of their own."

"Then I'll have to put them back in their place, but *neither* of you is coming with me. Alina's going to fly you both out of here. This is something *Cole* and I have to do alone. You have to accept that."

"I'm good with not having another ride on the dragon. I'll walk," Orin said.

Alina snorted. "Coward."

"I'm okay with that."

Brokk chuckled. "I'm okay with walking too."

"Fine, but you *are* leaving," Lexi said. "Alina will make sure of that, won't you?"

"I will, my queen," Alina replied.

Lexi wiggled her fingers at Brokk and Orin. "Happy walking."

Orin rolled his eyes, but Brokk sighed and squeezed Lexi's arm. "You'll need light for in there."

When Lexi lifted her hand, small flames flickered to life at her fingertips. "I bring the light with me now."

"You always have. Good luck, sister of mine."

Lexi smiled at him. "Thank you, brother. I *am* going to bring him home."

"I hope so," Orin murmured.

CHAPTER FIFTY-THREE

Lexi rested her hand against the cool rock wall as she made her way into the cave. The glow from her fingertips barely lit the way, but she kept the fire to a bare minimum.

If Cole saw it before she made it to him, he might retreat further into the caves. Or he could think an enemy was coming and go on the defensive.

The last thing she needed was for him to think she was the enemy and attack before he realized it was her. She might never be able to save him then.

What if he doesn't want to be saved?

That awful possibility niggled at the back of her mind like flies around a rotten piece of meat left out in the summer sun. But she didn't let it stop her as she forged onward.

The deeper she traveled into the earth, the cooler and damper the air became. Her shirt cleaved to her body as the rocks beneath her fingers became increasingly damp from the moisture there.

She didn't understand the source of all the moisture until she rounded a corner and came across a clear pool of mountain water. It took up almost all the walking space inside the cave, leaving only a small section of dry land for her to traverse.

She pressed her back against the wall as she crept around the pool's edge. Halfway around it, she knelt, doused her flames, and dipped her fingers into the water.

Shivering, she pulled her hand away and shook off the drops of icy liquid before rising again. The pool looked deeper in the middle, and as she relit her fire, it flickered across the pristine surface.

This is where Cole has been bathing.

Picturing him in this dark place and bathing in this frigid water made her sadder. It was all so lonely and dark and awful down here. She had to make him leave.

With every step she took, her heart raced faster, and sweat beaded her nape. She wasn't afraid of Cole; she was scared this would be her last chance to save him.

If she didn't reach him now, she never would. One way or another, this would be the end of them or the beginning of their new life together.

She rounded the corner and stopped when she encountered what must have been the source of the crash. Rocks had fallen from the ceiling and walls to clog the cave and block her way.

Burying the panic trying to rise, Lexi waved her hand over the rocks as she searched for some sign the cave-in buried Cole. She saw no sign of him but found an opening to her right. She could barely walk through it if she hunched down.

Carefully picking her way over the rocks, Lexi climbed up to the opening. Debris kicked out from under her feet; stones clattered and rattled as they hit the ground.

She winced at the noise; there was no way to hide her presence from Cole now. But he probably already knew she was coming; her fire created shadows, after all.

When she climbed down the other side, she stopped again to

search for him. She didn't see anything obvious but couldn't be sure.

Her fingers traced over the rocks as she looked between them and the rest of the cave. She couldn't leave him here if he *was* trapped beneath the rocks, but if he wasn't under there, then he was still in this cave, and she had to get to him.

Torn between tearing through this pile and exploring further, Lexi remained where she was as she debated what to do. Finally, she decided to explore a little further before trying to dig under the rocks.

If he was trapped under the rocks, he'd be trying to dig his way out by now. The cave-in could have knocked him out and broken his back, but he was a fighter; it wouldn't keep him pinned for long.

Reluctantly, she rose and turned toward the cave; she only made it a few more feet before her fire reflected off Cole's pale face as it loomed out of the shadows. Her fire danced over his high cheekbones and blazing silver eyes with tendrils of black surrounding them.

Thrown off by his unexpected arrival and the ferocity of his expression, Lexi staggered back a couple of steps. Before she could right herself, her heel connected with loose rock, and she nearly went down.

Lexi managed to stop herself from falling on her ass by throwing her hand out and bracing it against the wall. Her heart raced, and her breath came in pants as she tried to regain control over herself and the adrenaline flooding her body.

When Cole prowled closer, her eyes widened as she took him in. Only his face was visible as the shadows encompassed the rest of him. He was paler and gaunter than the last time she saw him.

Oh shit.

CHAPTER FIFTY-FOUR

She never expected to see Cole looking like this. She certainly never expected the animosity emanating from him.

"What are you doing here?" he snarled in an unrecognizable voice contorted by the shadows.

Lexi lifted her chin as she planted her feet and stared defiantly back at him. "I came to see you."

"We don't wish to see you," the shadows hissed in return.

Lexi gulped; she didn't know how to proceed. She hadn't expected a welcoming party, but she also hadn't expected him to be so angry about her arrival—or not him, the shadows who seemed more in control than ever before.

"The shadows don't scare me," she told him.

"Yes, they do."

When fire licked up Lexi's fingers and toward her wrists, it pushed the shadows back, but they laughed as they danced around her.

"We weren't here until you arrived," the shadows said. "You brought the shadows to the cave."

Lexi glowered at the shadows as they slithered through

Cole's skin and across his face. She *loathed* these things, but her heart yearned for the man she loved with all her soul.

She knew he was in there somewhere, but she couldn't see him now, and she had no idea how to break through these shadows to reach him.

"Cole—"

"The shadows can't exist without light, Arach."

"And light can't exist without dark!" she snapped. "What's your *fucking* point?"

"Arach magic gave us light and allows us to thrive. Arachs brought us forth, and now you intend to destroy us."

"I don't—"

"Don't lie!"

"I won't let you keep him!"

The Cole creature advanced on her, but she held her ground. When one of the shadows caressed her cheek, she involuntarily recoiled from its cool touch as another stroked her arm.

Unable to stand their touch, she retreated until her heels came up against the pile of rubble. When more of the shadows rubbed her cheek and arms, she retreated up the debris and through the opening.

Cole followed her as she descended the pile. When the shadows laughed, Lexi planted her feet and refused to give another inch. She wouldn't back away from them again.

The shadows jerked back as the crack and pop of his shifting joints filled the air. "Don't touch her."

Lexi kept her face composed but inwardly winced as a war waged across his face and throughout the muscles of his quivering body. She had no idea how to help him find peace, but she would try.

"Cole—"

"*Run*, Lexi."

This time Cole's voice issued from the creature across from her. The anguish in it brought tears to her eyes as she lunged toward him, but she pulled back when the shadows rose to block her.

Cole's face extended into a snout as claws erupted from his fingertips and the shadows hissed. Some of them slithered toward her, but the wolf's claws slashed through them. The shadows split but quickly reformed.

The flames on Lexi's hands and arms burned higher until they caught on the sleeves of her shirt and burned it away, along with her bra. The fire also caught on the waistband of her pants. Pieces of them floated in the air as her clothes dissolved until she stood naked before him.

Something flashed in Cole's silver eyes, and the half-transformed wolf growled as he stretched a paw toward her. Needing to touch him, Lexi extinguished the flames on one of her hands and reached for him.

Their fingers connected, and he gripped her tight. She stared at the entwined fingers and the claws resting against her hand as love and a feeling of coming home swelled within her.

They were *meant* to be together. They were stronger together and always would be.

Her attention shifted back to Cole's tormented eyes as his snout receded, his fangs retracted, and the beautiful Persian blue of his eyes flashed through the silver before black crept in to replace it. Her heart sank when she saw the shadows trying to control him again.

"Stay with me, Cole," she whispered.

From all around her, the shadows laughed and slid up her arm to whisper in her ear. "He's already gone; you can't change that."

They would lie; she knew they would. These things would do anything to keep Cole, but she couldn't stop the doubt radiating through her.

She had no idea how to save him; the Lord destroyed that

knowledge. The shadows leapt and danced through the air when Cole yanked his hand away from her.

"Fuck you!" Lexi shot back at them.

Insane, hideous laughter came from around her, and she was suddenly reminded of the Lord as he sat on the throne, laughing down at them. Pieces of her heart shattered, but she refused to give in to the sorrow choking her.

She could never let something like the Lord walk these realms again. She'd protect them, and the immortals living in them, until her dying breath.

"You better run, little girl," the shadows murmured.

"I'm not going anywhere."

When Cole advanced, she held her ground and relit the flames on the hand where she'd extinguished them. The fire chased the shadows closest to her away.

Lexi tipped her head back when Cole stopped directly in front of her. They stood chest to chest as Cole towered over her. This close, she saw the injuries marring his skin; most were nearly healed, but a few looked as if they'd been pretty bad.

When his hands stretched into the flames, his skin sizzled and popped. She jerked her hands away when he reached for her again.

"Stop that," she commanded as his hands seized her biceps.

And then, because the scent of burning flesh filled the air, she extinguished her fire. She refused to let the shadows torture him further, but she realized too late that was what they wanted her to do… or maybe it was *Cole* who did.

CHAPTER FIFTY-FIVE

M<small>ADNESS BATTERED</small> Cole's mind until he couldn't figure out who was talking to him anymore... the shadows, himself, or Lexi.

The agony of his blistering skin helped him break through the madness and gave him something else to focus on. Even after her flames went out, he cleaved to her as he held onto this moment of sanity.

And as he did so, a sudden understanding dawned on him.

"This is what the Lord felt like on the throne," he whispered. "He couldn't handle the arach magic, and it ruined him."

"But you *can* handle it," Lexi said. "The shadows and the magic that created them were set up as part of the trials. Only the strongest dark fae could activate the power. The arach designed the trials for *you*, Cole, and you can fight it; I know you can."

Her hands clamped onto his arms; when they did so, warmth spread through him. The discomfort in his hands eased as she healed him.

"No," he whispered. "Don't take the pain from me; it helps me think."

The warmth eased before fading as Lexi's hands tightened on

his arms. "Come with me, and we can figure this out together, because we can't do it separately."

Cole closed his eyes as the shadows whispered through his mind. "She seeks to destroy us. She seeks to destroy *you*."

Cole shook his head as he tried to clear it of the shadows' words. Lexi would never destroy him, but she was the only one who could.

"The power," the shadows whispered from him. "The power is *ours*. The host is *ours*."

∽

LEXI'S HEART sank when those monstrous things whispered from him again. She'd been getting through to him; she could feel it. She was making headway, but every time she did, those *things* reemerged to steal him from her again.

"I love you," she breathed as tears choked her throat. "I refuse to lose you."

"You already have. He's ours," the shadows replied.

Closing her eyes, Lexi dug her fingers into the thick muscle of his biceps. Her nails bit into his flesh as she gritted her teeth and blinked against the tears in her eyes.

She hated doing this to him; nausea twisted her stomach at the idea of it, but it was necessary. Pain had broken through the shadows before and brought Cole back to her. He said it helped him think, and she needed that.

"I'm sorry," she whispered before the fire erupted from her hands.

Tears spilled down Lexi's cheeks when Cole's skin sizzled and the stench of burnt flesh permeated the cave. She extinguished her flames almost immediately, but Cole's skin continued to crackle after the fire was out.

"You *bitch*," the shadows snarled.

"No," Cole said in a barely recognizable voice.

The change in his voice alerted Lexi that he was shifting again before soft fur sprouted beneath her hands.

"No," he said again.

Lexi realized he was battling the shadows inside him. They were trying to batter him down as his arms trembled beneath her hands, and the fur receded. She had to do something to keep *Cole* with her.

"I love you; I'll always love you," she vowed.

"You seek to destroy us."

She winced at the shadows' words.

"I seek to love *him*. My people created you; they gave him this power, and I can't take it away. I... I..." Her voice broke as she stifled a sob. "I don't know how."

She didn't hear him move, but suddenly his lips were against her ear. "It doesn't matter; you have the ability. *That* is what matters."

The shadows couldn't attack her, but terror crept down Lexi's spine. These things were monstrous, insane, and Cole was right... this *was* what happened to the Lord.

Maybe the shadows were a different kind of magic than the throne, and maybe the Lord couldn't control the shadows, but he could control the dragons, and it had eaten his mind until only a shell of the former man remained.

And if she didn't do something, that could become Cole.

Unable to stop them, tears dripped off her chin to land on the rocky floor with a small plop.

"We don't wish to be your enemy," the shadows said. "We are your protectors; that is why the arach created us. Stop fighting this and accept it. He is gone, we will rule, and you will live *many* years because of us. No harm will come to you while we live."

"I don't want this, and neither does Cole."

"Everyone wants something they can't have. Our needs must

be met; we are necessary for your survival, and you must live if the realms are to know peace."

Lexi's shoulders shook as more tears streamed down her face. She didn't hear Cole anymore; it was all those things.

"He is gone; we are your protectors now."

Her head spun as the shadows whispered, and her heart shattered. Maybe in these broken, battered, and far too often brutal realms, the best thing she could do for *everyone* was to walk away and concede defeat to these things.

They would protect her and the fragile peace they'd so recently established, but she could never let Cole go so easily. She couldn't leave him here to be devoured and driven mad by these things.

Unable to see him in the dark, she released his arms and grasped his face. Rising onto her toes, she inhaled the scent of rocks and earth clinging to him along with his natural musky, allspice aroma.

His beard tickled her palms as she leaned forward and kissed him. At first, he tried to recoil from her… No, not Cole; he would never do such a thing. The *shadows* tried to pull away from her.

They had taken control of him again, and she would wrest it back.

CHAPTER FIFTY-SIX

THE SHADOWS SCREAMED as they recoiled from Lexi's lips. They railed against her, against *this*, as they insisted she would destroy them and him.

But as the shadows resisted the warmth of Lexi's lips, her enticing strawberry scent, and the love she exuded, the lycan and dark fae parts of him surged to the forefront. They buried the wrath of the shadows as they were rewarded with what they desired most.

His claws extended as his arms encircled her waist, and he pulled her naked body flush against his. Lifting her off the ground, he slid one of his hands up the silken skin of her back to clasp her head.

As he did so, she opened her mouth, and he invaded to savor her taste as their tongues entwined. He was ravenous, hard, and desperate for everything she gave him.

Even as the shadows continued to rage against this, his other hand slid to her ass, and he squeezed it. Her legs wrapped around his waist, and she draped her arms over his shoulders as she kissed him like she would never kiss him again.

And if they stopped now, this *could* be their last kiss. Cole's arms cinched around her at the possibility. The lycan and dark fae had taken control from the shadows and wouldn't relinquish it while she remained in his arms.

Cole started to turn her into the wall to fuck her, but though he was nearly mindless with his lust for her, he still retained enough control to know it couldn't be *here*. He didn't want her in this horrible, dark place where he'd washed so much blood off himself and waged countless battles he'd repeatedly lost to his inner demons.

He didn't want to be in this place anymore. The stale air, the dank smell, and the countless whispered words that plagued him since finding this cave were a bane to his existence.

His erection made walking more difficult while he carried her up through the winding cave, and she continued kissing him. With every step he took, the head of his shaft slid across her wetness as she ground against him and her fingers bit into his nape.

Each stride was pure torture as he resisted plunging into her, but whereas he was willing to wait, Lexi wasn't. With a subtle shift of her hips, she took him into her.

Cole groaned when her sheath enveloped him, and he stopped walking as she rose over him before sliding down again. He shuddered as the familiar, amazing sensation of being inside her nearly brought him to his knees, but they were still inside the place where he'd exiled himself, and he had to *get out*.

When this was over and they separated, he would most likely retreat from her as the shadows seized control again, but he had control now and would exert it.

"No." He grasped her hips. "*Not* in here."

~

Lexi was so lost in the waves of emotion swamping her that it took a few seconds to process his words. When she did, her eyes flew open, and she pressed closer to him.

The brilliant silver of his eyes was all she could see in the darkness. It was difficult for her to remain still when his cock throbbed within her, but she didn't move as she buried her face in his neck.

Her fangs tingled as the beat of his heart awakened another hunger. Her fingers bit into his nape, but no matter how badly she yearned to taste him, she restrained herself.

He wanted to leave this place behind, and if she bit him now, she'd never keep herself restrained from fucking him until they both screamed in ecstasy. Beneath her hands, his body shook from the restraint it took for him to keep from finishing what they both desperately craved.

She'd vowed not to give herself to him again, that she wouldn't unless he would stay forever, but she couldn't fight this. It was her last chance, and she knew it.

"Not here," she whispered.

When he started walking again, she bit her lip to keep from riding him once more. A small whimper escaped as every step he took drove her a little crazier with anticipation.

Just when she thought she couldn't take it anymore, the sun burst over her eyes, and its rays warmed her from head to toe. Breaking the kiss, she tipped her head back to bask in its rays while it spilled over them.

When she looked at Cole again, his eyes remained the beautiful, vivid silver of the lycan as he studied her with a profound love that nearly undid her.

As she bent to kiss him again, he moved within her.

COLE REALIZED TOO late that taking her out of the cave might not have been his best idea. The shadows created by the towering mountains were more abundant, with the sun spilling down on them.

As they crept closer, their incessant whispering grew louder. However, the increasing aroma of Lexi's scent and the feel of her body moving against his drowned out the chatter of the shadows, but they refused to be completely quiet.

The shadows crept closer until they surrounded them while Cole brought her to the ground. He didn't break the kiss; he couldn't as he thrust into her with his shaft and tongue.

His mouth muffled her delicious sounds as her teeth scraped his lip and her fingers dug into his back as she urged him onward. He braced himself between her legs as he grasped her thighs and pulled her more firmly against him as their mouths broke apart.

Leaning over her, he sank his fangs into her shoulder and fucked her harder as all his control shattered. The shadows swirled around them as they encompassed them both.

He'd tried to keep them from touching her, but now, he couldn't stop them from brushing against her. And as the lycan marked its mate, the dark fae started to feed.

Power surged through his veins as he feasted on the energy their sex created. He was beyond reason, beyond any logical thought, as he existed solely on feeding, feeling, and *her*.

~

TURNING her mouth into Cole's neck, Lexi relished the pleasure Cole gave her as the dark fae feasted on her, the shadows caressed her, and the lycan marked its mate. Ravenous, she sank her fangs into his throat and started to feed.

Their joining had always been intense, but it had never been *this* intense. The strength of it was almost frightening as numerous sensations bombarded her at once. Her head spun as her body came alive, and all her nerve endings focused on him, the ecstasy he gave, and the joy of their joining.

Beneath the assault of those emotions, and as he pushed her closer to release, her control over her shield crumbled. It was impossible to keep it up when everything was falling apart and coming back together around her.

When the glow spread across her body, the shadows started to retreat, but there was nowhere to go as her light ensnared them. Cole relinquished his bite on her shoulder as the silver markings came to life across her skin.

He kissed her throat up toward her cheek. She craved more of his blood, but she released her bite and turned to meet his mouth.

She *needed* to kiss him again. It was what *had* to happen, and when their mouths met, a thrum of power, like a small jolt of electricity passed between them.

That jolt reverberated throughout her muscles and bones until it shook her soul. It delved deep as it swirled and combined with her until it flooded her with strength and became a part of the very essence of her soul.

As the kiss deepened, it changed a fundamental part of her until she felt something new seeping inside her. It caressed her skin and dug into her bones until it crept through every aspect of her. It didn't take much time to realize what it was either…

The shadows.

They passed between her and Cole until they became a part of them. When Cole's hand slid between their bodies and stroked her clit, Lexi screamed against his mouth as waves of ecstasy swamped her while the shadows pummeled her.

Despite their intrusion into her body, she didn't break the kiss as the shadows bound them together more than before.

CHAPTER FIFTY-SEVEN

COLE RAN his fingers up and down Lexi's arm while the dragons circled overhead. There were so many he couldn't count them as they choked out the sky.

"They've come to you," he said.

"Hmm," Lexi murmured as she nestled closer against his side.

Cole stared at the sky while he listened to absolutely *nothing*. It was so quiet for the first time in a month that it was nearly as maddening as the shadows' incessant whispers.

The quiet let him think about all he'd done and how out of control he'd been.

It allowed him to recall the horrible thoughts that constantly ran through his mind, his constant craving for blood, and how he'd sated it. But he would adjust to the quiet; he never would have adjusted to the endless chatter of the shadows.

The shadows were still there, slithering inside him and imbuing him with their strength, but they didn't whisper to him anymore. They didn't tell him that she would destroy him and that enemies lurked around every corner.

For the first time, they were nearly as at peace as the lycan and dark fae who had stopped warring against each other. *Finally*, the two parts of himself that were in complete opposition for six-hundred and seventy-two years were at peace with each other, and the shadows had calmed.

But for how long?

He ran his fingers through Lexi's silken hair as his eyes closed and he waited for the whispers to return, but they remained silent. It felt like some of them entered Lexi, but that couldn't be possible, could it?

Terror propelled him upright as he looked down at her. She smiled as she stretched languidly before him, showing off every inch of her splendid body.

"Are you okay?" he demanded.

Her fingers found his bicep and closed around it. He'd forgotten about his burns until her touch warmed him and the sting eased from them. Before, he didn't want her to take away the pain because it helped him think, but the easing of his discomfort didn't cause his mind to cloud again.

When she finished healing him, Lexi caressed his arm. "I'm fine. Are *you* okay?"

"The shadows...." He leaned closer to inspect her eyes, but they looked the same as always.

"Are gone. I don't know how to explain it." She bit her bottom lip as her attention shifted back to the dragons. "It's like I absorbed some of them, and they just... dissipated. It was the strangest thing ever. I felt them inside me, and then they were gone."

"Your light chased them away."

She rested her palm against his bearded cheek. "But they're still in you."

"They are. However, they're not in control anymore. You absorbed some of them and eased their presence inside me."

Lexi's attention shifted back to the dragons as her brow furrowed. "The arachs created the Shadow Reaver, and there is a way to control it, but I don't know what it is... or at least I didn't. We might have stumbled across it."

Lexi filled him in on what little they discovered from the arach archives; when she finished, his attention also went to the dragons again. They studied the sky while the sun sank lower.

"The shadows reported some of it to me," he told her. "They believed you were plotting against me."

When she rested her hand on his cheek, his attention returned to her. "Everything we did was to save you, but...."

Tears brimmed in her eyes, and she looked away. He grasped her chin before kissing her and gently stroking her face.

"I know," he said. "I understand."

"I thought there might come a time when I had to destroy you, or we would destroy each other."

"I know."

"I never wanted to do such a thing, but—"

"I know, Lexi, and it's okay. I understand. Some things can't be allowed to exist, and an out-of-control Shadow Reaver is one of them."

"But you're in control now."

"I am."

She closed her eyes and smiled. "Good."

"It makes sense the arach would create a way to control the Reaver, or at least ease the shadows from him. I can feel the shadows inside me; still, their power remains a part of me, but it's nowhere near as out of control as it was before. And my reach isn't as far with them as it was before.

"It was our kiss that drew them from me and weakened them. Or, I should say, your mark of the dragon. It's the first time your shield has completely crumbled and your mark has come out while we've been together like this. Your kiss and mark drew them from me. That must have been how the arach ensured some control over the Shadow Reaver would remain intact."

"It's such an intimate exchange for two immortals who could

have ended up hating or barely knowing each other. What if the last arach and Reaver never met?"

"I think that even with this Carleah's prophecy and the creation of the Reaver magic, they still didn't believe there would come a time when only *one* arach lived."

"Stubborn and arrogant to the end."

"Yes."

"I've never lowered my shield around you while we were having sex before. I was so determined to be normal again that I kept rigid control over it."

"And I always tried to keep the shadows from touching you before."

She rested her palm against his cheek, and he grinned when love filled her beautiful green eyes. "Are you really going to be okay?"

He leaned down to kiss her forehead and brush back her hair. "I will."

Lexi tried to believe him, but her breath sucked in when the prophecy came to life in a different way. "When the last light falls."

He pulled back a little. "Lexi—"

"No! We all assumed the rest of it would come true because if you lost me, your grief and anger would drive you to seek revenge. But it's *not* only because of your heartbreak and the loss of your mate. It's because, if I die, no one can take the shadows from you again."

Cole's eyes widened as her words and the truth of them sank in. "But we're going to make sure you never die."

"Yes."

But as her gaze searched his face, he saw her doubt and apprehension. "It's all going to be okay. Look at what we've already accomplished and learned."

"I know." She looked to the dragons again as she spoke her next words. "Will you be okay with what has happened since absorbing the shadows?"

"You mean all the immortals I've killed?"

"Yes."

"I'm more than okay with it."

"You used to have nightmares about the Lord's war."

"I did, but this is different. I regretted killing those immortals who fought against us in the Lord's war. Secretly, I believed in what they were doing, but I pretended to side with the Lord so we could try to bring him down from the inside.

"We failed in doing so, and I took a lot of lives that I shouldn't have. I had to live with the knowledge I killed what I believed to be innocent immortals. It was difficult to come to terms with, and I'm still not fully there, but if I chose the other side, I don't think we'd be here. So, I have to believe I chose the right path, even if I'll always live with the guilt of it.

"I will *not* live with the guilt of those I slaughtered to keep you safe. They were *all* the enemy, and they deserved to perish. I don't regret the violent and brutal ways they died; I'm sure knowledge of those deaths deterred some from trying to overthrow you. And I won't let up. If it means keeping you safe, then the shadows will still get their kills."

Lexi gulped before nodding.

"Do you think I'm wrong for that?" he asked.

"No."

"Becca is dead."

"I heard."

"I think you were right and she was in love with me."

"Oh, I was definitely right."

He smiled as he stroked her cheek. "She denied it, but after her treachery in that outer realm, she must have been the one reporting to the Lord."

"Maybe."

"Maybe?"

"She was in love with you; I'm not sure she'd risk telling the Lord anything if there was a chance you might get hurt."

"I don't think she believed he would hurt me. She wanted you out of the picture and would do whatever it took to ensure it happened."

"Maybe."

He traced the dark circles under her eyes. "Now, what about you? Are these because of me? Have I been keeping you up at night?"

"You... and other things."

"What other things?"

"I spent a lot of time searching for an answer to help you in the palace and then more time poring through those archives with the others. I snuck out at night a lot."

"I know."

She smiled at him. "I didn't like you watching over me with the shadows."

He grinned. "I know."

Her smile slid away. "I've also been having nightmares about the war, the Lord, and... and... failing. I'm so scared I'll let everyone down, do the wrong thing, get more killed, and be a completely inept leader."

"You're not."

"You can't be sure of that."

"I can. You would have killed me if it came down to it."

She recoiled from him, and her lips skimmed back to reveal her fangs. "Don't say such things!"

"It's true." She started to shake her head, but he clasped her cheek to stop her. "It's true, Lexi, and it's okay. You would have done it to save countless other lives. You would have sacrificed the one you love the most, and therefore yourself, to save them. That *is* a good leader.

"Are you going to make mistakes? Of course, but you'll recover from them, try to correct them, and learn from them.

You'll be fair and fight for your people. That is the best anyone can ask for from you, and you *will* do it."

Her eyes searched his face as she caressed his cheek. "I'll do my best to try."

"That is what counts."

"I ordered the death of the prisoners in the dungeons. It hasn't happened yet; it was supposed to be this morning, but something else came up."

"Me?"

"No, a new development in my abilities. I'll show you when we return to the palace. But more lives will be lost because of my command."

"Do you think it's the right one?"

"Yes."

"So do I."

"More blood will stain my hands."

He rested his hand over her hands. "It's, unfortunately, a consequence of ruling, but they have to die, Lexi."

"I know," she whispered.

"You won't have to carry it out alone; I'll be by your side for it now."

His fingers entwined with hers as she nestled against his shoulder and kissed his chin. Her lush breasts against his side reawakened his hunger. Knowing that he could help take her mind off those troubles, he kissed her and rolled her on top of him.

CHAPTER FIFTY-EIGHT

AT FIRST, Cole felt weird and out of sorts when he returned to the palace. It was strange to be amongst immortals and civilization again. He'd only been gone for a little over a month, but part of him felt like it belonged in a cave.

And maybe it did. While his lycan and dark fae halves were more at peace than ever, the shadows still inside made him more bloodthirsty. There was no changing that.

The shadows didn't whisper to him like they used to, but they made their presence known as they prepared to take down any threat to those he loved. He never wanted to be lost to the madness again, and as out of control as he was in the cave, but he'd gladly take more shadows into himself to destroy anyone who dared to plot against Lexi.

He would never hesitate to use the shadows, no matter the consequences to himself. But if he had to do it again, she could ease the burden from him when the danger passed.

He wouldn't be lost again.

The shadows didn't reach as far anymore; they didn't slither through all the different realms in search of threats and report back to him. He didn't like being cut off from this source of information, but after the death he'd unleashed, he liked to think the immortals wouldn't be so stupid as to try coming for her again.

But, after so many years of living, if there was one thing he could count on, it was the stupidity of others. They were still out there, and he'd destroy them when they made their move. They also didn't know his reach had lessened, so hopefully, they would be more hesitant to attack.

The day after he returned from the cave, he stood by Lexi's side and let the shadows help destroy the prisoners. At first, Lexi, his brothers, Del, and Maverick protested him doing so, but it was another show of the shadows' power as they encompassed the prisoner's necks and decapitated them.

The ones he didn't kill, the dragons slayed. Lexi was against the dragons' participation, but Alina volunteered them, and Cole agreed they should be involved.

She may not like it, but the death of these prisoners was a show of her power and control over the realms. So, while Cole decapitated some, the dragons torched or happily ate the others.

They were all quick deaths, something Lexi insisted on, but the display would be talked about in *all* the realms and make some immortals hesitate before attacking. Not only did this queen have dragons at her side and lethal powers, but she also had the Reaver.

No other had ever possessed so much combined ability to destroy. It was awing and frightening.

He was proud of the leader Lexi was becoming, even if she remained uncertain of her choices. The army was growing, the residents of Dragonia loved her, workers were returning to the palace, and she'd forged bonds with the sirens, giants, and dwarves.

Some of the other immortals would be more difficult to win over, but if she could make a giant smile, she'd win the others over too. It was only a matter of time.

Now, he stood beside her as they surveyed the lush, green garden. He'd seen it when they first returned to the palace, but after a week of being here, what she'd done here still amazed him.

When he glanced at the woman beside him, pride and love encompassed him as he clasped her hand. She was beautiful, strong, and *his*.

She smiled at him before shifting her attention back to the garden. "They removed the fountain yesterday and are planting a beautiful tree in its place today."

He slid his fingers into hers as he turned back to the gardens. "This would be a beautiful place to get married."

"It would."

"How about next week?"

Lexi turned her radiant smile on him. "Next week sounds perfect."

"Is that enough time to get a wedding dress ready?"

"I'd marry you naked."

He laughed as his fingers tightened on hers. "While I wouldn't mind that, I'd prefer not to have you naked in front of everyone else."

"I'm sure I can find something."

He bent and kissed her forehead. "I can't wait."

"Neither can I."

"Cole," Brokk said.

Cole turned as Brokk, Orin, and Varo strode through the trees toward them. His youngest brother still looked like he'd been hit by a truck and seen a dozen ghosts, but at least Varo was coming with them for this. It was some sign of life from a beaten-down man.

"Are you ready?" Orin asked.

"I am."

When Lexi opened a portal, they traveled through it to the

Gloaming. It had been a while since he last saw his kingdom, sat on his throne, and claimed the ruined land.

He would change that now. It was time to bring the dark fae home, rebuild the Gloaming, and fix everything the Lord destroyed.

They would also bury Niall's sword today. Lexi had put off doing it until he was back, and now, it was time to say goodbye to his friend.

He placed the sword in the ground with those of the other dark fae heroes. When the time came, he would build a monument to his friend, who gave everything to help destroy the Lord.

CHAPTER FIFTY-NINE

OVER THE NEXT FEW DAYS, Lexi wished she could spend all day with Cole in the Gloaming, but she couldn't spend that much time away from Dragonia. Things were calmer but far from perfect.

So, she went in the morning but returned a couple of hours later to deal with the petty arguments brought to her by the different realms, rebuilding the land, and the return of immortals who lived and worked within the palace.

She also had to deal with the different immortals who sought to pledge their fealty to her. When they knew someone was coming that day, Cole would also return to Dragonia to stand by her side as the immortals pledged their loyalty to them and Dragonia.

Most of the lycan packs had arrived, and many of the vampires had come alone or in small groups. Vampires mostly tended to remain alone unless they banded together to create havoc or help fight.

The witches, crones, sirens, nymphs, pixies, imps, gnomes, unicorns, sasquatch, pegasuses, light fae, giants, dwarves, and even some warlocks had sworn their loyalty. She still hadn't seen the demons, ogres, orcs, trolls, berserkers, zombies, mermaids, and many of the different immortals who existed, and she may never see them.

Many were solitary and preferred to be left alone in their groups. She was okay with that as long as they didn't try to cause any problems; if they did, they would pay for it.

While peace reigned throughout the realms, she would be happy.

In the afternoon, she worked with Amaris, Sahira, and Kaylia to prepare her wedding dress. It was simple and beautiful, and she never imagined she could be so excited about clothing.

She and Cole were already as bound together as they could get, but now everyone throughout the realms would officially know how tight that bond was. There were still those plotting to take them down, but together, they would defeat them all.

Lexi hummed to herself as she entered the sewing room Amaris had established on the second floor. Amaris was already there with Lexi's dress in her arms and a brilliant smile on her pretty face. Lexi turned to her guards and waved to them before closing the door on the lycans.

"This is our final fitting," Amaris said. "After today, everything will be all set."

Lexi bounced on her toes and practically clapped her hands in excitement as she walked over to Amaris. Sahira and Kaylia were finishing a potion and would be here soon, but she couldn't wait to put her dress on again.

"Let's get to work," she said.

After she undressed to her bra and underwear, Amaris helped her don the beautiful white gown. The lace front of it hugged her breasts before becoming more shear and turning into more lace around her shoulders.

The sleeves were sheer until another lacy pattern above her elbows ended them. A slit up the narrow skirt went halfway up her thigh. It was a relatively simple dress that flowed around her while she walked, and she couldn't wait for Cole to see it.

As she slipped the sleeves on, she felt beautiful and giddy. She could barely stand still, something Amaris scolded her for as she slid the buttons on her back into place.

"Almost ready," Amaris murmured.

Lexi tried not to tap her feet or bounce up and down while she waited, but it took everything she had to remain still while Amaris worked.

"There." Amaris slid the last button into place and smoothed the back of her dress. "Now, don't move while I get my sewing supplies."

Lexi stared out the window at the shadows of the passing dragons as Amaris bent and opened her kit. After her initial fitting, Lexi hadn't seen herself in a mirror in the dress, so while she had an idea of what it looked like, she hadn't seen the final product. She *finally* would today.

Amaris rose and stuck a pin in the dress before gripping the back, near her nape, and pulling it a little tighter. As she did so, something skittered onto Lexi's flesh.

The hair on her nape rose as the prick of multiple, tiny legs scampered over her skin. There must have been a spider in Amaris's sewing kit that hitched a ride onto her, but it was a damn big spider.

"What is that?" she murmured.

Burying her uneasiness over having the creature on her, Lexi went to brush it away as something jabbed her. Lexi gasped at the fleeting, piercing sensation that left a fiery burn on her neck.

"What was…?"

Her words came out slurred, and her question trailed off as the fire in her neck spread throughout her limbs. As it moved, her body felt heavier and less her own until she slumped. Her body sagged to the side like a deflating balloon.

Her legs trembled as she tried to remain standing, but it was impossible. It felt like she weighed a thousand pounds, and all of it was pulling her toward the ground.

Amaris's lips brushed her ear as she spoke. "That was for Andreas."

Lexi's mind spun in confusion. Andreas? Who's Andreas? Then she recalled the *Lord* was Andreas.

I don't understand.

She tried to look at Amaris, form questions, and *understand*, but it was impossible. Her tongue wouldn't move, and her legs refused to hold her anymore as her knees buckled and she slumped to the floor.

Amaris smiled as she stepped over her. For a second, the beautiful dark fae straddled Lexi as she smiled, an evil smile that would have sent chills down Lexi's spine if she was still capable of such things.

And then, it hit her. It was *never* Becca telling the Lord everything. That was always the simplest explanation, but it never fit quite right... at least not to her.

That's because it had always been *Amaris*.

She'd considered this woman her friend; Amaris was the first to welcome her into the Gloaming, accept her, and treat her kindly, but it had *always* been nothing more than an act.

Amaris was going behind her back and plotting against her the entire time. And she continued to do so.

How did I miss this?

"It won't be much longer, Lexi."

Amaris bent to brush the hair away from her face. Lexi yearned to slap her hand away, but her limbs refused to move.

"The bite of a noxus scorpion can only be counteracted by the milk of the crudue vine. Good luck finding that in the thirty seconds you have left to live."

CHAPTER SIXTY

LEXI'S HEART spasmed before clenching. It felt like someone was pushing against her ribs and tearing them open to wrap their hand around her heart.

That hand squeezed down as her heart lurched, twisted, and pounded spasmodically. Her arteries swelled to near bursting before releasing and engorging again. A choked cough wrenched from her, and the metallic tang of blood filled her mouth.

She tried to lift her hand to rest it on her chest. She could heal herself, but she couldn't fix a lethal blow, and she couldn't do anything when her hand wouldn't *move*.

Then her heart ached for a whole new reason as the awful reality of this situation sank in. *Cole.*

When the last light falls....

Tears clogged her eyes and blurred her vision. He wouldn't survive this either, but what would the Reaver do to the realms when he learned of this betrayal? What would he do without her there to ease the shadows from him?

The prophecy had already given them the answer.

Her heart pumped, stuttered, and compressed once more as blood pooled in her mouth before trickling past her lips. From the corner of her eye, she spotted a small, red scorpion skittering away.

Above her, Amaris grinned, but her grin faded when the door creaked open.

～

Sahira and Kaylia nodded a greeting to the guards outside the sewing room door. The man and woman stepped aside, and Sahira opened the door.

As she entered the room, Sahira's smile vanished. She stopped when she spotted Lexi lying on the floor in a pool of white while Amaris stood above her.

Did Lexi fall? Is Amaris trying some new, weird way to fit the dress, or had... had...

She had no idea what else could have happened for such a strange scene to unfold before her. And then, Kaylia entered the room and froze beside her.

As she stopped, Amaris cloaked herself in shadows and vanished.

"What the...?" Kaylia started.

Her voice trailed off when the skittering of tiny legs scampering across the floor drew their attention to the corner of the room. They saw the noxus scorpion at the same time.

And Sahira knew what had happened; it made no sense, but she knew the truth. "No."

Everything in her froze as she nearly sank to her knees. At the same time, Kaylia lunged forward. Her hands weaved an intricate pattern as she screamed, "Heart of stone. Heart of stone! I weave thee a heart of stone!"

Lexi inhaled one more time before freezing. The breath never left her lips; her expanded chest didn't release it, and her open eyes became unseeing as she stared blindly forward.

"Guards!" Sahira shouted. "The queen has been attacked!"

And where *was* her attacker? Her gaze flew around the room as she raced to her niece's side and collapsed next to her.

The blood trickling from Lexi's blue lips and trailing down her chin was the only part of her that still moved. Her skin was so pale it was nearly translucent.

When Kaylia cast the heart of stone spell over her, she'd frozen Lexi into this time and place. The spell stopped the poison from seeping through her body and destroying her, but she couldn't awaken, and she wouldn't move again until they found the antidote.

Sahira caressed her niece's cheek as she hunched protectively over her and searched the room. *Where is that bitch?*

For all Sahira knew, she'd somehow managed to slip past the guards or jumped out the window. Amaris could be gone, or she could be hiding in this room, waiting to strike again.

Does she have more of the scorpions? Noxus scorpions were rare, but if Amaris had one, she might have more. But in this condition, a knife through Lexi's heart would easily finish her.

Sahira hunched closer to Lexi, shielding her niece with her body. If Amaris came for her again, she would have to get through Sahira first.

They needed Cole or a dark fae stronger than Amaris to locate her, but they were all in the Gloaming. *No one* had expected this, not from someone they'd grown to trust so much.

Shouts echoed through the palace; the guards searched the room as they held their swords at the ready. The scorpion's feet tapping against the marble floor drew her attention as it retreated further from them.

They couldn't let that thing get free; it would kill anyone else it stung.

Kaylia spun in a circle as Sahira searched for a way to trap the scorpion. Dozens of glass bottles full of needles, threads, sewing tape, thimbles, and other assorted things lined the shelves on the wall.

Remaining protectively huddled over Lexi, Sahira waved a hand at one of those jars. Intricately moving her fingers, she spilled the contents across a countertop before the jar flew across the room.

The scorpion lifted its tail defensively and tried to scamper away, but Sahira slammed the jar down on top of it. The scorpion's tail clicked against the glass as it repeatedly attacked the jar.

"What happened?" the male lycan demanded.

Kaylia turned in a circle as she whispered, "That which I cannot see, let it be, let it be. That which I cannot see, reveal it to me."

Kaylia's fingers waved in a beautiful dance as the shadows around the room slid back to reveal Amaris. She clutched a dagger in her hand but must have decided to flee when Kaylia started her spell as she had one leg swung over the windowsill.

Amaris let out a startled cry as she threw herself to the side. She started to tumble out the window as the female lycan leapt forward. She transformed as she moved, but it was already too late… Amaris was beyond her reach.

The dark fae disappeared, and the dragons' bellows vibrated the walls and reverberated throughout the land.

They know.

And then a dragon rose to the window. Screaming and kicking, Amaris hung from its mouth. Pulling its head back, the dragon heaved the woman into the room.

She bounced across the floor before stopping a few feet away. The lycan planted a powerful paw on Amaris's chest and pinned her to the floor as the dragons roared.

Silence descended over everyone in the room as footsteps and shouts continued from the hall. A few seconds later, Maverick and Del burst into the room. A dozen more guards followed them, but it was too late for them to do anything.

And this was only the start of the horror about to unleash.

CHAPTER SIXTY-ONE

COLE STEPPED BACK and smiled as he surveyed the progress they'd made with rebuilding the Gloaming. The palace had remained untouched by the dragons' fire and the Lord's men.

The fencing around it still stood, but the buildings within the bailey were burnt-out rubble. All the homes on the once fertile land outside the palace were ash.

Underhill was still a mess, as were the other areas of the Gloaming, but inside the bailey, they'd removed all the debris and started rebuilding. The dragons' fires destroyed some of the lethal forests outside the walls, but much remained standing.

The dragons weren't overly concerned about the forests where the fae rarely traveled. A lot of the dark fae still hadn't returned after fleeing from the dragons' attack, but as word spread throughout the realms about the Gloaming rebuilding, more started to trickle in.

One of the first to return was Elvin, who dove into helping rebuild. When Cole and his brothers weren't here, Elvin oversaw the rebuilding.

They'd started with the homes inside the bailey, not because Cole wanted his soldiers housed first, but because it would be safer for those who returned to stay close to the palace and within the gates.

The dragons weren't a menace to them, but many other things out there were. He would do whatever it took to rebuild his homeland and keep its residents safe.

After they cleared away the debris from inside the bailey, they set to work chopping down trees along the woods line. The horses helped haul things back and forth, which didn't make his steed, Torigon, too happy, but he didn't balk too much at having to pull a cart.

They were careful not to go deep into the woods where rats larger than men thrived with all kinds of other creatures. As they progressed with the building and more fae returned, they moved outside the palace gates and started to clear the burnt land.

Though it looked desolate and barren now, the fertile fields of the Gloaming would once again yield crops next year. They'd seen no sign of the craz that resided in the mountains, but a couple of dragons now accompanied them to the Gloaming every day. Those far larger predators would keep the monstrous birds of the Gloaming at bay.

At first, Cole hadn't wanted the dragons here; he was concerned their presence would frighten the dark fae way; they had destroyed his father and the realm, after all. But now he saw them as the other piece of the puzzle that would keep Lexi alive.

It was time to work with them as the allies they would be from now on. He'd never forget that they'd eaten his father, and many of the immortals would harbor resentment toward them for the damage they inflicted, but they'd been under the Lord's control.

Now, they were freer and far less volatile without a madman pulling their strings. All the immortals would have to overcome it, as the beasts weren't going anywhere.

As more returned to the Gloaming, some ventured into Underhill to round up more wild horses that ran free there. Many of those horses had retreated to the mountains and caves when the dragons arrived and had survived.

None of those wild beasts were broken yet, but they would get to work on it soon. The dark fae knew horses and how to work the land. The Gloaming was blooming beneath their hands again.

He never wanted to be king of this realm, but he'd never been prouder to rule here. The dark fae were all coming to rebuild their home.

Cole wiped the sweat from his forehead and examined the wall he and Orin had lifted into place. Brokk and Varo hammered the nails into place and stepped back to inspect their handiwork.

"Looks good to me," Brokk said.

"It looks like it's time for alcohol to me," Orin said.

Varo remained taciturn like he often was these days, but at least he was helping. That help had brought some color back to his face and caused pride to glisten in his eyes.

"I could go for a drink," Cole said.

Lexi would still be in the fitting for her wedding dress, and they'd managed to get a lot done today. They all deserved a break and a bit of a celebration.

Orin flipped his hammer through the air as he laughed. "Maybe you're not such an uptight prick after all."

Cole scowled at him; leave it to Orin to irritate him when he was in a good mood. He decided not to let his little brother get to him as he turned to the others.

"Everyone, into the palace!" he shouted to be heard across the bailey. He'd send a crew out to gather those working in the field. "It's time to celebrate all of our work and a return to the Gloaming."

Cheers went through the crowd as one of the dragons launched itself into the air and took flight. The cheers died away as the dark fae staggered away from the beast.

They'd been here every day for a week and never once acted like this. The dragon's bellow was one of fury, but it didn't turn and come toward them. Instead, it opened a portal and vanished with one of the other dragons.

The third dragon paced outside the gates as it screamed. Its golden eyes shone with despair as it stared at Cole and screamed in suffering.

"Lexi," he breathed.

Cole had left shadows behind to watch Lexi; his control over the shadows wasn't as strong as before, but they would watch over and report to him. And now their whispers vibrated through his connection to them.

"She killed the queen."

Those words were like a blow to Cole's chest as they staggered him back a step. His heart shattered, and he labored to breathe as Varo rested a hand on his arm.

Cole tried to deny it, but the dragons' actions ended any of his protests.

"Brother, what's wrong?" Varo asked.

The dragon propelled itself into the air and swept over the gates as it soared toward him. Cole didn't fear the creature, but many of the dark fae screamed as they raced to find cover.

It was pointless for them to hide; the dragon was coming for him, and he was ready for it as his sorrow turned into a fury.

Grabbing his tunic, Cole roared as he tore it from him. He wanted to shred his flesh, tear open his bones, and rip out his heart to ease the misery battering him, but first, he would make whoever did this pay.

And they would suffer in the worst way possible.

From around the realm, he drew on the shadows and called them to him. They sped across the ground, zigzagged through the air, and raced toward him. Tipping his head back, he bellowed again as he opened his mouth to accept them *all* into him.

Cole's hair blew back, and dust rose from the ground as the

dragon landed before him. When the dragon opened a portal to Dragonia, the Shadow Reaver followed the beast through.

∽

"What was that?" Orin demanded.

Brokk was too stunned to move, never mind reply. He knew what that was; he suspected Orin knew too, but he refused to acknowledge it.

It was Varo who said the words, "Something happened to Lexi."

"Impossible," Orin stated.

"He's right," Brokk said, "and I think the prophecy is coming to fruition."

Orin shook his head as he paled visibly, but Brokk saw the resignation slipping over his brother's face.

"We have to go," Brokk said.

He plunged into the open portal before the dragon could close it and sprinted through the darkness in pursuit of his brother. They wouldn't run from what lay on the other side, but they'd probably be better off if they did.

CHAPTER SIXTY-TWO

"Is she dead?" Del choked out.

"No," Sahira assured him. "Kaylia cast a spell to freeze her heart before the poison could kill her. We have to find the antidote. We can save her, if we find it."

"No one has seen crudue vine in centuries," Maverick said.

Sahira spun on him. "You think I don't *know* that? Do you think I don't *realize* that? But we have to find it. This is my niece, and I won't lose her!"

Maverick held up his hands in a placating gesture. "We'll find it."

"It's too late," Kaylia whispered.

Her words caused Sahira's heart to sink. She'd been so certain Kaylia's spell had bought them time; they could save Lexi if they had time.

"The spell...."

Sahira's words trailed off when she realized Kaylia wasn't talking about the spell being too late for Lexi. It was too late because of *Cole*.

Outside the window, darkness seeped across the horizon as shadows rolled forth like towering thunderclouds. Unlike when he drew the shadows into him before to reveal more of the sun, they blocked out much of the light as they spread across the land.

Enough light remained for those shadows to thrive. Screams rang across the land, but they sounded more like panic than suffering. She didn't think the Reaver was killing... yet, but he'd come to rain down hell on those who'd failed Lexi.

"Shit," Maverick breathed.

The shadows rolled across the land until they pressed against the window and seeped inside. Sahira didn't dare move as their tendrils weaved throughout the room before brushing against Lexi.

Sahira considered wiping the blood away from her chin, it would only incense Cole more when he saw it, but she didn't dare move as the shadows created a blanket around Lexi. When some brushed against her flesh, she didn't jerk away from their cool touch.

As darkness descended over the realm, the shadows lifted Cole, and he rose to hover before the window. Sahira's breath caught in her chest and remained trapped there; breathing might trigger an attack.

Sahira had never seen anything like the man standing across from her. Not even when he absorbed the shadows to defeat the Lord had Cole looked so menacing and hell-bent on destruction.

When his gaze fell to Lexi, Sahira shuddered at the rage and grief in eyes so silver they burned brighter than the moon. Sahira could barely think through her sorrow and terror, but she knew one thing for sure...

Cole had come to exact revenge, and he would have it. The Shadow Reaver had been unleashed on the realms.

"She's alive, Cole!" Sahira blurted as the shadows carried Cole into the room. "Kaylia froze her heart before the poison could destroy her. She's alive!"

When Cole stopped beside Lexi, his silver eyes with the shadows creeping through them latched onto her, Sahira's bladder clenched, and she nearly pissed herself. She wasn't sure if she was getting through to him, didn't know if he understood her, and wasn't certain it would matter if he understood.

He looked ready to slaughter everyone as the shadows danced around him in a serpentine rhythm that would have made Medusa's snakes proud. They crept across his face and chest as they slithered through his skin.

"We can save her, Cole," Maverick said as he stepped in front of Sahira.

Cole's head swiveled toward him, and his nostrils flared. "Get away from her."

Maverick held up his hands as he edged away. Sahira was surprised to see the powerful, alpha lycan retreat from anything, but he had to know he wouldn't survive a battle with Cole, and his nephew's state of mind wasn't one for rationale. He would attack his uncle without a second thought.

Slowly, Cole knelt beside Lexi. Sahira retreated from her niece and grasped Del's hand when he extended it to her. Her brother helped her rise while Cole's fingers wiped away the blood on Lexi's chin.

For a second, emotion registered on his face as anguish radiated from him. Sahira could practically hear his heart screaming for her.

They'd just found each other again. Tomorrow was supposed to be one of the happiest days of their lives, and now... now... *this.*

"Who did this?" Cole hissed in a voice not his own.

More footsteps pounded down the hallway a second before Orin, Brokk, and Varo ran into the room. The three brothers skidded to a halt when they spotted Lexi and Cole.

"What the fuck?" Brokk blurted.

"Who. Did. *This?*" Cole bit out.

All their heads turned toward where Amaris lay with a lycan paw on her chest. She didn't move as she watched Cole.

A flutter of wings sounded a second before Alina grasped the sill with her talons and stuck her head through the window. When she saw Lexi, she issued a sound of raw grief as she bowed her head.

"Our queen," she whispered.

Cole rose and glided across the floor to Amaris. "Get away from her."

At Cole's command, the lycan retreated. Amaris pushed herself up and leaned against the wall as she glowered at Cole.

Cole hovered a couple of inches off the ground as he stopped before her. Sahira tried to look away; she wanted to kill the woman as badly as Cole, but she couldn't stand watching a bloodbath.

Her stomach churned as she glanced around the room, but she was too scared to move and wouldn't leave Lexi. Her eyes returned to Cole and Amaris as the shadows lowered him to the ground, and he bent to examine the woman.

His head tilted back and forth in an odd, creepy way that unsettled Sahira more. The shadows engulfed Amaris until they touched almost every inch of her.

CHAPTER SIXTY-THREE

"I'M NOT AFRAID OF YOU," Amaris stated.

Sahira could tell that wasn't true as the woman's fingers trembled on the ground. Sahira hated this horrible woman she'd come to consider a friend before this, but she had to give her credit for trying to act brave while death stared her in the face.

Cole moved so fast that Sahira never saw him until his claws were embedded under Amaris's chin, and he lifted the woman. When Amaris's mouth opened and a startled gurgling sound issued from her, the glint of Cole's claws was visible in her mouth.

Amaris's feet kicked against the wall as she clawed at his wrist. Blood spilled down Cole's arm, but he showed no sign of noticing it or his torn flesh.

"Why?" the shadows demanded.

The terrifying shadows coalesced around Cole as they filled the room and remained spread across the realm. Without Lexi, there was nothing to rein those shadows in again.

Sahira closed her eyes against the possibility of the prophecy coming true. The last light *had* fallen; Lexi wasn't dead, but if they couldn't find the crudue vine, the shadows would grow beyond Cole's control.

She didn't realize she was still holding her brother's hand until her fingers clenched around it. When she met Del's eyes, she knew he was thinking the same thing. If Cole tore the realms down around her, it wouldn't matter if they saved Lexi.

"Why?" Cole growled.

Amaris's teeth clacked together as she tried to talk, but Cole's claws had embedded her tongue to the bottom of her mouth, and only awful, gurgling sounds issued from her.

"She obviously can't talk with your hand in her mouth," Orin said.

Everyone in the room shot him a look, and he shrugged as if to say, *what else did you expect me to do?*

There were times when Sahira would love to choke the life out of him; this was one of those times. He was right, Amaris couldn't talk with Cole's claws in her mouth, but they were better off *not* having Cole's attention on them right now. And he *really* could have found a better way to impart this information to Cole.

When Cole retracted his claws and jerked his hand away, Amaris hit the ground with a thud. A hand flew to her throat as she tried to stop her blood from flowing. Shadows enclosed her wrist and pulled her hand away. They pinned it to the ground, along with her other hand.

"Answer me," Cole commanded.

For the first time, alarm flickered through Amaris's eyes, but she still lifted her bloody chin as she glared at Cole. "Lord Andreas is the one *true* ruler."

Due to her wounded tongue, her words slurred and bloody spittle issued from her lips, but she was understandable.

"He's dead," the shadows said. "No one can rule from the grave."

"And I still love him!"

Those words hung heavily in the room as the shadows tittered with cruel laughter. "You fool."

Sahira thought those words summed this woman up perfectly.

"How long were you reporting to him about what was happening in the Gloaming?" Cole demanded.

"From the second I entered the palace to work for you." Amaris's eyes remained defiant as blood coated her tunic. "I bet you don't know *when* that was."

Cole bent lower until their noses almost touched. "No, because I didn't give a fuck. You weren't worth noticing, and Andreas knew it. He only paid attention to you because he wanted something from you and got it. But you know who did notice you?"

He pointed a finger at Lexi's unmoving form. "*Her*. She was probably the only one who *ever* gave a shit about your worthless ass, and *this* is how you repaid her."

"She deserves to die, just like *you*. Andreas loved me, and you took him from me."

Cole sneered at her as the shadows yanked her hands to the side. "You're an idiot, and you'll die because of it."

"I welcome death to be with my love again. But you will continue to live with the knowledge *I* was the one who took your fiancée and mate from you. You'll never find crudue vine, which means she's as good as dead.

"Dragonia will fall, and you'll rot in your inability to save her. Isn't it fitting that you'll always get to look at her and see your bride-to-be in the wedding dress she never got to wear down the aisle? I think it is."

The bellow Cole released was so loud it rebounded around the room and echoed throughout the land. Sahira resisted slapping her hands over her ears as she recoiled from the raw anguish permeating his voice.

Her heart broke for him as tears burned her eyes. Lexi and

Cole had fought so hard for everyone. They'd been so close to the life of happiness they deserved, and this rotten *bitch* had stolen it from them.

Again, Sahira didn't see Cole move until both his hands clasped the sides of Amaris's face. Amaris struggled in his grasp, and her feet kicked against the floor as Cole squeezed until her head exploded and pieces of her showered the walls and Cole.

Sahira managed to restrain herself from making any noise, but Kaylia gagged before stifling the sound. Brokk rested his hand on her shoulder as Kaylia regained control of herself.

From below, shouts arose. Sahira turned to the window as Alina craned her head to peer down at the land.

"Invaders," Alina stated. "This traitor wasn't working alone."

Cole strode over to Lexi and carefully lifted her off the floor. He cradled her against his chest before kissing her forehead and walking over to Alina.

"Take her somewhere safe," Cole said. "Keep her protected."

Alina bowed her head before carefully lifting Lexi with one of her talons. The dragon nestled Lexi against her chest as she took flight.

Del stretched a hand forward to stop her, but it fell limply back to his side when Alina disappeared. Sahira squeezed her brother's hand as outside, metal clashed against metal and more shouts erupted

Sahira closed her eyes as she braced for another fight and more blood. When she opened her eyes again, Cole had climbed onto the windowsill.

"This won't last long," the shadows snarled before Cole leapt from the window.

Sahira and the others rushed over to look down as the shadows guided Cole to the ground. Before his feet hit the earth, more screams erupted, but these were different than the battle cries of war. These were the screams of those being tortured, dismembered, and strewn about.

The stone sill bit into Sahira's skin, and a breeze tickled her face as she leaned further out to see the portals where all immortals, other than dragons and Lexi, entered and exited Dragonia. Immortals were already trying to flee through those portals as the dragons and shadows descended on them.

But it was too late; no one escaped the wrath of the shadows.

CHAPTER SIXTY-FOUR

"Well, that was a quick fight," Orin muttered as the last of the invaders fell beneath Cole and the dragons' vengeance.

He stepped away from the window and turned to survey the wreckage of Amaris. If they weren't careful and didn't find the crudue vine, that would be *all* their heads.

Orin gulped as he rubbed his throat. He much preferred his head intact. It was far too good-looking a head to be anywhere else.

But if anyone could take it, it was the Reaver.

"Where do we find this crudue vine?" Brokk asked.

When the scorpion started tapping the glass again, Orin rubbed his throat again. Cole would return soon, and it wouldn't be pretty when he did.

"The last place anyone found it was Doomed Valley," Kaylia said.

Orin's eyebrows shot up as he studied the crone beside the window. She was far paler than normal, and dark circles surrounded her pewter eyes.

"Fuck," Maverick spat.

"And what other places has it been discovered?" Del inquired.

Kaylia closed her eyes and rubbed the bridge of her nose. "It's been centuries, but it's been located in some outer realms. I think most of those were by chance. There are rumors the merfolk might know where some is, but I'm not sure if they're true. You know how the merfolk can be."

"Secluded, judgmental, fish folk?" Orin suggested.

"Yes, they can... ah... be difficult."

"That's putting it mildly," Brokk muttered.

Kaylia continued as if he hadn't spoken. "Its milk is powerful and...."

Her voice trailed off as the scorpion tapped louder against the glass. They all turned to look at the red scorpion as it poked the glass with its black stinger.

"And the only way to counteract the venom of a noxus scorpion," Kaylia continued. "It's only ever saved one immortal before. Most of those stung by a noxus don't live long enough to receive the antidote. It's pure luck we walked through the door when we did, or else...."

Her attention shifted to the window. She didn't have to finish her words; Orin knew what she'd been about to say... or else they'd all be dead.

And Cole would have been the one to unleash death on all of them. Orin rubbed his very pretty throat again.

Before anyone else could say anything more, Cole reappeared in the window. Covered in blood, he glided into the room and stopped before Kaylia.

"We will split up to find the vine," he said.

Orin somehow managed to restrain himself from looking nervously at the shadows when he realized they'd been reporting their conversation to Cole. He should have known they were listening.

"I think—" Orin blew out a breath before continuing. "—you

should stay here. Someone has to protect Dragonia from another possible invasion."

Cole didn't speak as the shadows slithered beneath his flesh. Those things made it look like his ciphers moved and flexed, but Cole didn't. The shadows were working to take him over, seeping through him and creating a madness that would destroy his brother if they didn't save Lexi.

"The dragons can ensure the realm stays safe," Cole replied in a voice mostly his own, though the shadows distorted it a little. "No one can sit on the throne and control them while Lexi still lives. And they won't find her."

Orin suspected his brother knew exactly where Alina had taken Lexi. The shadows would have tracked their every move.

"We *will* find that vine," Cole stated.

Orin nodded, but when he looked around the room, he saw apprehension and doubt on the faces surrounding him.

CHAPTER SIXTY-FIVE

BROKK STEPPED into Doomed Valley with Kaylia, seven lycans, three dwarves, and two dark fae guards. Over the centuries, he'd heard many stories about Doomed Valley but never expected to step foot in it.

Mainly because most of those stories were about those who *never* survived this realm. Some of the stories came from those who did survive the lethal valley.

Many believed those stories were lies and the immortals who spread them never stepped foot in this forsaken land. Or, if they did, they fled almost immediately afterward.

He looked to Kaylia and the guards spread out around them. So far, he couldn't see what was so awful about this place as the valley spread out before them in rolling hills so green and vibrant the color almost seemed fake.

But it was real and dazzling and so beautiful it stole his breath. How could something be so green and so ripe yet so... *doomed*.

They said the creatures of Doomed Valley moved so fast an immortal couldn't get a portal open in time to flee. Countless immortals had entered this realm and never returned. Their deaths had turned into horror stories that frightened children under their beds.

He'd been one of those children. For a time, he was obsessed with the tales from Doomed Valley; he read everything he could get his hands on about it.

He'd daydreamed about opening a portal out of the Gloaming and into the Valley so he could explore and conquer it. Throughout much of his childhood, he was certain that he would come to the Valley as soon as he came into all his dark fae powers.

Then, he read a story about a lycan *known* to have survived. The man wrote of a creature so horrific its red eyes lit the night and its fangs sliced through flesh as easily as a warm knife through butter. He was the last to bring the rare, coveted, crudue vine from this valley.

He spoke of endless whispers, monsters that hunted day and night, and moving forests. There was never a moment of peace in the Valley.

The man was so haunted by what he witnessed here that it drove him mad. His pack had to destroy him to ensure the safety of its other members.

As the lycan's story unfolded, Brokk felt his eagerness to explore the valley dwindling more as the hair on his nape rose. His room's shadows became monstrous as they shifted and swayed around him.

He couldn't run to his father and explain why he was frightened. The dark fae didn't fear shadows; the dark fae *were* the shadows.

So instead, he threw out the story of the lycan, crawled under his bed, and slept on the floor for the next two weeks. It was one of the most humiliating experiences of his life.

A dark fae who feared the shadows was an embarrassment. He'd considered himself a coward and never told another living soul about it.

Eventually, he talked himself into not being a weakling and returned to bed, but the Valley stopped being as appealing afterward. And soon after, women became a much more fun pastime than reading.

He'd forgotten about the Valley until Kaylia mentioned it. The second she did, he knew he had to be the one to come here.

Since this was the last place crudue vine was known to exist, it had taken time to convince Cole of that, but his brother would go to the merfolk while they started here. If the merfolk couldn't help them, Cole would split up the ones with him and meet him and Kaylia here with more enforcements.

Looking down at the vast, doomed land stretching endlessly below them, Brokk questioned if they'd ever find anything here. There was *so* much of it, and it seemed endless, but if the lycan had succeeded, so could they.

Somehow, it was only fitting that he was here now. It was as if his life had come full circle, and he couldn't help feeling like this was where he was meant to be.

He didn't quite understand why he felt that way, but he hoped it didn't mean his life was soon coming to an end. Even if it did mean that, he wouldn't turn back. They had to save Lexi and the realms because they would all fall if they failed.

Without Lexi, nothing was holding Cole back, and he'd taken far too many shadows into himself again to keep them controlled for long.

He looked to Kaylia and the others. "Are you ready?"

"Damn right," a dwarf said as she tapped her battle-ax on the fertile earth.

Most of the others didn't look as enthusiastic. They'd all volunteered to come here, and their faces remained stoic, but alarm shone in some of their eyes. He suspected they would be the first to fall.

With a sigh, Brokk started down the hill and into the land where many other immortals were lost.

CHAPTER SIXTY-SIX

Over the next three days, Orin made his way rapidly through as many outer realms as he could before having to take a break from opening portals. Many of the realms he encountered were barren and useless, but some held immortals who were mostly content to stay as far from the civilized realms as possible.

He understood their desire.

He would be content to live amongst the outer realms, free of the burden of responsibilities and birth. Alas, as long as he had brothers, it could never be. They kept screwing up and requiring his help.

The others had all broken into groups to search for the vine, but he insisted on going alone. It was how he worked best, and he didn't need anyone else with him, slowing him down or screwing shit up. They didn't have time for that.

Varo and Brokk weren't happy with his decision, but Brokk had gone to Doomed Valley, and Varo remained with Cole. Orin doubted Varo's calming presence would have much effect on the Reaver now, but they needed all the help they could get to keep Cole from killing them.

If it took too much time to find the vine, Cole might lose

control of the shadows even with Lexi still alive in her strange, stone-like state.

When the last light falls....

At first, they'd all taken that to mean Lexi's death, but it could be *this*. Orin rubbed his throat again as he recalled how Amaris's head exploded.

Cole hadn't applied that much pressure, or it hadn't *looked* like he did. His muscles barely flexed when he squished her head like a bug.

And the rebellion that followed was a pathetic attempt, as only about a hundred immortals entered Dragonia. The dragons alone could have taken them out easily enough, but Cole had helped destroy at least half the army.

It was easy enough to tell who did what in the aftermath. The dragons either left smoldering remains behind or ate them. Decimated body parts followed Cole.

He had no idea what those fools were thinking when they tried to invade, but their plans were cut *very* short. They must have assumed Amaris had succeeded in killing Lexi and Dragonia would be in a state of chaos after the fall of its queen; they paid dearly for their mistake.

But without Lexi to rule, it was only a matter of time before word got out and more tried to invade. While she lived, they couldn't take the throne, but they could cause a lot of damage and throw all the realms into chaos. And if Lexi didn't wake....

Well, he didn't like thinking about what would happen then.

Orin gulped as he stepped onto a barren realm he'd never seen before. The rocky outcroppings were desolate, no sun shone upon the cold land, and the icy breeze sent a chill down his spine.

The crudue vine could grow anywhere, though it rarely did, but *nothing* lived on this realm. He retreated into his portal as he tried to think of somewhere else to go.

He'd visited a couple of the outer realms he knew. He was

aware there was no crudue vine in those realms but hoped for a lead on where to find some, and maybe some details about outer realms he didn't know. With those details, he could picture them and go there.

He'd already exhausted all those leads and was now picturing barren rocks while he opened portals, as that's what most outer realms consisted of. He was discovering new places this way, but many lacked any life.

The opening of so many portals was starting to beat him down, but he had enough strength to keep going for a few more. He'd have to take a break after that.

Eventually, his destination-less portals would either take him to the vine, to some realm where he'd never been, and to other immortals who could help him or try to kill him. Or, he might run out of places to go.

That last option seemed highly unlikely as many hypothesized the outer realms were limitless. Orin believed that.

Sooner or later, he would have to stop picturing barren rocks simply because there were probably outer realms without these rocks. But for now, it was what he knew and where he went.

Finally, when he was about to call it a day and find somewhere to crash, he emerged from a portal and into a town with a busy center street cutting through the two and three-story buildings shading the dirt road before him. The craggy rocks known throughout the outer realms rose in the distance.

Those rocks loomed over the land and blocked what remained of the setting sun. Colors streaked across the darkening sky, but those colors faded as the sun lowered.

Music and laughter came from a building further down the road, and a woman squealed in delight. The collection of immortals walking the street varied; they all got along as dwarves stopped to talk with warlocks and vampires emerged from some of the buildings.

At the end of the road was a large lake, a rare find in an outer realm. That meant witches were most likely here too, and they'd started breathing life into this place.

A pegasus soared overhead, and water flicked from her tail as a mermaid dove beneath the water. The buildings were an eclectic mix of shabby wooden ones that tilted a little or had lopsided windows, brick, and elegant, sweeping ones bordering on being mansions.

Storefronts and homes blended, and when Orin turned to look behind him, more of the street unwound before taking a corner and vanishing. It was rare to find an outer realm as well established as this one, but more homes were nestled into the craggy face of the black rock rising beyond the end of the street.

The immortals here had really settled into this outer realm. Shrugging, Orin turned away from the end of the road.

While he was here, he could gather information, recharge, and feed on some of the women dancing on the balconies of the stately brick building at the end of the road. He smiled as he sauntered toward the party.

CHAPTER SIXTY-SEVEN

THE SHADOWS WHISPERED INCESSANTLY to Cole as they begged him to unleash the death and brutality the realms deserved. He and Lexi had brought them peace, given them a stable environment, and were working to rebuild.

They would be fair rulers who wouldn't unleash brutality on the realms like the Lord had, and *this* was how they were thanked. The ungrateful pieces of shit kept plotting against them and trying to steal the throne from Lexi.

They kept plotting and attacking, and now they'd succeeded in taking down the *one* immortal who deserved it the least. While Lexi remained frozen, and they couldn't find the crudue vine, then she was as good as dead.

And they would keep coming. Her absence would only embolden, not deter them.

His claws bit into his palms. Blood welled against his fingers, but he didn't feel it as he stalked forward.

And he'd never seen Amaris coming; neither had the shadows. The devious bitch had been smarter than their other adversaries; thankfully, not smart enough to succeed… yet.

Amaris wasn't the last of their enemies either. Plenty more of them remained out there, scheming, and he'd never be able to locate them before they tried to strike.

They would continue to go after her and him as they sought to destroy everything he loved. But not if *he* killed *them* first.

Cole closed his eyes as he struggled to shut out the whispers. He'd experienced peace from the insistent bloodlust since Lexi took the overflow of shadows from him, but now, without her, they strove to take over again.

The only thing keeping them at bay, and him from slaughtering, was his mission to find the crudue vine and the fae and lycan parts of himself that were finally working together.

They remained rational… for now. Eventually, the lycan would break down over separation from its mate, and the dark fae was already seeking the one it loved.

Lowering his head into his hands, his claws scraped skin as he massaged his temples and tried to calm the rampaging voices. Something had to silence them, but the only one who could was lying in a dragon cave, hidden away, and protected by the things Cole once hated so much. The dragons were the only ones he trusted to keep Lexi safe while away.

He'd left some shadows to keep an eye on Dragonia, and the dragons now resided in the throne room and outside the portals. If any threat dared to enter, they would slaughter it.

While Lexi lived, they would protect her and the throne. If something happened to her….

Cole shook his head against the possibility. He *would* get through this and save Lexi. They *would* be married.

"Are you okay?" Maverick inquired.

"Fine," Cole grated through his teeth.

"There's water ahead," Sahira said.

"Finally," Skog muttered.

Cole understood the dwarf's irritation as they'd spent three days walking through Atlantia. He'd opened a portal to where he last visited in the mermaid realm only to discover the Sea was gone and broken shells, brown seaweed, and purple, blue, and yellow coral in its place.

It was rumored the Indigo Sea shifted and changed its location depending on the whims of the merfolk, but this was the first time he'd ever seen proof of it. And since he was the last to visit Atlantia, they decided against portal hopping to try to find the Sea—which could cause them to miss it—and set out searching for it.

The last time he came to Atlantia was with his father, and one of the mermen escorted them through a portal he'd created. That was a few hundred years ago, and things had changed since then.

Cole lifted his head and opened his eyes as they drew closer to the Indigo Sea, which was the color of its name. The water lapped against the sandy shore speckled with boulders the size of buses and smaller rocks where some of the merfolk basked in the sun.

A sneer curved his lips as he studied the merfolk. They weren't known for their willingness to help unless it benefited them, but if they knew where to locate crudue vine, he would do everything in his power to get the answer from them.

Beneath the sun's rays, the merfolk's tails had become golden as they occasionally flicked into the air while they stretched languidly on the rocks. Neither the men nor women wore tops. All their hair spilled over the stones and toward the ground.

In the sea beyond, their deep blue tails came out of the water and sprayed rivulets of ocean water around them as more swam toward shore. The merfolk's tails changed color depending on their environment.

Cole studied the creatures while they approached. He'd never had much interaction with merfolk before. Often, these sea dwellers spurned other immortals, and Cole couldn't have cared less about ever returning to Atlantia.

Some immortals came here hoping to find the treasures it was rumored the mermaids protected. Whether true or not, Cole didn't know, but many came hoping to gain riches.

And still, other immortals came with the hope of bedding a merfolk. They were said to be wild, but Cole had entertained plenty of wild women and had no desire to catch one.

One of the women noticed them first. She flipped on her rock, propped herself up on her elbows, and lifted her golden tail as she gave them a smile that set Cole's teeth on edge.

"We have a whole treasure trove of immortals who have arrived to chase their riches," she said in the accented voice of the mermaids that resembled the Greek accent of mortals.

The mermaid's words drew the attention of the rest of the merfolk. They all turned to watch while Cole and the others approached.

"We're not here for your riches," Cole told them.

The merfolk chuckled, and their tails flicked in the air.

"Ah, then you've come for sex, dark fae," the mermaid said. "I can assure you the rumors are true. Once you have one of us, *no one* else will ever satisfy you again."

"We're not here for that either."

The mermaid giggled, and a ripple went through her tail before it vanished to reveal a pair of slender legs. Her white-blonde hair shone in the sun as she turned on the rock, spread her legs, and smiled.

One hand ran leisurely down her body to between her thighs. "You're famished, dark fae; I can sense it. Let me ease you."

Some of the others chuckled, and another mermaid, this one with hair the color of garnets, rose. As she glided toward them, everything in Cole recoiled from the naked woman. Even the shadows wanted no piece of her.

"We can make all of you so happy," the redhead murmured.

Cole sensed the attention of the others on him as they waited to see how he would react. The dark fae part of him was ravenous, but he'd rather starve than touch another woman. The idea of it made him sick.

Before the woman could get too close, a wall of shadows rose to keep them separated. More shadows slipped across the rocks and encircled the blonde's legs, sealing them together.

"We're not here for that," Cole snarled in a voice mingled with those of the shadows.

The smiles faded from the merfolk as they exchanged uneasy looks. Everyone came here looking for sex, riches, or flecks of their tails for spells; that was what the merfolk counted on. They could predict that and torment those who arrived here.

They didn't know how to react to someone who didn't seek those things.

CHAPTER SIXTY-EIGHT

"We're looking for crudue vine," Sahira stated.

The merfolk exchanged another look as another merman emerged from the water, pulled himself onto land, and draped himself over a rock. He lifted his head to stare curiously at the newcomers before glancing around at his brethren.

"There's no crudue vine here," another merman said.

"It's rumored you know where to locate some; if it's not here, then *where* is it?" Cole demanded.

"It's a rumor, so how would we know?"

A chuckle ran through all of them.

"Silly dark fae, don't you know better than to listen to rumors?" the redhead taunted.

A shadow rose to her throat so fast that it was barely visible until it cinched around her neck and lifted her onto her toes.

"Don't fuck with me," Cole warned. "You have no idea what I'm capable of doing. I could kill you all and not feel remorse for it. I'm not here for your games, and I'm not here for sex or your treasures. I'm here to save the woman I love. The woman who rightfully rules over *all* of you. If you know something, and you're not telling me, I'll kill every last one of you."

"We live in the sea. You can try, but you'd never kill us all," the blonde replied.

"Do you think there aren't shadows in the sea?"

"Okay, okay." Sahira waved her hands in a calming gesture as she jumped into the conversation. "I think we should all take a deep breath and start over. We're not here to fight you. We're here to save the new queen of Dragonia."

All their tails stopped flipping up and down as a hush descended, and the merfolk became immobile. They didn't blink while they watched Sahira.

Gulping, Sahira looked at him before continuing. "She was stung by a noxus scorpion. We froze her heart before the poison could kill her, but we have to find the vine before we wake her."

The merfolk studied them before shifting their attention to each other. No one spoke, but Cole saw the conversations running through their minds as they seemed to communicate wordlessly.

Finally, as if they were one, their attention shifted back to them. "There's nothing we can do to help you," one of the mermen said. "We don't bother ourselves with the affairs of other immortals. This realm is peaceful; other immortals only come here when they seek to take from us. We don't reward those who do."

When Cole stepped forward, Varo reached for him, but his younger brother's hand fell away before it touched his arm. Cole focused on the merfolk while sending shadows beneath the sea to uncover what he needed.

"She is the queen of all the realms, including *yours*," Cole said. "She rules you, and you *will* do whatever you can to save her."

"We have not acknowledged her as our queen. We didn't swear fealty to her, and as you know, we have a king and queen here."

"Do you?" Cole growled.

The shadows had sought something to use against these things, and now he had it. A scream went through the ocean, but the sound didn't pierce the day when the shadows seized on the woman with a crown made of shells adorning her black locks.

Someone else roared beneath the water, but Cole didn't care as the shadows dragged the woman from the depths. The shadows chattered excitedly around him and darted to and fro as they frolicked like dolphins.

They sensed a fight coming, the blood that would spill, and the death they incessantly craved. A bloodbath was at their fingertips.

The merfolk tried to maintain their nonchalant air, but uneasiness grew as they stirred and looked at each other again. The blonde tried to break the shadow's hold on her legs, but they laughed as they squeezed. The redhead tried to claw at the shadows; it was useless.

More shadows erupted from the ocean while they dragged the merfolk's queen from beneath the sea. Her scream drew the attention of the others as the shadows held her above the water like the sacrifice she would become if these assholes didn't help him.

Some of the merfolk transformed and leapt to their feet while the queen clawed at the shadows around her neck. The merfolk were renowned for their abundance of riches, sexuality, and fighting ability. Many who came to capture one didn't survive. Those who did were often tricked out of the things they'd gained.

"Don't do anything foolish, Cole," Del cautioned. "We're not armed for a war, and Dragonia can't take another one right now."

"I'll slaughter all of them before they ever step foot in that realm," Cole vowed.

"They may be a bunch of assholes, but we need the merfolk," Sahira said. "They might not know where there's some crudue vine, but their scales are precious and necessary for spells. Not to mention, they're living, breathing creatures. You can't slaughter them because they won't work with us."

"If they continue to fuck with me, then yes, I can."

"You have to calm down," Varo said in his soothing tone. "Violence won't help us here."

"Reasoning wasn't helping us either. So now, it's time to make them understand I'm *not* fucking with them. If they can help us, then they better do so."

The queen thrashed in the shadow's grasp as the other merfolk crept closer. The thunderous expressions on their faces said they'd gladly kill him if they got the chance.

More of the merfolk transformed while some jumped into the water and swam out toward their queen. Before they could reach her, the shadows formed a wall between the two to keep them away.

A torrent of water burst from the sea as the merking erupted from the waves. Kept aloft by a fountain of water, he held a trident in his hands as he searched for his queen.

For a second, the king calmed when he found her, but his face clouded with rage when he spotted the shadows around her neck. Twisting inside the fountain of water, the king's eyes found Cole's.

Cole smiled in return.

CHAPTER SIXTY-NINE

"Hello, King Firth," Cole greeted.

Before he could say anything more, the king of the merfolk lifted his trident, waved it at the sea, and swung the trident toward them. A giant wave of water rose from the previously calm, crystalline, blue water and surged toward them.

Not even the shadows could fight against that wave. "Run!" Cole commanded.

As the shadows pulled the queen toward Cole, the others scattered behind the boulders. Leaping forward, he wrapped his arms around her before diving behind a group of boulders.

The wave crashed over him with a thunderous roar. Water pummeled his body and battered his muscles and bones until it flattened him into the ground. He kept the queen beneath him to ensure she didn't break away and swim back into the sea.

And when it finally ended, the queen squirmed in his arms, clawed at his flesh, and kicked against him, but he refused to let her go as he spit out water. Keeping hold of her, he waited until the shadows reported the others were safe before rising and emerging from behind the boulders.

When he turned to face the king, he wasn't surprised to discover the merfolk advancing on them with weapons. They'd either had those weapons stashed behind the rocks or the sea swept them into their hands. Either way, Cole wasn't backing down.

"This doesn't have to be a fight!" Cole shouted as he planted the squirming, pissed-off queen down. She'd lost her crown and tail, but she was still volatile. "I came here looking for help that your merfolk refused to give, so now I'm asking *you* for it."

"Diplomacy could have gone a long way with that," Sahira muttered from where she hid.

"Fuck off," the shadows hissed.

When the king pulled his trident back again, the shadows surrounded it. The king struggled against their grip on his weapon, but they wouldn't relent.

More shadows encased the approaching merfolk, halting them in their place. Cole's joints popped as the lycan sought to break free. The dark fae sought to take control of the water, but though he could manipulate the elements, the merfolk had far more control over water than him.

"Listen to me!" Cole shouted.

The shadows sought blood and didn't understand why he was holding back. He could easily destroy these fish, but enough reason remained for him to know he couldn't kill *all* the merfolk. They couldn't help him if he did.

But he'd gladly flay them all if they didn't smarten up.

Until then, he would *not* be the prophecy. Not yet, anyway. The shadows were back, louder than ever, but he retained some control. He could keep them at bay while he had a chance of saving Lexi… at least for a little longer.

He didn't kid himself into thinking that, as more time passed and the whispers grew louder and the shadows stronger, he'd retain this amount of control. But for now, he could.

And he had to. He and Lexi were working to bring the realms together; they couldn't do that if he started offing the residents.

But they also couldn't do it if Lexi didn't have the cure.

"Listen!" Cole shouted again. "We came here for crudue vine; it's rumored you know where it is. I asked your merfolk for help, and they refused. Now, I'm asking you."

The queen tried to kick him again, but he easily sidestepped the blow as the drenched and irritated-looking others climbed out from behind their boulders. Sahira pulled a yellow starfish from her hair and tossed it toward the sea. Skog scowled at him before shifting his attention to the merfolk.

"You do *not* come to Atlantia and demand our help!" King Firth roared.

"I asked for your help to save *the* queen of the Shadow Realms."

"We don't concern ourselves with the business of other immortals."

Cole's hand tightened on the queen's throat. "She's to be my wife. She *is* my mate. Concern yourself with that; understand *that*."

The king's face remained impassive as his queen stood with her chin raised and defiance emanating from her slender body. The king's gaze met his wife's. This was the woman he loved and would do anything to save.

"You know what I am," Cole said to the merking. "Which means you must know the only reason your wife and *all* your followers are still alive is because I have chosen *not* to kill them."

"The Shadow Reaver," the queen stated.

"That's right, and we didn't come here to fight or make enemies. If you help us, we'll repay the favor. I came here to save the woman *I* love and will marry, but I need your help. She's also the only one who can keep the Reaver at bay. Without her, it's only a matter of time before the shadows let loose."

"You came here and not only threatened my people but also my *wife,* and I'm supposed to help you?" the king demanded.

"Yes."

A stunned silence followed Cole's simple word. And then the queen spoke.

CHAPTER SEVENTY

"We know where to find some crudue vine," the queen said.

"Mira," King Firth said in a warning tone.

"You would do this and more to save me, Firth. The queen of the Shadow Realms is trying to make them all a better place, and at least we don't have to fear her killing us for no reason like we did the Lord.

"If she dies, do we want some other immortal taking the throne and leaving us with another madman to deal with? Or worse, are we going to be the reason the Reaver destroys all the realms? I'm assuming he'll start with us."

"I will," Cole confirmed.

Firth didn't look happy about his wife's words, but the funnel of water he'd been riding lowered him onto the shore. "Let my wife go."

Cole debated this for only a second. He could easily reclaim the queen if necessary, but releasing her now would be a sign of good faith. Letting her go, he kept the shadows in front of the other merfolk as he cleared a path to let her glide toward her husband.

The king grasped her arms and looked the queen over before

pushing her behind him. Mira looked more irritated by this than Cole's capture of her; she immediately stepped out from behind her husband.

Cole almost laughed over the exchange. The woman reminded him of Lexi, but he'd stopped finding anything funny the second the shadows whispered to him about Lexi's downfall.

"Where is the vine?" he asked.

"On the other side of Atlantia is the Malignant Waters, a salty lake full of ocean creatures. *All* of them are ruthless, and no one has successfully taken the vine from them in centuries, but there's crudue at the bottom of the lake," Mira said.

"And I'm supposed to believe you're telling me the truth?"

He required their help but didn't trust a damn thing they said. However, they didn't have any other options.

He had no idea if Brokk or Orin had been successful. They hadn't returned to Dragonia yet—the shadows told him as much—which meant they most likely hadn't found crudue either. He couldn't take the chance of leaving here without the vine. This could be their only option.

"You're going to have to," the queen said. "If you'd like, I'll take you to the lake."

"Mira!" the king snapped.

"The sooner they're out of our land, the happier we'll all be."

No one could argue with that.

"Besides, he most likely won't survive the lake, and then we won't have to worry about the Reaver." The queen turned and opened a portal. "You can follow us."

"Hold on," Cole said.

He sent the shadows into the portal to see what lay on the other side. When they reported back there was nothing more than a lake, Cole nodded to the queen.

King Firth scowled but followed his wife through the portal. Some of the other merfolk went with them, but the king commanded the others to remain behind.

"Go ahead," Cole said to the others. "It's safe. I'll go last and make sure no one attacks from behind."

Del and Sahira exchanged a look before entering the portal. Skog followed, but Varo and Maverick remained at his side.

"We'll go together," Maverick said.

Cole didn't argue with him, and he kept the wall of shadows behind them as they strode through the portal and on toward the Malignant Waters. When they arrived on the other side, the queen shut the portal.

The brilliant sun shining down on the lake emphasized its clarity; he could see to the bottom. The lake was about three hundred feet in diameter and nearly a perfect circle.

A hundred feet below, purple, yellow, orange, gold, and silver seaweed clung to the gray rocks lining the bottom and sides of the lake. The seaweed swayed in a current that must have come from the multiple caves burrowed into the sides of the rocky lake.

Nothing moved through the water, but Cole spotted a thick, neon-red vine at the very bottom. He'd never seen crudue vine before, but he'd heard tell of its unique color and the thick thorns lining the rare plant.

There was so much of it down there, yet the merfolk had none? Surely it was worth a few horrible creatures he didn't see.

"Why haven't you harvested it?" he demanded.

"Because we value our lives," the queen replied.

Cole frowned at her before turning his attention back to the water.

"I don't see anything down there," Del said gruffly.

"And you won't until you're *in* the water with them," King Firth replied.

Cole studied the dark caves lining the lake. There were dozens, if not more of them; some were a good thirty feet high and thirty feet wide.

Skog tapped his battle-ax on the rocks lining the shore of the lake and rubbed his grayish-brown beard. "What are they?"

"So many things," one of the merfolk murmured.

The queen waved her hand at the serene, beautiful lake. "There are Cetus, kraken, sharks, and horrible, small fish who rend the flesh from your bones. There's a reason the merfolk aren't bathing in crudue vine. Only one has ever survived going in there to retrieve the vine."

"And I won't do it again." King Firth's eyes were full of challenge when they met Cole's. "I barely survived the first time, and I did it for my wife. I won't do it for anyone else."

"Understandable," Cole murmured. "And I will do it for my mate and fiancée."

"You can't go in there, Cole," Varo said. "It's almost certain death."

"So were the trials, and so was drawing so many of the shadows into me, but I'm still alive, and I *will* save Lexi."

"Brokk and Orin could still find the vine. We can leave here and split up as we planned. Some of us can also start searching the outer realms while the rest join Brokk. There's more vine out there… somewhere."

"And all of it will be somewhere perilous. There's a reason crudue vine is so rare. Besides, the sooner we have it, the sooner Brokk and Orin can give up their missions too. They can also return to somewhere safer."

"This is a bad idea," Del said. "Who will protect Dragonia if you die?"

"The dragons and, then once she wakes, Lexi. But that doesn't matter because I'm not going to die."

"You're a stubborn fool," Maverick murmured.

"A fool in love," Mira said.

"King Firth had a tail and can breathe underwater; he could move through that lake a *lot* faster than you, and he doesn't drown," Maverick said.

"The dark fae have some control over water," Cole reminded him.

"Not that much control," Del said. "The shadows can kill from a distance; maybe they can bring the crudue vine to you."

"Perhaps," Cole murmured.

He sent the shadows through the water to the vines, but though they could encompass flesh and tear it apart, they couldn't free the vine from the rocks.

"No. Maybe if I was closer to the vine, the shadows could tear it away, but I doubt it. The shadows seek blood; the crudue vine isn't blood."

"Crudue is also magical and powerful; it doesn't obey the same laws as other plants," Sahira said. "It grows from trees and lakes and out of rocks. But it never grows where I seek thee. Or at least that's what I've heard others whisper about the vine."

Cole kicked off his boots and pulled off his pants. "Then there's only one option."

CHAPTER SEVENTY-ONE

"I'm leaving shadows here to watch over my friends. If you try anything, they *will* kill you," Cole said.

To prove his point, the shadows surrounded the merfolk's feet. Two of them stepped back before realizing they were on the shadows and jumping a little forward.

"Point taken," King Firth said.

Completely naked, Cole didn't hesitate before diving into the crystal clear lake with the monsters lurking within. All the seaweed attached to the rocks stopped moving as soon as he entered the water.

They went straight as an arrow before recoiling and closing in on themselves as if trying to hide from the monsters about to emerge. Cole kept his attention on the vine as he kicked through the water.

The shadows he'd left behind reported no sign of hostility from the merfolk, but he didn't think the king and queen would harm them. It hadn't started well between them, but he'd earn their respect if he survived this, and if he didn't, the others weren't a danger to them.

If he died, the merfolk would return to the Indigo Sea while the others would continue their mission to save Lexi. Since he had no intention of dying down here, he'd earn their respect and get that vine.

He'd always been a good swimmer, strong and confident. As an immortal, he could hold his breath for extended periods, on average, at least twenty minutes, but that was if he was lying in a pool relaxing, not swimming, and not about to fight monstrous creatures who had the advantage of living in this lake.

However, he had the shadows, and they were already sliding into the water in anticipation of the attack to come. They didn't care what creature they spilled blood from as long as *they* spilled it.

He could also manipulate the water. Not enough to push this much out of his way, but he could use it to his advantage when the time came.

From the corner of his eye, Cole caught a flash of silver. Before he could see what was coming for him, blood erupted into the water, and the shadows' laughter drifted through his mind.

He was closing in on the crudue vine; he continued to have the shadows try to break it, but they failed. He kicked harder when more movement erupted into the lake and the water rippled around him.

Cole couldn't see what was coming, and he didn't look. He remained focused on the crudue while he trusted the shadows to protect him.

If he'd been this close to an immortal, or something else with a pumping heart, the shadows would have ripped it apart and brought him the pieces by now. But much to his irritation, they couldn't tear into the crudue vine.

His lungs didn't burn, and his legs weren't growing tired, but he felt a sense of time slipping away. He'd been underwater for too long; the darkness around him was growing as more creatures filled the lake, and while shadows danced across the rocky bottom, there wasn't a whole lot of them to draw on.

And the creatures were increasingly choking out the sun and causing those shadows to dwindle.

When his fingers wrapped around the crudue vine, he avoided the thorns. He was certain the creatures guarding this lake already knew he was here, but his blood in the water would entice and excite them further.

Once he succeeded in ripping a section of vine free, he turned to discover blood choking the water as the shadows continued to slaughter. Between the blood and the increasing presence of the creatures, the sun was rapidly fading.

And without the sun, the shadows couldn't thrive.

Cole twisted the vine around his bicep. He stopped caring about the thorns; they didn't matter anymore. They bit into his flesh, dug into his muscle, and embedded there, but he didn't feel their prick as he studied the monsters swirling above him.

There was no pathway through them, and even if there was, they'd close it before he made it to the surface. He'd have to go through them, and he had no problem with that.

Smiling grimly, and with the vine locked securely around his arm, he planted his feet on the rocky bottom and shoved upward through the blood and water. He still wasn't tired, and his lungs didn't burn, but the trip up wouldn't be as easy as the one down.

He only made it ten feet when the monsters confirmed this. From out of the increasing darkness of the water, a tentacle the size of a tree unfolded.

He darted to the side in time to avoid one of the suction cups attached to the tentacle. The razor-sharp teeth within the cup clacked loudly as it missed his waist, but just when he believed he was out of its reach, it swung to the side and snagged his ankle.

Cole inwardly cursed and swung down as claws erupted from

his fingers, and those teeth bit into his flesh. With a pull he felt to the center of his heart, those things started feasting on his blood.

With one, two, three hacking slices, he succeeded in slicing off the end of the thick appendage. He had no idea where the monster that belonged to it was in the water, but the tip of its tentacle remained embedded in his ankle as Cole kicked again.

He didn't see the shark that crashed into him a second later. The tip of its rough nose abraded the skin on his chest a second before its multiple layers of teeth sank into his flesh.

Unprepared for the searing pain accompanying the crunch of his ribs and the crushing of his lungs, Cole grunted out a shout that released what air he still had inside him. Bubbles erupted before his eyes as the shark propelled him into the side of the lake and bashed him into the rocks.

Cole waved his hand at the water and drew enough to slam it into the shark's face, but it did little good. The massive beast's tail swung back and forth in the water as it opened its jaws a little before biting down again.

Cole suppressed a scream as he plunged his claws into the shark's nose. He ripped through its cartilage and down toward its nose. Its black eyes were too far away to get at them, but he shredded the creature's nostrils as he hacked into them.

The shark's tail waved faster as it smashed him repeatedly into the rocks until blood erupted from Cole's mouth. The darkness of the creatures spreading through the lake and the blood had choked out most of the shadows, but there were enough left to encircle the beast.

He gathered his dark fae abilities to shove more water at the creature as he pushed it back. The lycan half of him continued to batter the monster while the shadows worked to pry it away.

For once, he could feel all the parts of himself working together. Their strength flowed through him as all the pieces of who he was, finally clicked together while they worked as one to keep him alive. They'd *finally* found common ground as they came together inside him.

The shadows pried open the shark's mouth as he continued to carve into the beast. Finally, the shadows succeeded in tearing its mouth open. Cole swam out of the creature's mouth as the shadows tore off its bottom jaw.

Desperate for air and finally able to feel a little relief in his crushed chest, Cole couldn't control his instinct to breathe anymore. As soon as he did, water flooded him.

His lungs contracted and tried to expel the liquid filling them, but it was impossible. His heart lurched, and his entire body spasmed. He was drowning, and it hurt like a motherfucker, but it wouldn't kill him.

He'd survive, but it would weaken him. And without oxygen to fill his muscles and brain, his strength waned as disorientation crept in.

Stars burst before his eyes, and his head spun as he tried to recall where he was and why. His head bobbed as unconsciousness briefly pulled him into its oblivious depths, but the shadows jerked him awake again.

Shaking his head, Cole stopped feeling the burn in his lungs and the jabbing stab of his ribs digging into his body. Trying to orient himself, he rested his hand against the crudue vine on his arm.

Though little compared to what the rest of his battered body felt, the thorn's prick reminded him why he was there. *Lexi!*

He required both hands but pressed his finger onto that thorn in the hopes it would keep him grounded and focused on saving his mate. He had to get the vine to her.

He clawed at the water with one hand as he kicked and struggled to the surface. The weight of the liquid in his lungs tried to drag him back to the bottom. It was slow going, but he refused to give in to the agony and confusion trying to destroy him.

Shadows wrapped around his arm, drawing him upward, but

he felt the weakness in their grasp. When a mammoth creature passed overhead, the shadows dissipated as darkness reined in the lake.

When another tentacle slithered toward him, Cole realized the creature, still partially twisted around his leg, had come for its revenge. And without the shadows, it was just him and the monster above.

CHAPTER SEVENTY-TWO

Sahira took a lurching step toward the lake that had gone from pure, crystalline beauty to a revolting mass of the most grotesque things she'd ever seen. The water was almost entirely black and red as blood and the creatures churned within it.

There were so many different monsters and shredded parts, she could barely tell one from the other. Silver fish flashed to the surface, and as they did, their hundreds of misshapen, dagger-like teeth clacked loudly.

Tentacles rose and fell out of the water. Blood dripped from those appendages with their hundreds of suction cups filled with teeth.

Nausea churned in her stomach as her hand went to her mouth. They couldn't lose Cole.

"What do we do?" she breathed.

"There is nothing for us to do," King Firth said.

"Use your fucking trident!" Del commanded. "Push those things away, electrocute them, create a wave, or do *whatever* else you can with it."

King Firth lifted his trident from the ground and gripped it in both hands while his sea green eyes narrowed on Del. His pale blond hair waved around his broad shoulders as he looked about to use the trident on Del.

"Merfolk do *not* take orders from vampires," Firth stated, "or anyone else."

"We understand," Varo said in that calming way he had.

Sahira wondered if the merman realized Varo was using some of his light fae ability on him or if he didn't know Varo was part light fae. Either way, some tension eased from the king's shoulders as Varo continued speaking.

"But there must be something you can do to help. The king of the Gloaming and the queen of the Shadow Realms *will* repay your kindness."

"They're both about as good as dead," one of the mermaids muttered.

Mira shot the mermaid a dark look before turning back to the lake. "He still lives."

"How do you know?" Skog inquired.

"Because the creatures haven't returned to their caves. If he were dead, they would have fed and moved on by now."

Sahira twisted her hands in her shirt as she looked pleadingly at the king. "You must be able to do something."

Firth sighed before turning to the lake and resting the prongs of his trident on top of the water. A ripple ran across the lake, but it didn't do anything to stop those ugly little fish from flapping across the surface or the kraken as it spread further through the water.

"This lake is in Atlantia, but I have no control over the Malignant Waters." King Firth lifted his trident from the water and set the bottom on the ground. "Our home is the Indigo Sea. While I have some effect and control over other oceans and bodies of water in other realms, this lake of monsters is beyond my capabilities. I have no idea why, but it has been this way for every king of the merfolk."

"How do we know you're telling the truth?" Maverick demanded.

The smile King Firth gave him was more a baring of his teeth as the air around him wavered and a blur started around his legs. After the man shifted, he lay on the ground with his trident at the ready, and his beautiful, golden tail spread out behind him.

The sun glistened off his tail as Firth lifted it to reveal the fins at the end. No, not fins... it was more like a fin and a half, as part of the left fin was gone. Only a jagged line remained.

"I was already king of the merfolk when I entered these waters to gather the crudue vine necessary to save my wife from a warlock's poison. As you can see, I didn't escape the waters unscathed. If I could control this lake, do you think I would have allowed *this* to happen?" Firth demanded with a shake of his tail.

Before any of them could respond, Firth shifted again and once more stood naked before them. It was then that Sahira noticed that half his left foot was missing.

While coming here, she hadn't noticed it as the man didn't walk with a limp and she wasn't looking at his feet. She had much more to focus on than feet... like being surrounded by enemies and a lake of death.

Now, she marveled over how well he maneuvered with an injury like that. It must have taken him years to adjust to walking so easily on half his foot.

"Okay, so you can't help," Maverick muttered.

"What is that thing doing?" Skog inquired.

Sahira's attention shifted to the black blob hovering twenty feet beneath the water's surface. It was so large it blocked out half the lake; it resembled a giant octopus or squid, and its large, pink beak occasionally broke the surface as its black eyes rolled.

"That's the kraken," Mira said, "and it's looking to eat."

Del ran a hand through his pale blond hair and tugged at the ends while studying the behemoth. "Wonderful."

The kraken's gigantic tentacles spread out over half of the lake. Some waved in the air while others delved deeper into the blackened, bloody depths. When those tentacles rose again, bloody water dripped from the ends and splashed back into the lake.

Where is Cole? Sahira's heart raced as she leaned forward to see better through the water, but it was pointless. She couldn't see beyond the monster below them.

While the kraken looked like it would be mushy and cold to the touch, she suspected its skin was thicker and tougher to destroy than it seemed. It would be difficult to kill this monster, and she had no idea where to start.

She ran through all the water spells she knew, but none of them would help in this situation. She could part the water a little, letting them get closer to the creature, but she didn't know what they could do after that.

The kraken's tentacles shook, and when fresh blood welled from beneath it, the silver fish jumped in and out of the water more enthusiastically. Sharks rolled as they flopped around the surface, eating some of the smaller fish, which in turn caused them to go after the sharks.

None of them attacked the kraken. She suspected they knew it was pointless. But if those tiny monsters, with teeth that could easily shred flesh, couldn't do anything against the kraken, what could they do?

How do we get Cole out from under there? And is he still alive?

Her blood ran cold at the possibility he might already be gone and these things were finishing their feast before retreating.

A strange ripple went through the kraken's tentacles and across the water as some of its appendages curled inward. She didn't know if it was reacting like this because Cole was doing something to it... or the creature was devouring her friend.

CHAPTER SEVENTY-THREE

Del couldn't tear his eyes away from the monstrosity floating in the water as its tentacles curved in and the kraken shuddered. He had no idea what was happening beneath the surface of the lake, but their chances of saving Cole, and his daughter, slipped further away with every passing second.

There had to be something he could do, but though his mind spun through a dozen different scenarios, he couldn't settle on one. He was a general in Cole's army; it was his job to devise plans.

He'd plotted to help defeat the Lord; he'd taken out countless enemies over the years with his strategies, but standing here, watching the blood and turmoil, his ability to see a way out of almost anything had deserted him. He had no idea how to fight sea monsters.

What can I do to stop this?

He tugged at his hair again as the beast convulsed. When it did so, it floated closer to the surface.

Del's heart raced as his brain uselessly stuttered over possibilities. He'd always prided himself on his ability to think under pressure and come up with answers others couldn't see.

Now, when he needed it most, that ability failed him, but he couldn't move past the possible loss of his future son-in-law and daughter. Even if they could find crudue vine somewhere else for Lexi, it would devastate her if Cole died trying to save her.

His beautiful, loving girl would never be the same again. She would continue to breathe and function without Cole, but she'd never truly *live* again.

He didn't doubt Lexi would become the greatest ruler the Shadow Realms had ever known, with or without Cole, but her life and heart would always have a hole in them. He could hope for her to find love again, but it wouldn't happen.

She had agreed to marry Cole; he was the man she intended to spend the rest of her life with. While they weren't married, he knew no immortal who lost their love and went on to love again.

It just didn't happen. Immortals could do many things but not fall in love twice.

He couldn't stand here and let that happen to his Andi. Not only was she his daughter, but Cole was his best friend and son-in-law, even if it wasn't official yet.

He had to do something, but what?

The kraken jerked again as it floated closer to the surface. Now that it was only five feet below them, its black eyes were more visible as they broke the surface before going under again. Those eyes were the size of a man.

Del's heart raced as he looked around for anything to help him. His gaze settled on Skog's battle-ax as the dwarf studied the kraken with disdain and awe.

"Give me your ax," Del commanded.

Skog gave him an affronted look as he tapped the bottom of his ax against the ground. "Dwarves do *not* give their battle-axes to *anyone* unless they're pried from our cold, dead hands. And I don't intend to die today."

Del ignored his words as he waved his hands impatiently at

the stubborn dwarf. "And I don't intend to watch my family die today. Give me the ax."

Skog scowled, but before he could say anything more, Maverick yanked the ax from him. Skog spun on the lycan who towered over him. The dwarf pulled back his arm to launch a punch at him.

Skog may not intend to die today, but hitting a lycan was a good way to set off that chain of events. Despite their small stature, dwarves were incredibly strong, but they weren't stronger than a lycan.

Before Skog's fist could fly, Varo stepped between them. "Easy," the light fae coaxed. "Del must have a plan and needs your ax to see it through. Do you?"

The hopeful look Varo gave him was far too optimistic for Del's liking. Normally he did have a plan, and on more than one occasion, some brilliant ones.

Today was not one of those days. This was more of a wing and a prayer.

Despite that, he still replied, "Sure."

Skog's scowl deepened as he looked from Maverick to Del and back again. "This isn't over, wolf."

"Anytime, dwarf." Maverick tossed the ax to Del. "How are we going to save my nephew?"

"Luck."

With that, Del backed up a few feet before sprinting toward the lake's edge. With a fierce shout, he launched himself off the ground. His feet kicked in the air as he flew over the water.

When the kraken's eyes rolled toward him, he considered too late the possibility one of those tentacles might hit him as they lashed out of the water. One whipped past his head with enough speed and strength to shatter his skull, but he ducked it.

Water poured over him and sprayed his face as he dodged another tentacle while keeping a firm hold on the ax. With a thud, he landed on the monster as the tip of a tentacle streaked across his cheek, welting it almost instantly and causing his head to ring as his vision blurred.

He'd made it past the tentacles, but the monster was much more slippery than he anticipated. Adjusting his hold on the ax, he scrambled to right himself when he started sliding toward the monster-infested water.

Unable to maintain his precarious position on the monster, Del lifted the battle-ax over his head and swung down to embed it in the kraken. The creature bucked and flailed as tentacles whipped through the air and water sluiced off to drench him.

An almost melodic screaming issued from the kraken as the water churned faster, and those silver fish flung up water as they flapped against the surface. Eager to devour him, their chattering unleashed a cacophony of noise.

With the battle-ax firmly embedded in the kraken, Del kept himself from sliding to the side, but even with his legs spread wide, they didn't cover an eighth of the beast. The kraken dove a little deeper, and water poured up to the soles of his boots.

One of the silver fish leapt from the water and bit into his boot, but its teeth didn't pierce the leather. More of them hovered closer, and another leapt out to grasp his arm.

Del gritted his teeth against the pain and grasped the slippery body. He tore the fish and a chunk of his flesh away. It flapped and clacked in his grasp as he threw it back into the water.

But as the kraken sank lower, threatening to turn him into fish food, its melodic screaming increased, and it rose back toward the surface. What Cole did to this beast was more painful than anything he did as the kraken sought to escape Cole.

Once he was sure the kraken wasn't about to take him under, Del ripped the ax free and inched his way through the kraken's slippery blood toward its head. When he was closer to its head, he positioned himself behind the beast's eye.

Another tentacle lashed out of the water and smacked him in

the head. It knocked him to the side and momentarily blinded him.

He couldn't let his suffering deter him; if he did, he and Cole were as good as dead.

Lifting the battle-ax, he dodged another tentacle trying to take off his head and yelled as he brought the ax down. He sank it into the creature's eye as he ducked a tentacle swinging at his back.

It whistled as it lashed over his head; its passing created a wind that pulled at his clothes and hair. He pulled the ax free when the tentacle splashed back into the lake.

As he did so, he slid toward the monster's other eye. Just as he plunged the ax into its second eye, another tentacle smashed into his back.

With a crack that briefly drowned out the chatter of the silver fish and the melodic screams of the kraken, his spine snapped. As Del's fingers and legs went numb, he lost his hold on the ax.

He glimpsed the brilliant blue sky for a second before plunging into the water.

CHAPTER SEVENTY-FOUR

Cole punched rapidly as he continued to bury his claws into the underside of the kraken. He sliced through its flesh, shredding it and spilling blood until it clouded the water between them so much, he barely saw the creature anymore.

Its blood obscured the silver fish darting through the water, but they hadn't bothered Cole... yet. He suspected the wrath of the kraken was keeping them at bay. That wouldn't last.

From out of the opaque water, a tentacle snaked toward him. Before he could stop it, the thing slithered around his chest in a vicelike grip. His bones ground together as it further battered his broken ribs into his punctured lungs.

No air or water remained in his lungs; it was all crushed from him. He didn't think any water remained either as the kraken squeezed it from him.

The teeth inside the suckers sank into his flesh, and with a big pull, the kraken drank his blood, further weakening him. Despite his determination to get to Lexi and *save* her, his strength waned as the monster feasted on him.

The water muted the sound, but he heard the suck of the kraken draining him. And with each of those pulls, its teeth dug deeper into his flesh. But that wasn't the worst of his problems as, with each draw, the monster maneuvered him closer to its mouth.

Through the bloody water, he saw the gaping orifice filled with teeth taller than him and sharper than the honed edge of a sword. *Lexi!*

He could *not* die down here. Not when he was this close to saving her; he had the crudue vine wrapped around his bicep!

More white stars blurred his vision, and visions of his dad and mom flashed through his head as his brain misfired from lack of oxygen and blood. He clung to her name and repeated it to keep himself focused on the reason for this fight.

He *refused* to let this thing win.

Cole turned his attention to hacking off the tentacle embracing him. So far, he'd cut away three of these things, but as soon as one fell, another came out of the darkness to ensnare him. And it was no different this time. As the tentacle fell away, a new one coiled around him.

He'd hoped by punching and slicing into the kraken, it would relinquish its hold on him and consider him not worth the effort. He'd been mistaken.

Then, as the new tentacle fell away and he drifted back into the bloody sea, the creature reeled back. A strange, music-like screaming vibrated through the water as its tentacles lashed around him.

Dredging his last remnants of strength from the depths of his soul, Cole avoided the tentacle that would have broken his back. He gritted his teeth against the agonizing grind of his bones digging into his flesh as he kicked backward.

Though his body instinctively sought breath, his lungs were so brutalized, he couldn't even inhale the water clogging his nose and mouth. The inescapable liquid was everywhere, yet he had to escape it.

As the kraken continued to make that sound while pulling

back, a sliver of sunlight hit the water. His disoriented mind clicked into place when he saw he was closer to the surface than he'd realized.

That slice of sunlight also allowed the shadows to break free again. They screamed for blood and vengeance as some grasped his arms and pulled him toward the surface while others went for the kraken.

Cole kicked harder as some of the shadows sliced into the tentacles. The kraken screamed louder as blood poured from its missing appendages. That blood blocked out the sun once more.

The shadows unraveling from his arms took away his momentum toward the surface, but he refused to give in. He'd glimpsed freedom, was nearly to it, and would *not* be denied it.

Lexi! An image of her, so still and unmoving as she remained frozen in that awful state, formed in his mind. He couldn't let her down.

Every movement sent stabbing pains throughout his body. Everything inside him scraped and dug and grated, but he shoved his discomfort aside as he pushed past his dwindling strength from blood and oxygen loss.

His father's hand floated to him out of the water. A golden glow behind him highlighted his face.

Forgetting what he was here to do, Cole stretched his hand toward his father and sighed when his father's hand gripped his. It wasn't until the teeth bit into his fingers and his blood was sucked from him that his vision cleared and he saw the tentacle encircling him to his wrist.

A scream reverberated through his head, but no sound issued as he sliced the tentacle away. When the kraken's head came down again, Cole kicked back and flattened himself against the wall to avoid it.

Through the blood and the white stars obscuring his blurred and nearly pinpoint vision, he watched the beast sink lower into the lake. Tentacles whipped around its head; it seemed to be trying to protect or wipe at its eyes, but Cole couldn't be certain.

But it was no longer above him, which meant... *freedom!*

He pushed away from the wall and swam toward the surface. While his fingers clawed at the water, he ignored the hands stretching toward him and his mother's laughter ringing in his head as he strained to break free.

The shadows returned to pull him toward the surface when sunlight streamed over him again. As the sun grew brighter through the water, he could almost feel the air on his face and its warmth.

He was nearly there when something tore a chunk of flesh from his calf. The first blast of agony was followed by more as small teeth ripped into him.

Cole refused to look back as more blood flowed into the water. He knew what was feasting on him; he didn't have to see it.

While the silver fish ate, the shadows spread out and laughed as they encompassed the silver creatures, tearing them in two. More shadows grasped his arms and lifted him faster as his dark fae abilities pushed forward to help part the water.

CHAPTER SEVENTY-FIVE

"Help me grab him!" Sahira shouted when her brother's body floated to the surface.

Del wasn't moving, and blood coated the water around him, but he *had* to be alive. She couldn't lose him.

Tears clogged her throat and burned her eyes as she twisted her hands in her shirt while kneeling at the water's edge. When she stretched a hand over the water, some of those silver fish leapt toward her.

She snarled at them but refused to snatch her fingers away as her brother's broken body floated closer. "Del," she whimpered.

Maverick rested a hand on her shoulder before kneeling with Varo beside her. Taller than her, they had longer arm spans as they leaned over the lake and grasped Del's outstretched arms.

Despite his stillness, Del's body jerked as they dragged him closer, and more blood spilled into the water. Those damn fish were *feeding* on him.

But they were the least of her concerns as a dark shadow rose from the depths of the bloody lake. It cut through the water with a speed she never could have imagined. Even before she saw its fin, wide-open mouth, and multiple layers of teeth, she knew it was a shark.

"Hurry!" she gasped as she leaned toward Del.

She still had no idea where Cole was, but they could help her brother. Finally, he was close enough that she could hook her fingers into his shirt, and as the smaller fish continued to feed, they hauled him onto the shore.

The shark leapt out of the water a second later. Its massive jaws clacked shut with a bang that echoed around them before it plummeted beneath the water again.

Blood and water spilled around Del as Maverick set him down. It drenched Sahira's feet as she leaned over her brother.

"Shit," Maverick breathed.

Sahira's hands frantically ran over Del as she gently rolled him over. Two gray, scaly fish with lower jaws jutting out from their upper mouth and teeth the size of her fingers, snapped at her as she tore them off Del.

When they started flopping against the shore, Skog booted them into the lake. "He had a pretty *shitty* plan."

Sahira shot him a look before focusing on her brother again. Grasping his cold, pale cheeks in both hands, she leaned over him as he coughed. His fingers twitched against the ground, but his feet remained unmoving as water spewed from his lips.

That awful, racking cough filled the air as Sahira wiped water from his lips and turned his head to the side so he could spew out more water. He coughed a few more times before going still.

"Del?" Sahira ran her hands over his chest before settling them against his cheeks. "Del, can you hear me?"

Finally, her brother's bright, blue eyes met hers; he coughed again before smiling. In a voice made rough from the coughing and water, he spoke. "I can hear you. You're not exactly quiet, you know?"

Sahira laughed loudly as she bent to kiss his forehead. Only her brother would consider her noisy, but he was the only one who knew there was a time when she was quite loud.

For most of her adult life, she'd been reserved, but by then, she'd learned to accept her fate as an immortal who never truly fit in. Because of her lineage, she was trapped between witches and vampires, two species who despised each other.

When she was a kid, she hadn't realized how much that would leave her in limbo. As an adult, she'd learned how unwelcome she was throughout most realms.

Back then, if the humans had known the truth about immortals like they did now, she wouldn't have been welcome in their realm either. Now, the mortals were so badly beaten that they had no choice but to accept immortals.

But, as a child, before she encountered countless hate and disdain from others, she'd been loud, vivacious, and outgoing with the people she met in the human realm. Her dad and Del used to tease that giants were quieter than her, and she'd laugh… loudly.

Then time wore on, her dad died, and as an adult, she learned she was a rare, shunned, oddity amongst immortals. Not even her mother wanted her.

Now, she laughed while hugging Del against her and winced when he groaned over the jostling of his wounds.

"We'll fix you up soon," she promised.

Skog stepped beside them and planted his hands on his hips. "You lost my ax."

"I'll get you a new one," Del croaked.

"You can*not* simply get a dwarf a new ax. It took years of death and beheadings to hone my weapon into the fine killing machine it was. Are you going to behead thousands of immortals for me?"

"Like it's been thousands," Del muttered.

"Excuse me?" Skog's accent grew thicker as he became more riled up. "I have killed *countless* enemies."

"Yeah, yeah, yeah," Maverick said as he clasped Skog's shoulder. "You're a warrior, and we'll ensure you're rewarded with a fine new weapon since you sacrificed yours for a great cause. You helped destroy the kraken."

Skog rolled his eyes. "I'd like one made from fae metal this time."

"I doubt the fae will allow that, but first, let's save my nephew."

"Cole?" Del asked.

No one answered as their attention shifted to the lake. There was still no sign of him, and though the kraken was gone, other horrors filled the water.

CHAPTER SEVENTY-SIX

"There!" a merfolk shouted and pointed at the lake.

Sahira held her breath as she frantically searched the water. The silver fish continued churning, a shark fin circled near the shore, and she couldn't see the other horrors below.

She also couldn't see Cole. Biting her lip, her fingers bit into Del's shoulder as she tried to keep her crushing disappointment and sadness at bay. If the monsters haunting this water were still all riled up, then he had to be alive... didn't he?

She hoped so, but she had no idea how to help him. Del had taken care of the kraken, but what did they do about these other things?

And then, just when she was about to look at Del and shake her head, Cole broke free of the water. Blood dripped from the hands stretched into the air and ran down his face in dark red rivulets.

Shadows enclosed Cole's wrists while they dragged him forward with impossible speed. His body and legs jerked as they trailed him in the water, but he was *alive*! The shadows wouldn't exist if he was dead.

When Cole was closer to the shore, Maverick and Varo

grasped his hands and yanked him onto land. More of those hideous, silver fish followed him onto the shore.

Their bodies slapped against the ground as they flopped back toward the lake. They splattered with a sickening crunch when Maverick stomped on them before kicking their remains into the water.

Maverick knelt at his nephew's side and clasped his face; from Sahira's position, she saw his chest was so broken it was concave. Water trickled from his lips, but his chest didn't rise and fall with air.

He was too crushed to breathe.

Bile clogged her throat. Cole had survived the water, but at what cost, and could he heal from this extent of injuries?

"He has the vine," the queen said and pointed at Cole's arm.

Unexpected tears burned Sahira's eyes as she spotted the vine wrapped securely around Cole's arm. After everything he'd endured, he managed to keep the vine. His love for her niece robbed Sahira of her words, before she finally found them again.

"We have to get that to Lexi. She can help heal him," Sahira said.

Maverick carefully lifted his nephew as Varo and Skog hefted Del between them. Cole's eyes remained closed and his breathing nonexistent as his head fell against Maverick's chest.

She twisted her hands together while hoping it wasn't too late to save him. Not only was his chest crushed, but dozens of gashes lacerated his body; he had so little blood left that it barely trickled from his injuries.

As the others hurried toward the portal Maverick created, Sahira remembered the merfolk. She had far more important things to worry about now, but they couldn't leave without thanking them.

"Your kindness will be repaid," she vowed to the king and queen.

Mira tilted her head to the side as she studied Sahira. "Who are you to promise such a thing?"

"The queen of the Shadow Realms is my niece; she won't forget that you helped save her life. I promise you that."

"Make sure of it," the king said.

Sahira nodded and followed the others into the portal and onto the human realm. From there, they traveled to Dragonia.

CHAPTER SEVENTY-SEVEN

As soon as they returned to Dragonia, Sahira saw Cole and Del settled into the infirmary before going to work on the potion to save Lexi's life. Maverick and Varo hovered near Cole's side while Skog stood over Del, grumpily describing the kind of ax he expected. Del gave him the finger.

While Sahira worked, the light fae and witches created poultices and potions to help Del heal. Only a few short months ago, she never would have believed a witch would work to help a vampire, but they were doing everything they could for her brother.

Even more astonishing, she trusted them to keep him alive.

She didn't fear they would poison or try to kill him when she wasn't looking. They would save his life; she was certain of it.

And while the fae and witches also worked on Cole, she was certain he was beyond their abilities. She'd sensed it before she saw the sad looks on their faces and the covert glances they exchanged.

He required Lexi's healing ability to get him through the worst of this. She just hoped it wasn't too late and would be enough to save him.

Sahira steadied the tremor in her hand at the possibility and lowered the bottle full of nutmeg, cloves, pixie dust, and a single unicorn hair. When she felt more in control, she poured the bottle into her cauldron.

This had to work.

While she added more ingredients, the young witch, Melisandra, stirred the pot. Her black hair rested in a knot against her nape while she worked.

It took a few hours, but as soon as Sahira finished the potion, she leaned out the window to shout to the dragons. "We have the potion to save the queen! Bring her to me!"

Leaning back from the window, she stretched her back while she wiped sweat-dampened hair from her forehead. She'd give anything for a shower to relax her tense muscles and a bed, but first, she had to save her niece.

She glanced back out the window as the dragons soared past. She wasn't sure if they understood her, but ten minutes later, Alina arrived... without Lexi.

Sahira blinked at the dragon as she lurched toward her. Had Kaylia's spell failed? Had something happened to Lexi while they were gone?

"Where is she?" Sahira blurted.

"I will take you to her, but I won't bring her here while she and the Shadow Reaver are so vulnerable," Alina said.

Sahira didn't ask how Alina knew about Cole's injuries; word got around fast with immortals and probably faster amid dragons. She bit her inner cheek while she pondered Alina's words, but what choice did she have? Lexi needed her, Del was in good hands, and Cole....

"We have to bring Cole with us too. Lexi will recover from the poison once she drinks the antidote, and he needs her healing ability."

Alina bowed her head in agreement. "Bring him to me."

Maverick and Varo didn't look happy about this new arrangement, and the witches and light fae muttered disapprovingly about moving him, but Cole required more than they could do for him. Reluctantly, Maverick lifted Cole, and Varo rested a hand on his brother's leg as Maverick carried him to the window.

Alina extended her talons and carefully plucked Cole from Maverick's arms. She curled him protectively against her chest.

A low, barely decipherable moan issued from Cole at the movement, but he still wasn't getting enough air for anything more than that small sound. She'd never expected to see Cole so frail, and as she glanced around, she realized it was best to get him away from here.

The dragons couldn't hurt the Shadow Reaver, but she couldn't say that for all the others here. They would keep Del alive, but Cole represented a threat to *everyone*. He was prophesized to destroy the realms; some might decide to eradicate him first.

And what better time than now?

"The potion?" Alina asked.

Sahira lifted the small bottle and gave it a little shake before tucking it securely into the inner pocket of her shirt. She buttoned it closed afterward. As a witch, she often had little hiding spots for any required things.

"I'll bring it with me," she said.

Glancing around the room, she contemplated bringing more healing potions and poultices for Cole. She didn't know how she'd carry them all and couldn't waste time gathering them. The best thing for Cole now was Lexi.

She ran over to tell Del what was happening and kissed his cheek before returning to the window. Sahira rested her hand against the stone sill and climbed onto it. The wind tickled her face, and she resisted her impulse to look down. *Nothing* good would come of *that*.

Without looking down, Sahira scrambled onto the dragon's neck and edged lower until she was secure against her nape and could grasp the lethal spikes. Poking her head out, she looked at Maverick and Varo in the window.

"Watch over Del for me," she said.

"We will," Maverick promised.

"Of course," Varo said.

Sahira clung to Alina as the dragon pulled away from the window and turned to fly over the land. At first, Sahira kept her eyes closed against the wind battering her face and the distance she sensed between her and the ground. Eventually, curiosity won out, and she pried them open.

She'd never been a big fan of heights, but the clouds drifting past astonished her, and the earth below was a beautiful, vibrant green with splashes of reds, oranges, and yellows from the turning leaves. As they traveled, Sahira smiled while she took in the beauty around her.

The dragon was powerful and confident as her wings cut through the air, and Sahira found a new appreciation for heights as she drank in the world below.

CHAPTER SEVENTY-EIGHT

It wasn't long before Alina touched down. She kept Cole securely tucked against her chest, and her head lowered as she crept into the cave on three of her legs.

Sahira flattened against the dragon's back as the walls closed in and the rocks above nearly scraped her. Moist and dark, the cave smelled of minerals and fire. Though, she realized the fiery scent was Alina as she inhaled the dragon's aroma.

Like riding a horse, each of the dragon's steps had her shifting from one side to the other as they traveled deeper into the cave. Finally, they arrived at an area that opened into a large, circular space.

When Sahira sat up, her eyes immediately fell on Lexi, settled securely on the nest in the middle of the cavern. Alina's three wyrmlings snuggled against her side. Two of them lifted their heads and yawned, but the little orange one remained sleeping.

Sahira was so focused on Lexi, she didn't notice the two dragon heads emerging from the shadows until their warm breaths billowed over her. The rest of the dragons' bodies remained cloaked in darkness.

Gulping, Sahira tried not to let her distress over the seemingly free-floating heads show. The dragons wouldn't hurt her if she didn't hurt Lexi.

Alina set Cole down near Lexi. "What happened to the Reaver?"

Sahira scrambled off Alina's back and hurried toward the couple. "Love."

"It does get us all."

The orange dragon woke when Sahira knelt at Lexi's side. A tiny puff of smoke spiraled from its nose as it sniffed Sahira.

Alina nudged her children away with her snout. "Shoo."

Disgruntled noises issued from them, but they leapt out of the nest and scrambled to settle around their mom's legs as Alina sat to watch Sahira. Sahira caressed Lexi's cheeks and tried not to wince over how cold she felt.

The spell made her heart stonelike, and it did the same to all of her. The color had leached from her face, making her paler than paper. Her lips remained slightly parted, but no breath issued from her.

It was such a disconcerting thing to see from someone she loved so much. She ignored the twinge in her heart as she reached into her shirt, undid the button, and removed the potion.

This has to work.

Sahira took a steadying breath as she removed the stopper from the bottle. She'd never made a potion with crudue vine before—few had *ever* worked with the rare vine—but she was confident she'd made the antidote right… or at least, as sure as she could be.

The spell came from the Book of Shadows her mother gave her; she'd *never* had a problem with a spell in it before. Her mother didn't want anything to do with her, but she'd left behind a powerful book.

It was the *only* thing her mother gave her besides life. For years, Sahira believed the book was a sign of her mother's love, but it wasn't.

After she left the foolishness of her childhood behind and met her mother, she realized the woman left the book for other reasons. Sahira didn't know those reasons and doubted her mother would ever reveal them, but it *wasn't* love.

It never had been. And she learned that lesson the hard way when she foolishly searched for her mother, only to be met with a woman who wanted nothing to do with her.

Even after all these years and all the distance from that awful encounter, the memory caused a pang in Sahira's heart. *It doesn't matter if that woman loves you or not; you have plenty of others who do.*

And she *had* to save one of them.

With tender care, she started prying Lexi's mouth open further. It took more time than she anticipated, but she finally got it open enough to pour some potion in.

When there was enough inside, she clamped Lexi's lips shut and removed her hand. Lexi didn't move, and none of the potion spilled out.

And now came the tricky part. Kaylia had cast the spell that saved Lexi's life, but she could break it.

Sahira had heard Kaylia's words for the spell, and that was all she needed to break Lexi's heart of stone. But she had to make sure Lexi swallowed the potion as soon as she woke, or the noxus's poison would kill her before she could counteract it.

Waving her hands over Lexi's body, Sahira repeated Kaylia's spell. "Heart of stone, heart of stone, I weave thee a heart of stone."

When Sahira finished repeating the spell, she took a deep breath before uttering the words to wake her niece... and possibly kill her.

CHAPTER SEVENTY-NINE

"Heart of stone, heart of stone, I break your heart of stone."

Sahira clamped her hand over Lexi's mouth and nose while she used her other hand to shove her chin up. Lexi's fingers dug into the nest and tore away pieces.

Her feet kicked as her body twitched from the poison. Behind her closed lids, her eyes rolled as her back arched off the nest.

"Swallow!" Sahira shouted at her. "You must swallow the potion, Lexi!"

She hadn't needed to yell at her as Lexi had no other option but to drink the antidote if she was going to breathe. When Sahira saw her niece's mouth and throat work, she released her hold on Lexi.

She pried her mouth open again as Lexi continued to seize and her heels kicked against the sticks that created the nest. Once she had Lexi's mouth open enough to get more potion in there, Sahira poured it inside.

When some of the precious drink spilled out of the corners of Lexi's mouth, Sahira shut it again. Despite the small trickle, more liquid went down her throat when Lexi swallowed.

Her fingers tore out chunks of feathers and cloth from the nest as her head thrashed. The dragons edged closer as Sahira cradled Lexi's head while her body flopped.

Bending over her niece, tears streamed down Sahira's face as she whispered, "Please come back to us."

Lexi flopped a few more times before her back bowed off the ground until only her head and feet touched the nest. Time stood still for Sahira as her heart stopped, and ice seeped through her veins until it permeated *every* part of her.

Then Lexi hit the ground with a thud before going completely still. Sahira watched for any sign of life as Alina's warm breath billowed over her.

Please, Hecate, please let her live.

So many lives rested on Lexi's shoulders, and now, Sahira's. If she messed this up, countless humans and immortals would die when the realms inevitably fell into chaos at the hands of another monster whose mind would rot on that throne.

Not only that, but she would have killed her niece. A woman she'd helped raise since birth and someone she loved deeply. A fracturing started in her iced heart as tears spilled onto Lexi's cool cheeks.

"Lexi," she breathed, the word little more than a croak. "Please."

She'd never be able to live with herself if she failed and killed one of the two immortals she loved most. She'd never be able to look at her brother, Cole, or anyone else again.

And that was *if* Cole survived. Without Lexi's healing ability, there was a good chance he'd die too. Which meant her failure could condemn two immortals to death. And if Cole lived, but Lexi didn't, she could be condemning countless others to death.

She should have waited for Kaylia to give Lexi the potion, but she had no idea when the crone would return or *if* she would. Doomed Valley wasn't a place many escaped. And if she'd waited, they might have had to watch while Cole worsened and died.

She had no other choice.

A sob rose and lodged in her chest as she stroked Lexi's cheeks and wiped her tears away. When she leaned over to kiss Lexi's forehead, her niece's eyes flew open. Lexi sat up so fast, her head nearly smashed off Sahira's, but she jerked back in time to avoid the collision.

For a second, Lexi sat in the cave, her hands planted behind her as her eyes darted around the walls, and the baby red dragon leapt into her lap. Too stunned by the abrupt change in events, Sahira could only sit and gawk.

And then, with a relieved cry, Sahira threw her arms around Lexi and crushed her niece against her chest. "Oh, thank Hecate."

Lexi trembled as her hand gripped Sahira's arm. "What happened?"

"Something horrible, but you're okay." Sahira brushed the hair back from Lexi's face as she leaned back to take in her niece. She remained pale, and her eyes were haunted and shadowed, but she would survive. "I'll fill you in while you work."

"Work?" Lexi croaked.

Sahira reluctantly released Lexi, but she blocked her niece's view of Cole and had to move away. She turned to reveal where Cole lay near them in the nest.

When Lexi gasped, the dragon hopped out of her lap, and she scrambled over to her fiancé as the other dragons crept closer. Tears spilled down Lexi's cheeks as her fingers hovered over Cole's face, broken chest, and battered body.

Though he'd been cleaned and some poultices applied, she could see the chunks missing from his legs through the paste. Blood had stopped seeping from the wounds, but it had given some of the poultices a pink hue.

The light fae and witches had done their best in the short

time he was with them, but many of his injuries remained raw and visible. And there was no hiding the damage done to his chest. What little breath he took was barely visible, and he sometimes made a little rattle that sounded like death.

"What happened?" Lexi cried.

"I'll talk while you heal," Sahira said. "I didn't bring any other potions or healing things with me; I'll gather them in a little bit, but right now, you're his best hope."

You might be his only hope, but Sahira kept that to herself. Lexi had gone through enough without having that possibility dumped on her.

Lexi placed her shaking hands against Cole's broken frame and leaned over to kiss his forehead. Sahira said another silent prayer to Hecate as she told her niece about what happened.

CHAPTER EIGHTY

Over the next week, Cole remained in Alina's cave while Lexi traveled back and forth to Dragonia on the dragon. It took him far more time to heal than she would have liked, even with her ability and the numerous potions and poultices Sahira brought to the cave after she woke.

He'd been so badly battered and broken that, for the first few days, Lexi was sure he'd die. Now, she expected him to survive, but his battle in the lake came at a steep cost. He would never be the same again.

None of them would. They were all different from the immortals they were six months ago. They could never return to who they were before all this started, and she could never regain the innocence of her life before the Lord's war began. She didn't want to either.

Things were different; *she* was different, but also right where she was meant to be and surrounded by love. There was no greater gift in the world.

While Cole healed, she insisted he remain in Alina's cave, no matter how much he and the dragon didn't like it. He was getting stronger every day, but too many immortals had more reason to kill *him* than her.

Without him, they would consider her more vulnerable and easier to take out. She would prove them wrong, but she'd had enough fighting and couldn't picture her life without Cole. No matter what it took, she would protect him.

Their wedding date had come and gone, but it didn't matter; they couldn't get married without Brokk, Kaylia, and Orin present. And, so far, *none* of them had returned.

She'd sent a group into Doomed Valley, but most of them quickly returned with stories of beasts and no sign of Kaylia and Brokk. Two of those she sent didn't survive the adventure, which didn't bode well for those who went out to save her.

After losing those two, she decided against sending anyone else. She couldn't risk the lives of any more immortals when Kaylia and Brokk might already be dead.

She'd also sent out dozens of guards to search for Orin. So far, they all remained alive, but who knew if that would last.

There was a reason Orin hadn't returned yet. And if those guards stumbled across that reason, they could either wind up dead or in trouble.

She'd put out word for him to return and offered a reward for any valid information leading to his whereabouts, but nothing had come of it so far. It was as if he'd vanished.

And while she wouldn't put it past Orin to become distracted in his search for the crudue vine, he wouldn't have stayed away from his brothers for this long without at least checking in on them. Plus, no one had reported seeing him for almost two weeks.

Lexi had no idea what he'd gotten into, but it wasn't good. She was sure of that. She hoped he was still alive... even if she wanted to kill him most of the time.

No matter how much he irritated her, she wouldn't get married without him. And neither would Cole.

Lexi ignored the sadness trying to take over when she contemplated the possibility her friends, immortals she'd come to consider her family, had died because of *her*.

No, not me… Amaris.

Her blood still boiled when she recalled the betrayal and deception of her friend. During those first few days in the cave, huddled by Cole's side, she constantly replayed every interaction she ever had with the helot while she worked to save him.

All the things they'd said and done ran through her mind as she tried to figure out how she could have missed this. But no matter how often she replayed it, she never sensed any animosity or deception from the woman.

But she now understood Amaris's kindness to her when the other dark fae were distant and cold; it was a way to get closer to Lexi and learn more. The woman was so excited when she learned of her and Cole's engagement and excited to make Lexi's dress, but that was so she could tell the Lord and attack Lexi when she least expected it.

All of Amaris's actions had come across as kind and sincere. She'd seemed like a good friend, someone Lexi could trust and someone she had come to care about.

And it was *all* a lie.

The whole time Amaris was running back to the Lord, feeding him all their actions, and monitoring them. The *entire* time, she was helping to plot their demise.

And when the Lord fell, she took matters into her own hands.

Lexi rubbed her nape as she recalled the scrape of the scorpion's tiny feet against her flesh before the creature struck. She shuddered at the memory as the betrayal burned like acid in her gut and throat.

The whole time, Cole believed it was Becca, and while that woman also had her dark moments, and Lexi would never mourn her death, she had been loyal to Cole… for the most part. She was devoted to the Cole she *wanted* him to be, not the one who existed.

She'd paid for that with her life.

And Lexi was terrified Amaris's betrayal had cost some of those she loved their lives.

CHAPTER EIGHTY-ONE

On the seventh day after her return from the nearly dead, when Alina flew her back to the cave, Lexi wasn't surprised to discover Cole standing outside it. She was annoyed and concerned, but she'd known this day was coming. He was too stubborn to listen to reason.

Trying to act as if the wall wasn't helping to support him, he leaned casually against it while he kept his arms folded over his chest. He'd been increasingly frustrated with her insistence to remain hidden while she traveled back and forth to the palace.

She'd been able to keep him at bay, mainly because he could barely stand, let alone walk or fight. That had changed, and no matter how much she didn't like it, there wouldn't be any stopping him now. The set of his jaw made that abundantly clear as she slid from Alina's back.

The shadows slithered around her as some drifted across his face and through his eyes. Now that she knew she could help control them, they didn't unnerve her as much as they once did, but she still didn't like seeing them like this. It meant his control was wavering.

She hadn't taken the shadows from him since Amaris

ambushed her. They made him stronger and offered an extra layer of protection while he was barely coherent, but it was time for her to do so again. If she didn't do it soon, they would start driving him mad again.

"You shouldn't be up yet," she said while she rubbed Alina's snout.

"It's time, and I feel great," he replied.

"Liar."

He smiled as he stepped away from the wall. Without missing a step, he strode toward her with the grace he'd always possessed and the confidence that came from who he was.

If Lexi hadn't known him as well as she did, she *might* have believed he wasn't still hurting, but she saw the slight difference in his gait as he leaned a little more to the left. His right leg had taken the brunt of the attack from the horrible fish Sahira told her about.

Lexi had done her best to heal him completely, but she couldn't regrow missing things. Though the chunks taken out of his legs had mostly healed, the scars and some indents in his flesh remained. They probably always would.

Those scars would serve as an everyday reminder of how much he loved her and everything he was willing to endure for her, but she hadn't needed them to know that. She simply needed him.

She was grateful and happy he was still here when he'd been so close to death. What he'd done to save her only made her love him more, something she hadn't believed possible. But then, she grew to love him more every day.

"Excuse me, my children are hungry," Alina said when Cole stopped before Lexi.

Lexi supposed that was true, but Alina couldn't have missed the hunger in Cole's gaze as it roamed over Lexi. The dragon wasn't in the cave before his arms wrapped around her waist and he pulled her closer.

"I've missed you," he murmured.

"I've been with you all week."

"You know what I mean."

That she did, as the evidence of his arousal prodded her belly. She planted her hands on his once-again-solid chest. It was a relief not to feel his bones grinding beneath her palms like she did those first two days.

"You should be resting," she chided.

"I've rested enough. Now, I should be returning to the realms, but first, sex will help revitalize and strengthen me further."

She couldn't argue with that. As part dark fae, it was true, and his wolf was probably seeking to connect with its mate, but... "I'm not sure you're up for it."

He took her hand and held it against his erection. "I'm more than *up* for it."

Lexi started to protest, but his kiss cut her off. She'd expected his kiss to be demanding, but it was so gentle it nearly brought tears to her eyes.

He maneuvered her behind some boulders near the rocky mountains surrounding them as he stripped away her clothes. His fingers grazing her flesh sent shivers through her as her shield crumbled and her glow lit up the day while the shadows entered her.

Power swelled between them, and by the time she was naked and hidden in a rocky alcove, she was wet and trembling with need. It had been *far* too long since they'd experienced this, and she craved more.

He wasn't the only one who was ravenous; she hadn't fed from him in a couple of weeks, and hunger thrummed through her veins as his pulse beat against her lips. His skin was salty and warm against her mouth; it was familiar and loved as her nails grazed his back.

When he lifted her off the ground, she encircled her legs

around his waist and took his cock into her. She gasped at the familiar sensation of him stretching and filling her as rightness stole through every inch of her body.

Nothing felt as right as when she and Cole joined. It was beautiful and poignant and made each of them stronger.

She took more shadows from him while he feasted on the energy their sex created. And when the shadows lessened, she broke the kiss, sank her fangs into his throat, and came while his blood filled her.

CHAPTER EIGHTY-TWO

After another week passed, she and Cole started talking about their wedding again. They wouldn't get married until their loved ones returned, or they had answers, but they decided to prepare for that day... whenever it came.

Her time in Alina's cave, and the memory of what Amaris did to her while wearing it, had ruined her dress. However, the witches and light fae had gotten together to weave a beautiful creation; Lexi cried when she saw it.

The ivory-colored dress had a sweetheart neckline and bell sleeves that almost fell to the ground. The bodice hugged her upper body and narrow waist before spilling down to become a simple skirt flowing around her when she walked. The small train trailed a couple of feet behind her, and silver embellishments of flowers lined the edges of the sleeves and decorated the skirt.

More silver strands ran throughout the bodice in such a detailed, intricate way that they gave the impression of vines weaving throughout the material. It was such a beautiful yet earthy dress that all blended beautifully together.

It was so much more elegant and fancier than her first dress, something she'd sworn she didn't want, but she loved *everything* about it. And she'd be much more excited about wearing it if they had some answers about their missing loved ones.

The Lord broke much of the arach's things when he took over the palace, but he hadn't destroyed their jewels. Why would he when they were worth so much?

It pissed her off that he'd been so careful about preserving the things worth money in this place but so careless with the lives of many immortals and humans. The throne really had rotted his brain.

Amongst those jewels, she and Sahira had found a beautiful silver headpiece. On her wedding day, it would lay flat against her head before winding back into two long trails down her back.

The top of the headpiece was two dragons facing each other. Their mouths were open, and the rubies coming from them looked like a small plume of fire.

Emeralds made up the dragon's eyes, and their tails entwined to create the flowing trails that would weave throughout her hair. She planned to wear her hair in an intricate twist Sahira had perfected. She had no idea when she'd be able to wear it, but one day, she would.

Once he was strong enough, Cole sent shadows into Doomed Valley, but like the guards she sent, they reported nothing about the missing group.

That could mean the shadows hadn't gone into the region where Brokk, Kaylia, and the others were now, or they'd all left the Valley and were searching somewhere else for the crudue vine. She doubted they would have done that without coming back to check in with all of them first.

It could also mean they were dead.

But the shadows hadn't reported bodies either, so that gave them all hope. And she needed that hope. They *all* did.

Without it, there was only more loss and sadness, and they'd had enough of that.

She didn't kid herself into thinking it would be all sunshine and roses from here on out, but things would get better; she and Cole would make sure of it. They would give everyone in all the realms a better life.

But she wanted her loved ones here for it. And she would do everything she could to ensure that happened or to bring their bodies home to be mourned as they should be.

The shadows hadn't just gone into Doomed Valley; they were also in some other outer realms. But since she and Cole were keeping them under control and there were fewer inside him, they weren't as strong as they used to be and couldn't reach as far.

Plus, there were countless outer realms to explore; the shadows could never search them all. It was slow and steady, but hopefully, there would be some answers soon. The not knowing was tearing her up inside.

Despite the uncertainty gnawing at her belly, life had to go on, and neither of them could go in search of the others, though she'd like to go with some dragons into Doomed Valley. She couldn't leave Dragonia after everything that happened and everything *still* happening.

The other immortals would see it as a weakness and try to strike if she and Cole weren't here to defend it. *But no one came for the realm when I was nearly dead.*

Still, she knew that leaving the realm unprotected, other than the dragons and her growing army, was the wrong move to make for any length of time. However, she hated waiting for her friends and family to return when they put their lives on the line for *her*.

But far more lives, in *all* the realms, depended on her. So instead of going into Doomed Valley, she asked some dragons to go, and three did.

There'd been no sign of them since, though Alina didn't believe they were dead and neither did Lexi. She thought she'd feel a severing in the connection that developed when she took the throne.

She suspected it was only a matter of time before Cole went after his brothers, but for now, he focused on helping her maintain control of the realms and rebuilding the Gloaming. Like her, he felt trapped by the weight of responsibility and all the lives resting on his shoulders.

She went with him in the morning, and in the afternoon, while she went through a new series of dress fittings in Dragonia, Cole remained to help the dark fae rebuild the Gloaming. They were making great progress because, while Cole was away trying to find the crudue vine and recovering, Elvin continued the building.

Many of the dark fae had returned to the Gloaming, they'd cleared more ruined land for the spring crops, and their attention had shifted to building outside the palace walls. The Gloaming was coming back to life.

Yesterday when Lexi journeyed back to the Gloaming with Cole, they returned to the palace again. Every time she entered the large, mysterious palace, it felt like the building was enfolding her in a warm embrace.

Even with the palace's amazing hospitality, much to her disappointment, the locked rooms remained that way. She pondered if the palace would one day reveal them to her, but she doubted it. The palace loved being an enigma; it was part of its personality.

Standing inside the palace's grand ballroom, with the rest of the dark fae surrounding them, Lexi had watched Cole ascend the dais to his throne. Once settled on his seat, Elvin placed the king's crown on his head.

Cole's hands gripped the ends of the arms as he stared at the cheering dark fae surrounding him. They'd already crowned him king, but this was a renewal of his position in this realm.

When he beckoned her forward, Lexi smiled before climbing

the stairs and settling onto the throne beside his. He smiled at her and claimed her hand.

Once they were married, she would officially become his queen, and he would become her king of the Shadow Realms. But the crowd loved this show of their unity. They clapped and cheered so loudly it reverberated off the walls and echoed all around them.

Lexi's hand tightened around Cole's as she realized they were doing it. They were bringing all the realms together and bringing peace to the lands. It was more than she'd ever dared to hope for when this journey started.

When she first arrived in the Gloaming, she never expected the dark fae to welcome her here, but they embraced her now... and many of them had done so before they knew of her arach heritage.

Today, Lexi smiled over the memory but was drawn back to the present as the lycans standing outside the doors in the hall opened them before she and Sahira arrived. Lexi thanked them before descending the steps into the expansive throne room.

Some dragons, Cole, Maverick, Varo, and her dad, already waited for her and Sahira near the dais. They were meeting with the merfolk soon; she and Cole owed them, the king intended to collect, and they would repay the debt if they could.

Before then, they'd agreed to gather to talk about their next steps in finding Orin, Brokk, and Kaylia. She was beginning to fear they were out of ideas.

CHAPTER EIGHTY-THREE

When they made it to the others, she stopped beside Cole, and he slid his arm around her waist before kissing her temple. They finally had everything they'd fought for, but it wasn't complete. While his brothers remained missing, he couldn't settle into his new life.

For the first time in his life, he was finally content with who he was. The lycan and dark fae parts of himself no longer clashed against each other but worked in unison as they strove to keep the realms and Lexi safe.

And the shadows, as long as he didn't take too many into himself, didn't try to overwhelm him. While in the lake, the three pieces of himself worked together to keep him alive and connected in a way they never had before.

That connection remained, but he couldn't know peace without his brothers. He wanted to open a portal and dive into Doomed Valley, but he'd just gotten Lexi back, and he didn't dare leave her without a lot of shadows to watch over her.

For that to happen, he would have to draw more of them into himself again, which could push him to the brink of madness once more. He couldn't take that risk while in the Valley and away from Lexi.

He also couldn't start jumping through all the outer realms. He could travel through some of them daily but couldn't spend weeks or months searching through them. There were far too many of them for that to do any good.

Their best bet was to raise the reward for info on Orin and have more immortals hunt for him. That was more likely to turn up answers than his realm hopping would.

So, while he wanted to rush out in search of his brothers, he couldn't. The not knowing was tearing him apart inside, and his inability to do anything about it was maddening. He *hated* it.

He'd finally found peace with himself, but there was no peace in his heart, and there wouldn't be until he had answers.

"There's still no word, and the shadows haven't found anything," he reported.

Lexi's head bowed. "What do we do now?"

"Keep the shadows and dragons searching Doomed Valley." With a sigh, Sahira added, "And I'll find Orin. I still have the tracking spell on him."

She'd offered to do this before, but Cole and Lexi both voted against it. They were running out of options, but Cole didn't like it.

"No," Lexi said. "If he's gotten into trouble, or is dead somewhere, you could be walking into a trap. We can't lose you too."

Sahira waved her hand dismissively, but Cole didn't miss the flicker of unease in her eyes. However, he didn't know if that unease was from Lexi's words or because she would have to deal with Orin.

"It will be fine. I'll go quickly and leave the portal to him open. If there's any hint of trouble, I'll come back immediately."

"Sahira—" he started.

"We have to find at least *one* of them. This absolute *nothing* we've been living with is exhausting. Something has to change;

we can't keep living in this limbo, and I *can* find Orin, which means we'll at least have answers about one of them."

"I'll come with you," Del offered.

"So will I," Varo said.

"No, all of you should stay here. I won't be gone long. Besides, we must show a strong, united front against the merfolk. I don't believe they mean any harm, but a strong display of unity is necessary to show to *all* immortals. Word of that will spread through the realms."

"You're part of that strong, united front," Lexi said.

Sahira took her hands and squeezed them. "And if I can get Orin back here before the merfolk arrive, it will be a stronger front."

"How much time do you think it will take?" Maverick asked.

"Not long at all."

"Where do you plan to open the portal to go to him?" Del asked.

"I'll travel to the human realm and, from there, open a portal directly to him," Sahira said.

"We'll send guards with you too," Cole said.

Sahira pondered this before relenting. "Okay."

CHAPTER EIGHTY-FOUR

"I'll be back soon," Sahira said to the lycan guards. "Stay here. If there are any signs of trouble, you can follow me, but for now, I'll go alone."

She wouldn't have anyone else getting hurt or in trouble if they didn't have to. Lexi and Cole would disagree with her, but they didn't order the lycans to follow her every move. They just requested for them to accompany her.

It was a fine line; for a second, she thought they might argue with her, but the lycans bowed their heads in agreement. They stepped to either side as she turned away from the portal that led them into the mortal realm.

She'd prefer to never deal with the annoying dark fae again, but she couldn't leave Orin's absence hanging over Lexi, Cole, and Varo. It was draining them all.

Knowing Orin, he'd gotten sidetracked by a piece of ass and completely forgotten what he was supposed to be doing.

That's not fair of you.

And it wasn't. No matter how much she disliked Cole's brother, she had to admit he loved his family... in his twisted way.

Taking a deep breath, she drew on the tracking spell she'd cast over him while she pictured Orin. Normally, an immortal couldn't open a portal to another immortal; they could only do it to other realms, but the tracking spell allowed her to find him anywhere.

When she got a bead on him, she smiled and looked at the lycans. "I've got him."

One of them bowed their head in acknowledgment; the other remained stone-faced. Closing her eyes, Sahira continued picturing Orin as she waved a hand in front of her to open a portal to him.

When it fully formed, she entered it. Despite what might lie ahead, she strode confidently through as she erected a shield around herself.

If something tried to attack her, they wouldn't get close enough to kill her before she fled back into the portal. She'd only take one quick look to ensure all was safe and either go back for the lycans, for an army, or drag Orin out of wherever he was by his ear.

She was almost to the end of the portal when giggles drifted to her through the darkness. Sahira frowned as the girlish laughter swirled around her.

She hadn't expected that he'd been distracted from his mission by sex, but the laughter…? What was going on?

At first, it wasn't Orin's laughter, but then a deeper, more masculine chuckle reached her. That had to be him, but something was off here.

Orin was a selfish asshole, but he loved his family. So why, if everything was fine and he was *laughing,* hadn't he returned?

She almost turned around and went back. She didn't want to walk in on him in bed with some woman, but her growing anger propelled her forward. After everything Cole and Lexi had been through, after they almost *died*, all their worry for *him*, and

Brokk and Kaylia's absence, Orin deserved to have his fun ruined.

Ready to kick his ass, Sahira stepped out of the portal and into a room with a large, opulent, king-sized bed. White sheets were tangled on the mattress, and sheer red gauze draped over the top of the posts.

In the middle of the bed lay Orin and three women. One woman straddled his face, another had her head between his legs, and the third rode his hand.

For a second, Sahira could only gawk at the hedonistic display. She knew the dark fae were insatiable, but this was... was....

She couldn't think of the right word for it, and it didn't help that though she was disgusted, she couldn't tear her eyes away. She'd never seen anything like it. There were *three* women, but he must be satisfying them as two cried out in wild abandon.

Sahira blinked at the scene before reality returned, and she tore her eyes away. It took her a few seconds to form words as she tried to scrub her mind of everything she'd witnessed and what she was still *listening* to.

She didn't think that would ever be possible. This scene would haunt her until she died.

"What are you *doing*?"

She instantly regretted the question. The answer was obvious.

The sounds of ecstasy stopped as gasps filled the room, but Orin's low chuckle caused her to glance at him from the corner of her eye. She looked away again.

A hand slapped lightly against skin, and Sahira pictured him patting one of the women's asses as he said, "Excuse me, ladies; I have some business to deal with."

"Who is she?" one of them demanded.

"An old friend."

"Hardly," Sahira retorted.

Orin chuckled. "As you can see, she's testy. So, please excuse us, ladies; this shouldn't take long."

They moaned in protest, but the mattress crinkled as the women climbed off the bed. "Don't finish without me," he instructed.

"We can't make any promises," one of them pouted.

"Then you'll be punished."

The women giggled, and Sahira rolled her eyes, but she couldn't deny a part of her was... intrigued? What kind of punishment?

She tamped down any curiosity as fury and revulsion warred to the forefront. Lexi was on her deathbed the last time Orin saw her, yet here he was, acting like a disgusting pig.

That's because he is *a disgusting pig!* She'd never doubted that, but she hadn't realized she could think any less of Orin before coming here; she'd been wrong.

She wanted out of this room and away from this revolting man and these fawning idiots. And she hoped she never saw Orin again after this. He'd always been selfish, but this was a whole new level.

The man was infuriating! Sahira's hands fisted as she imagined punching the arrogant smirk off his face. She couldn't see him, but she knew it was still there.

The naked women giggled as they scurried past Sahira and out the door. Once the door closed behind them, Sahira chanced a glance at Orin.

He sat upright in bed, his hands behind his head and the sheet draped casually across his waist. The sheet obscured his dick but didn't conceal the tent his erection created.

His pointed ears poked out through his disheveled black hair, and his black eyes glistened with amusement as they surveyed her. The ciphers across his upper chest and arms were on full display, and they shifted when the muscles in his arms flexed before relaxing again.

"Helloooo, little witchy witch," Orin purred. "I was wondering when you would come looking for me. You missed me a lot sooner than I expected. That warms the cockles of my heart."

CHAPTER EIGHTY-FIVE

His casual, amused attitude only ratcheted up her ire. "You don't have a heart!"

He chuckled again as his eyes gleamed with amusement. "Ouch, little witch, you wound me."

The look on his face stated she'd done the exact opposite. "*What* are you doing?"

"Judging by your uptight nature, I can tell it's been a long time since you last had it, but you *do* know what sex is, don't you?"

Sahira planted her hands on her hips. "That's not what I mean."

"Then pray, enlighten me; what do you mean?"

"You're here screwing around while your brother nearly died! I always knew you were a complete asshole, but this... this..." She sputtered as she tried to form words. "This is a whole new low, even for *you*!"

Orin's casual demeanor vanished, his hands dropped, and he sat straighter on the bed. Sahira looked away when his movement caused the sheet to shift enough to reveal the glistening head of his cock.

"Don't be such a prude, little witchy witch. And which brother?" Orin asked.

His chiding tone set her teeth on edge. "Cole."

"Is he okay?"

"Yes, no thanks to you."

"And Lexi?"

"Awake and ruling the realms again." She glared at him as she ignored the fact he hadn't bothered to cover himself. "Cole saved her but nearly died in the process. It was *horrible*! Thankfully, Lexi was able to save him, but they could have used *your* help."

With a casual wave of his hand, he dismissed her words. "It's good they have each other. What of Brokk and Varo?"

Sahira rolled her eyes. She'd known him for far longer than she would have liked, but she still couldn't believe how *small* his conscience was and how easily he could dismiss his brother's near death.

"Varo is fine. No one knows where Brokk or Kaylia are. They haven't returned, and there's been no sign of them; it would be nice if you returned to help us search for them."

Orin smiled as he settled against the headboard and propped his arms behind his head once more. "Well, you see, little witchy witch, that's where the problem lies. I'd be happy to return, I've been trying to do so for weeks, but I'm stuck here."

Sahira glanced around the large, well-appointed room. "What do you mean you're *stuck* here?"

His casual demeanor vanished, and his eyes glinted with a barely simmering fury that unnerved her more than walking into his orgy did.

"Welcome to the Cursed Realm, Sahira. Once you come here, there's no turning back."

Sahira shook her head in denial. "That's not true. You're making it up so you can use it as an excuse to fuck around while everyone else worried, suffered, and nearly died."

His smirk returned. "You know me so well, but you're wrong on this. I asked you to take the tracking spell off me, and you refused. Now, you'll pay the consequences of that as, like me, you're stuck here too."

"I have a portal—"

Before she could finish speaking, Orin interrupted her. "Do you?"

Sahira spun to find the portal she'd created was gone. She gaped at the wallpapered wall with its wood-paneled wainscotting.

Her portal should be *right there*. "What happened to it?"

She waved a hand while envisioning the area of the human realm she had left behind. A new portal should open, but nothing happened.

Then she pictured the crone realm as her hand waved and... nothing. She moved on to *any* other realm she could think of, but still, no portal materialized.

"You're wasting your energy and time; believe me, I get why you're doing it, but I'm telling you, it's pointless," Orin said. "I did the same thing when I learned I couldn't leave, even after the others trapped here told me it was useless.

"I've learned it's pointless since then, but, I will admit, I still try it every day. We're trapped here, Sahira. There is no escaping the Cursed Realm."

Sahira's blood ran cold as she spun back to Orin. "You could have stopped this!"

He quirked an eyebrow at her. "How?"

"You could have found some way to warn me or anyone else against coming here! You could have run into my portal if you weren't so busy getting your rocks off!"

His harsh bark of laughter sent ice through her blood as that steely glint returned to his eyes. "There is nothing *I* could have done, but there is something *you* could have done... if you'd broken your tracking spell, you wouldn't be here. You doomed yourself, witch.

"As for running into your portal, it's been tried. No one here can enter a portal created by another. Now, like the rest of us, you're trapped here. So, sit back, relax, and enjoy your stay. I suppose it's not too bad, once you get used to being unable to leave."

A thousand questions pummeled her, but she didn't utter them. She tried to reject his words and that this was partially *her* fault, but she couldn't.

She *could* have taken the spell from him. Sahira told him she would wait for Cole's approval before doing so because she enjoyed irritating him by keeping it in place.

And now, she was paying dearly for it.

But they couldn't be *stuck* here.

She tried to deny it, but the truth was slapping her in the face. She couldn't open a portal, and Orin, the biggest asshole she knew but who also loved his family, had been gone, with no sign of him, for weeks. He would have returned to check in, or someone would have reported seeing him in an outer realm if he could leave here, but he couldn't.

Her heart fell as reality sank in. She was trapped here too.

CHAPTER EIGHTY-SIX

The blood drained from her face, and she rested her hand against the wall to keep from swaying. "How is this possible?"

Orin shrugged. "You tell me, little witch, because I have no idea."

"I've never heard of magic like this before."

"Maybe it's another little trap the arachs designed before slaughtering each other."

"Maybe, but…"

"But what?"

Sahira bit her bottom lip as she looked around. "Why would they do this? They had a reason for hiding their magic in the trials, but what reason would they have for this? But I don't know; I can't think of any other way a place like this would exist."

Maybe she could figure it out when she wasn't so confused and panicked, but right now, she wanted to run screaming from this realm. And she couldn't.

"You've tried everything to escape?" she croaked.

"As have all the other immortals trapped here."

"How many are here?"

"I didn't bother to count them, but quite a few. Now"—Orin patted the mattress beside him—"I've had enough of this depressing talk. You can either call them back in or join me yourself. There were three of them, but I think you've got enough pent-up sexual energy to equate to three, and you'd be a fun enough ride to satisfy me."

Sahira gawked at him. "How can you think about sex at a time like this?"

"What else am I going to do to pass the days? They get a little tedious around here."

She was sure they did, but still... "I'd die before I *ever* fucked you."

Orin's eyes shimmered with amusement and intrigue as he tilted his head to study her. "To each their own, but I think you'll be a fun little shell to crack. And since I have nothing else to do around here...."

His words trailed off as he gave her a suggestive little smile. Sahira extended her middle finger before spinning away and flinging open the door. The three women jumped when she stormed out of the room.

"If you kill him, I won't blame you," Sahira said.

"I make them *way* too happy for that," Orin called after her. "And one day, little witch, you'll find out exactly *how* I do."

Sahira shuddered at the possibility and stalked down the balcony she'd emerged onto before abruptly stopping. Gripping the rail, she tried to steady her nerves and apprehension over Orin's words.

She would never crawl into *that* man's bed, but he'd marked her as someone he would conquer while here. He would go out of his way to punish her for keeping the tracking spell on him. This place should be punishment enough, but he wouldn't see it as such.

He was a dark fae; they loved to play games and conquer or

break all those who stood in their way. Outside this realm, he had plenty to keep him entertained.

Here, he had only orgies and toying with *her*. And he was probably already growing bored with the numerous women who had rotated through his bedroom since he arrived here.

She had to get out of this realm and away from him before his attention turned to *her*.

But how do I do that if I can't open a portal?

Gazing at the elegant room below with its crystal chandeliers, stately bar, and multiple gaming tables, she strained to calm the pounding of her heart. A vast assortment of immortals gathered in the room, drinking, playing games, and flirting.

She searched for answers in the crowd but found none. These immortals were going about their normal, everyday lives, but she sensed tension in the room and an edge to their laughter that belied their outwardly happy demeanor.

Her hands curled around the balcony railing as she blinked away the tears of frustration and hopelessness in her eyes. She would *not* cry. She would talk to them and learn more.

Throwing back her shoulders, she descended the stairs. If she was going to get answers, she'd have to start with those who had been here longer than her.

If there was a way in, there had to be a way *out*, and she would find it because being trapped here with Orin was a fate worse than Hell.

And since she had no intention of burning for the rest of her life, she would do whatever it took to get free.

∼

Read on for an excerpt from *Wicked Curses* Book 7 in the series. It's available now for preorder:

brendakdavies.com/WCwb

Visit the Erica Stevens/Brenda K. Davies Book Club on Facebook for exclusive giveaways and all things book related. Come join the fun: brendakdavies.com/ESBKDBookClub

Stay in touch on updates and new releases from the author by joining the mailing list!
Mailing list for Brenda K. Davies Updates:
brendakdavies.com/ESBKDNews

SNEAK PEEK
WICKED CURSES, THE SHADOW REALMS BOOK 7

S<small>AHIRA</small> <small>GLIDED</small> through the crowd filling the elaborately appointed bar. Conversations swirled around her, but she was still too shell-shocked by her current situation to register anything they said.

She'd never seen this eclectic a mix of immortals in one place or getting along so well. Being trapped in this forsaken realm had bound them together, instead of pitting them against each other.

Though, she imagined there were times when they turned on each other like rabid dogs. She'd only been here for ten minutes and was already feeling claustrophobic; being trapped with all of them would make her crankier.

She rubbed her neck as she resisted pulling at her collar. *I'm trapped.*

The words ran through her brain on a continuous loop. It couldn't be true. It *had* to be some sick joke.

Orin wasn't the most trustworthy guy in the world; he could be lying to her. She wouldn't trust him to walk across the street without first throwing someone in front of a car.

And he'd gladly push her out there or run her over.

But if he's lying, why can't you open a portal out of here?

Just recalling her inability to do so made her throat tighten; she tugged at the collar of her peasant shirt. She had to resist tearing it off so she could breathe easier, as it was becoming increasingly difficult to draw air into her lungs. Sweat beaded her forehead and trickled down her back.

I'm stuck here. I'm stuck!

Oh, shit. Oh, shit.

"Easy," a deep voice rumbled from beside her.

Sahira hadn't realized she was hyperventilating until the words came from beside her, and a large hand rested on her shoulder. She looked up at the towering figure beside her and almost fell over as she had to *keep* looking up.

Standing at least seven-feet-tall, the demon was over a foot and a half taller than her. Her neck hurt from craning it to see his face.

"You're new here," the demon said. "It gets easier, but it's a shock to us all at first."

"It can't be real," she muttered.

"It is. Here, have a drink."

Sahira blinked at the drink he slid toward her as it sloshed a little over the side. The amber liquid blurred before coming back into focus and blurring once more.

Get your shit together, Sahira.

She downed the contents in one long gulp. The demon chuckled as he took the glass from her and set it on the bar. The dwarf behind the bar refilled the glass before pushing it toward her.

"Make sure she knows there's no freeloading in this realm," the dwarf said in an accented voice that resembled an English accent.

"Give her a minute, Duribelda," the demon said.

"It's Belda, and you know it," the dwarf muttered before walking away.

"Are you okay?" the demon asked.

Sahira downed the alcohol and winced when it burned her throat. She hadn't tasted the first glass, but this one left an impression.

"Fine," she said and coughed into her hand as she blinked away the tears burning her eyes.

She set the glass on the bar, and this time the demon grabbed a bottle from behind the bar with his long arms and claw-tipped hands. He refilled her drink before setting the bottle beside it.

"Keep drinking," he said. "I'm Drozeth or Zeth, as most call me."

"A demon," she murmured.

"You're very observant."

Despite her shaken status, Sahira chuckled. "I just meant it's not often you run into a demon. You're a rarity in the realms."

"That's probably why I'm the only one here."

"And what of witches?"

"There are some here."

"And vampires?"

"They're here too. Are you going to have a problem with that?"

She laughed humorlessly. "Not me."

But some might, and she didn't give a shit about that. She had way bigger fish to fry.

"How long have you been here?" she asked.

"Ten years."

Sahira pulled at the collar of her shirt as the world blurred again.

"Easy," Zeth said.

She tilted her head back to take in all of him. His broad nose, strong cheekbones, and jaw accentuated the handsomeness of his face. Two red horns curled out from the sides of his bald head; they hooked toward the middle.

His yellow eyes shone with concern as he leaned a little

closer. He had a narrow waist, and his broad shoulders blocked the bar behind him. Two sharp, bony hooks rose from the tops of his shoulders and curved toward his neck.

"It does get easier," he told her.

"Does it?"

"In some ways, but you adjust."

"That doesn't sound encouraging."

"Not much is around here."

Sahira laughed bitterly as she downed her drink.

∼

ORIN HAD a little extra spring in his step when he opened the door and closed it on the three sleeping women. He strolled along the balcony as he resisted the urge to start whistling. Ever since getting stuck here, he hadn't had much to look forward to, but now...

Well, now he had a witch to hunt and play with. Rubbing his hands together, he grinned as he contemplated how he would torment his little witch.

She couldn't run and hide from him here, and she deserved everything she got after refusing to take her tracking spell off him. Being trapped here should be punishment enough for her; it wasn't.

He was going to devise something much more painful. He'd break her, bed her, and make her pay for everything.

His smile widened as he glanced down at the tavern below. He stopped smiling when he saw the demon standing with *his* witch.

No one was going to play with his witch but *him*. Rubbing his hands together, Orin descended the steps. He'd find a way out of here, but until then, he would make her pay.

∼

Preorder *Wicked Curses*, releasing 2023:
brendakdavies.com/WCwb

∽

Stay in touch on updates, sales, and new releases by joining to the mailing list: brendakdavies.com/ESBKDNews

Visit the Erica Stevens/Brenda K. Davies Book Club on Facebook for exclusive giveaways and all things book related. Come join the fun: brendakdavies.com/ESBKDBookClub

FIND THE AUTHOR

Brenda K. Davies Mailing List:
brendakdavies.com/News

Facebook: brendakdavies.com/BKDfb

Brenda K. Davies Book Club:
brendakdavies.com/BKDBooks

Instagram: brendakdavies.com/BKDInsta
Twitter: brendakdavies.com/BKDTweet
Website: www.brendakdavies.com

ALSO FROM THE AUTHOR

Books written under the pen name Brenda K. Davies

The Vampire Awakenings Series

Awakened (Book 1)

Destined (Book 2)

Untamed (Book 3)

Enraptured (Book 4)

Undone (Book 5)

Fractured (Book 6)

Ravaged (Book 7)

Consumed (Book 8)

Unforeseen (Book 9)

Forsaken (Book 10)

Relentless (Book 11)

Legacy (Book 12)

The Alliance Series

Eternally Bound (Book 1)

Bound by Vengeance (Book 2)

Bound by Darkness (Book 3)

Bound by Passion (Book 4)

Bound by Torment (Book 5)

Bound by Danger (Book 6)

Bound by Deception (Book 7)

Bound by Fate (Book 8)

Bound by Blood (Book 9)

Bound by Love (Book 10)

Coming 2023

The Road to Hell Series

Good Intentions (Book 1)

Carved (Book 2)

The Road (Book 3)

Into Hell (Book 4)

Hell on Earth Series

Hell on Earth (Book 1)

Into the Abyss (Book 2)

Kiss of Death (Book 3)

Edge of the Darkness (Book 4)

The Shadow Realms

Shadows of Fire (Book 1)

Shadows of Discovery (Book 2)

Shadows of Betrayal (Book 3)

Shadows of Fury (Book 4)

Shadows of Destiny (Book 5)

Shadows of Light (Book 6)

Wicked Curses (Book 7)

Coming 2023

Historical Romance

A Stolen Heart

**Books written under the pen name
Erica Stevens**

The Coven Series
Nightmares (Book 1)

The Maze (Book 2)

Dream Walker (Book 3)

The Captive Series
Captured (Book 1)

Renegade (Book 2)

Refugee (Book 3)

Salvation (Book 4)

Redemption (Book 5)

Broken (The Captive Series Prequel)

Vengeance (Book 6)

Unbound (Book 7)

The Kindred Series
Kindred (Book 1)

Ashes (Book 2)

Kindled (Book 3)

Inferno (Book 4)

Phoenix Rising (Book 5)

The Fire & Ice Series
Frost Burn (Book 1)

Arctic Fire (Book 2)

Scorched Ice (Book 3)

The Ravening Series

The Ravening (Book 1)

Taken Over (Book 2)

Reclamation (Book 3)

The Survivor Chronicles

The Upheaval (Book 1)

The Divide (Book 2)

The Forsaken (Book 3)

The Risen (Book 4)

ABOUT THE AUTHOR

Brenda K. Davies is the USA Today Bestselling author of the Vampire Awakening Series, Alliance Series, Road to Hell Series, Hell on Earth Series, and historical romantic fiction. She also writes under the pen name, Erica Stevens. When not out with friends and family, she can be found at home with her husband, son, dogs, cat, and horse.

Printed in Great Britain
by Amazon